the silent series book two

SILENT
GUILT

N. E. HENDERSON

Sign up for Nancy's mailing list where you'll get the latest news, sales, and more by visiting www.nehenderson.com

Edits by Mo Sytsma (2022)
Edits by Charisse Spiers (2020)
Proofreading by Beth Hale (2022)

eBook ISBN: 978-0-9912444-4-7

For Joe

You are the ultimate alpha male and my muse for Nicholas. You put up with a lot, but then so do I so I guess we even each other out. I love you, babe!

PROLOGUE

NICHOLAS

What have I done? Those words silently pound inside my head over and over like a bad pop song on repeat. To top it off, I have a tsunami-size migraine trying to kick its way out of my skull as I stand, staring down, watching this strong, beautiful woman sleeping soundly in her bed.

Shannon is finally asleep after hours of crying on my lap in the living room. Some were soft, silent tears that wet my shirt. Others were loud, ugly cries that made her pound her small fists into my chest. They all made me want to rip something apart. No, not something, I remind myself . . . someone.

My father.

Towering above her, I bend and pull the covers over her, tucking her in tightly. She was exhausted when I brought her in here and is now passed out on her side, her head resting on her pillow with her hands tucked underneath. I hope she's out for the next few hours. She needs all the sleep and comfort she can get. Too bad I'm not someone who can give her what she needs.

Because I'm the someone who caused all that's happened to her in the first place. I've messed up in more ways than I ever imagined possible. But I can't think about myself right now. I need to concentrate on fixing the mess I've caused.

Righting myself, I continue peering down at her. She's everything I've always wanted but knew I could never have—at least not long-term. Pinching the bridge of my nose, I close my eyes, only to reopen them immediately. I can't shut them. Every time I do, I see red, and I can't breathe. I should have killed that bastard ten fucking years ago. If I had, she never would have been raped once, let alone twice.

I'm a real piece of shit for letting that happen to her—letting him happen to her.

I don't deserve her. I'll never deserve her.

Moving quietly, I grab her cell phone from the nightstand next to the bed. Bringing the screen to life, I notice it's a little past midnight. Quickly, I locate her music app and find her favorite Papa Roach album, *Metamorphosis*. After hitting play, I put the album on repeat. Shannon is one of the few people, like myself, who can sleep peacefully while lyrics are being screamed in the background. Still, I set the volume down to a low beat. Before setting the phone back on the bedside table, I flip the switch on the side of her phone to silent so it doesn't ring while I'm gone.

I take my own cell phone out of my pocket, silencing it as well, then place the phone next to hers. I make my way into her closet as quietly as possible and grab my extra gym bag. Walking back into her room, I take one last look at the sleeping beauty before exiting the room just as "Lifeline" filters through the small speakers.

I don't have a plan, not really, anyway. I know I shouldn't confront my father. It's a bad idea, a very bad idea, but I've never been one to listen to the voice of reason.

I grab Shannon's car keys from a basket next to the front door, then quietly slip out, locking the door behind me. Looking down, I remember Niko lying dead when I arrived hours ago, and I ball my hands into tight fists. His blood stains the concrete under my feet. The motherfucker killed my dog. I don't have proof, but I know he did it. It's too coincidental. This was personal. I also know what the message behind it meant, and I'll be damned if I let him hurt her a third time.

Not a chance in hell will I allow that to happen again.

Jase has probably already handled Niko by now. Knowing him, he buried him in my backyard before he headed to his fight. A fight I had every intention of going to until my sister had to be bailed out of jail and then demanded to be taken to Shannon's house. Nikki had been frightened, unusual for my sister. She never shows weakness, which is why I didn't put up much of an argument with her about coming here.

Hitting the unlock button on the key fob, I open the driver's side door, toss my gym bag into the passenger's seat, and sink into the car. I adjust the seat to accommodate my long legs, but there still isn't quite enough room, causing me to mutter a slew of curse words under my breath. She needs a bigger car, I think to myself as I ease the door shut. *Who the hell enjoys driving this box of shit?* I shove the key into the ignition, turning it so the engine comes to life. Simultaneously the radio starts blaring "Had Enough."

"Fuck!" I shout.

Startled, I turn it down as quickly as my fingers will move. I know it's not going to wake her with the music already playing, but she has neighbors. I don't need to wake them. Luckily, her house isn't as close to her neighbors as most in this neighborhood are, so I think I'm in the clear. I have no idea what I'm about to do, but I'm smart enough to know I don't want anyone to see me coming or going.

Throwing the gearshift into reverse, I ease out of the driveway.

I could almost laugh at the song coming through the speakers if the lyrics weren't so dead-on at this very moment. *Almost.*

Once on the highway, I head south. I know where I'll find my father—at his on-again, off-again mistress's townhouse. My dad doesn't know I know about her, but I do. I have for a long time. It's only a twenty-minute drive, and with next to zero traffic, I can probably make it in fifteen.

Red flags continue to flash in front of my eyes. I need to listen to Jase and not do something stupid, but I can't stop myself. The beast inside rages and wants free. There aren't enough chains in the county of Los Angeles that could hold me back from ripping that monster apart. Not after everything I learned tonight. I've never been this on edge before—not even before or during a fight. Not any of the times I've watched or heard him hurt my mother. It should scare the shit out of me, but it doesn't.

I've always known my good-for-nothing father was an evil bastard, but never in a million years would I have thought he was capable of what he did to Shannon. The lyrics to the song that just finished playing repeat in my head. *We have had enough.*

By the time I make it to the small community my dad's girlfriend lives in, I only have one thing on my mind: hurting the man who damaged my beautiful girl. I honestly don't care what happens to me as long as he pays for everything he's done. I'm not stupid. I know people rarely get away with the shit I'm about to do, but it has to be done. I'll be damned if I let her feel unprotected another day. If that makes me a bad person, well, I don't give a flyin' fuck.

Parking the car in a small, deserted parking lot a block from Harper's townhouse, I turn off the engine, but I can't bring myself to get out. I have a death grip on the steering wheel as I lean my head back against the headrest. The rational side of me is still trying to talk myself out of it. I know there is no going back once I step out of this car. The other part of me knows if I don't do this, I won't be able to live with myself.

Releasing the grip on the steering wheel, I reach over and unzip my gym bag. I take out my sparring gloves and put each one on, noticing a few scratches on my left arm and a small cut above my knuckles on my right hand. At least if I'm questioned, I have my training as an excuse. Once my gloves are secured tightly, I open the door and get out of the vehicle, then make my way down the set of steps next to the parking lot.

Noticing the dark car in front of me, I feel a sense of relief; he's still here. Once I make it past his car and to the end of the pavement, I jog down another set of steps to the private beach. Her house isn't far. My father thinks he's slick because he doesn't park in her driveway. No, that wouldn't make good headlines if an LA county judge were caught having an affair, now would it?

Once my feet hit the sand, I slow my pace. This is a quiet community, many of the townhouses are rentals for vacationers. I don't need anyone to see me. At least, not until I'm finished doing what I came here to do. If someone saw me now, I'd look out of place with my fighting gloves and a button-down shirt and jeans. I certainly don't need the cops called before I settle the score with my father.

After a few minutes of trekking down the beach, I notice a figure in the distance, causing me to stop. A large fence is wrapped around what I assume to be a dumpster on my left. I quickly hop behind it and wait. My heart pounds a tattoo in my chest. After what feels like an eternity, the person passes me. There's enough moonlight to identify the figure. I know it's him, my father, but I can't move. My feet are frozen to the ground.

How can I do this? I'm not like him. Even with all the shit I've done over the years. I'm not evil. Only evil people kill, right?

Shit.

I don't need this right now. I don't need a conscience.

"Goddamn it." I hear him say as he halts and pivots. I think he's seen me, but he doesn't look in my direction. He walks back in the direction he came from. After he passes me yet again, I follow him. My heart rate accelerates. All the hate I have for this man boils to the surface. My body begins to heat, making my fists clench together. I can't see anything but the color red when I take a deep breath.

"You sick fuck," I spit out in a disgusted tone, causing my father to stop dead in his tracks.

A small moment of silence passes before he speaks.

"Nicholas?" His voice shakes. It's not the confident tone that normally pours from his mouth. He slowly turns, facing me, and his eyes grow wide as they dip down to my hands.

He doesn't have a chance to say another word before I tackle him and sit on his chest, effectively pinning him. I start to pound, releasing everything I feel into him. The sound of my fists hitting flesh and bone echoes in my ears. Over and over, I punch him in the face. It drowns out the waves crashing to the shore a few feet away from where I have him on the ground. I always suspected my dad wasn't a fighter, and now I know for sure. He doesn't know how to fight me off or even how to flip me over.

He is a sorry excuse for a man, let alone a father. He doesn't deserve the breath he takes. This man deserves to burn in hell. And that's exactly where I plan on sending him.

When I can't punch anymore, when all the fight in my body is gone, I sit back. Looking down, his face finally comes back into focus. My father lies motionless, limp, and bloody. He looks broken. A sight that echoes the way I feel. Quickly looking up and around, I see no one in the area but the two of us.

Shit.

What have I just done? I'm letting my conscience get the better of me.

Fuck.

I jump up and off his body. I don't know if he's dead, but I can take an educated guess.

Fuck.

Isn't this what I wanted? Yes, it is, but hell. I take a step back and rub my gloved palm over my face. That piercing feeling in the center of my chest hasn't gone away. Did I think it would? Did I think killing him would ease my own guilt?

I wanted it to.

Without thinking too long, I bend down and gather his body up. I make my way to the ocean, my father thrown over my shoulder. Going thigh-deep into the water, I let his body fall from my shoulder. I walk backward as I watch his body float face down.

Once I'm out of the water, I turn and jog to the stairs, making my way up and over to the next set. Before I know it, I'm back at Shannon's car and ripping the gloves off. Walking to the passenger's side, I swing the door open and pull out a towel and spare clothes from my gym bag. I place the gloves inside. As quickly as I can, I strip out of my soaked clothes, toss them into the bag, and then towel myself off. After placing the dirty, wet towel in my bag, I pull on a pair of gym shorts and a sleeveless workout shirt. Shutting the car door, I jog around to the driver's side and hop in.

Holy shit. What the hell have I done? What if he's dead? What if he's not dead?

Shit.

I should've at least made sure. Should I have weighed his body down? Hell, I don't know. I've never killed anyone before.

"Fuck!" I yell, hitting the steering wheel. I start the car and slam the gear into drive.

CHAPTER ONE

Pregnant? *She's pregnant. Shannon is pregnant. Oh, God . . .
I'm . . . We're . . .*

Making my way to Nikki's car, I pull the door open
and then plop into the seat in a daze. I feel like the air has been
sucked right out of my lungs. I slam my head back into the
headrest, frustrated, as I pull the door closed.

I'm hot. It's too damn hot inside this car. Why am I so hot?
My body is on fire. Must be, but it's not.

"Why isn't there any goddamn air running in your fucking
car?" I yell at my sister before turning a nasty look in her
direction.

"Don't you fucking yell at me. The air is running, asshole,"
she spits out, gesturing toward the A/C vent in the middle of the
dashboard.

Leaning forward, I rest my forehead in my palms while
attempting to bring in air through my mouth, but it's a struggle.
I can't think straight.

Pregnant?

"Are you okay?" Nikki inquires, and I almost want to laugh

only nothing about this is anything to laugh about. My sister's voice sounds so far away with everything else running through my head. I can hear the rapid pounding of my own heart beating in my chest.

She's pregnant. We're having a baby. What have I done?

"Nick?"

"Just get me the fuck out of here. Take me to my house," I demand, throwing my body back into the seat. My heart may not have any sympathy for the man I killed, but my brain knows what I did was wrong—so very wrong. I'm not sorry, but hell . . . Everything changed with two simple words: *I'm pregnant.* I'm going to be a father. I was fine with going to prison for killing a man, but not if I'm having a kid.

"Fuck. Fuck. Fuck," I yell as loud as my voice will push the words out. I hear Nikki put the car in reverse, and I'm jerked farther back into the seat as she accelerates. My sister isn't exactly the smoothest driver.

I close my eyes, but I feel every jerk and pull as she makes each turn. She turns the volume on the radio up, but not loud enough that a conversation can't be had over the music. Before I know it, she pulls into my driveway and parks. I open my eyes before swinging my head in her direction. She's biting her fingernails and giving me a pleading look. *Damn that look.*

"Please tell me you didn't kill him," she says with a sigh. I've never lied to my sister. I've never had to, and if anyone could see through me, it's her. I turn my face, peering out the window. I can't look her in the face if I'm forced to lie.

"Drop it, Nikki. I have enough shit to deal with today," I say as I reach for the door. I can't tell her. Even if she despised the man as much as I did, I can't tell her I killed our father. I certainly can't put the burden of that on her conscience.

"Nick, I really need you to tell me it wasn't you. Please, Nick." Her voice is soft, and I can tell she's on the verge of tears. It's been a long time since I've seen my little sister cry. The last time, it almost cost me my best friend. I can't take my sister's tears. I drop my hand from the door handle and relax back into the seat, feeling defeated. Before I can answer, she says, "I punched Dad yesterday morning."

"What?" I ask, turning in the seat to face her, instantly on alert.

"I took a swing at him yesterday morning in his office. Several people witnessed it, and the whole office watched me be escorted out by the cops."

This is not happening. I take a deep breath through my nose and then blow it out through my mouth.

"That's why you got arrested yesterday, and you're just now telling me?" I tried to keep my voice calm, but I'm anything but calm at this moment. "Fucking Christ," I scream. Shit. What if people think she did it? No. I'd never let that happen.

"It's only a matter of ti—" she starts, but I cut her off.

"Where were you last night after you left Shannon's? Jase had a fight. Tell me you were with him the whole night."

"Nick, you don't thi—" I cut her off again.

"Just answer me, dammit," I shout.

"I was at the fight until midnight. Afterward, Jase and I and a couple of other fighters went to Club Blue until three in the morning. I talked Charlie into letting us stay after the place closed at two. Jase and I went home, then went to bed. Mom called, waking me up around seven this morning."

Thank God she has an alibi. It was somewhere around one when I killed the bastard. I sigh as relief washes over me. There's no way in hell I would take a chance of my sister getting accused.

"Stop worrying," I tell her in a calmer voice. "People saw you last night. No one is going to think you did it." She relaxes into her seat like a weight has been lifted off her. She's smart, but I don't think she even realized she had an alibi. An idea hits me, and I look at my sister. She knew what our father did to Shannon before I did. The memory of her telling Shannon to tell me or she would rushes back. How did she know?

"Why did you take a swing at Dad?"

Nikki tenses and looks away. She can't lie to me either.

"Nikki?"

She reaches forward, turning the volume down on "Blood Empty Promises," the song giving me a bad feeling about what she's going to reveal.

"Because of what he did to her," she huffs.

"You knew?" Realization dawns on me. "Shannon told you before she told me?" It comes out more of an accusation than a question. A flash of anger mixed with hurt floods me from head to toe.

"No, Mom told me," she clarifies.

Say what?

"How the hell did Mom find out?" Did everyone know before I did? Nikki leans forward, pressing her face against her hands wrapped tightly around the steering wheel.

"Two days ago. Mom let it slip two days ago."

Did she just say two days ago? Surely I'm not hearing this correctly. There's no way they both knew that long and hadn't said one word to me about it.

Before I form any words, my sister continues. "I immediately went to see Shannon. When I got there, she was puking her guts out. I didn't get a chance to talk to her about it. I made her go to the doctor, where she found out she was pregnant." Nikki pauses, panic crossing her blue eyes. "Oh, God, please tell me she told you about the baby?"

Two days.

Two fucking days ago.

My body heats, and I can feel my blood coming to a simmer. I only nod and wait for her to continue. Why didn't my sister tell me then?

"When I dropped Shannon off, she said she was going to tell you about the baby. Then later that day, when I saw you at Knocked Out, I knew she hadn't told you. By the next morning, I just lost it. She wouldn't answer her phone, so I confronted Dad about it. Then everything went to shit, and I got arrested. He fucking had me arrested," she tells me, rushing her words out all at once. I stare at my sister in silent disbelief. She's known for two days and never said a word. Not one damn word.

"Nick, say something." She's looking at me with wide blue eyes, panic blazing back at me. She knows I'm about to light into her ass.

"Let me get this straight," I say through clenched teeth. "You knew for two goddamn days, and you didn't bother to tell me?"

"Nick?" she questions in a low voice, placing her hand on my forearm. This is her calming technique for me.

"Don't you fucking *Nick* me!" I yell, slamming my palm down on the dashboard. She flinches and removes her hand from my arm quickly. My body is scorching hot, and the sting I should have felt from smashing my hand against the plastic doesn't even register.

"It wasn't my place to tell you," she declares.

"The hell it wasn't. You're my sister. I should've been the first person you came to after finding out," I continue yelling at her. I can't believe she's known this long and didn't say anything. My own sister.

"I'm sorry," she whispers. I hear how much she regrets it in her voice, but that doesn't change anything. She left me out in the dark.

"Sorry doesn't fucking fix it, now does it?" I say and fall back into the seat. Propping my elbow on the ledge of the door, I lean my head into my right palm. My skull feels like it's about to explode. My entire family knew. My mother. My own mother knew, but how? I don't understand.

"How did Mom know?" I ask, forcing my voice to come out calmer.

Nikki sighs heavily. "Apparently, she suspected it the first day she met Shannon, when we went to their house for dinner, the Sunday before Memorial Day."

This isn't happening. I'm dreaming, and I'm going to wake up from this nightmare.

She blinked quickly at me. "Mom went to see Shannon last week. I guess she asked her and Shannon confirmed it."

Wow. My mom knew even longer and didn't have the decency to tell me either. A great family I have.

"There's something else you should know," she says in a defeated tone.

Nice. More shit I'm not going to like.

"What else is there?"

"Mom asked her not to tell you. She asked her to walk away and never see you again." Nikki's voice is so soft that I want to question what I just heard. Why would my mother do that to me? My own mother. Because of me, my father hasn't hurt her in a decade. I've protected her, and this is the thanks I get. "Nick, I'm not saying what Mom did was right, but in her defense, she was only trying to protect you."

"You're kidding me, right?"

"She isn't stupid, Nick. She knows you. She knows what you're capable of. She knows how fast you can lose your head and do something you'll regret."

Regret? I don't regret what I did to my father. I regret not doing it sooner. I regret fucking someone else up instead of the person I really wanted to hurt. That's what I regret. I take a deep breath, trying to let everything sink in. This is one fucked-up mess I don't know if I'll come out of.

I reach for the door handle and pull. Before I can get a leg out, Nikki stops me with a hand on my arm.

"Nick, that was a lot of information to process. I think you need to go work some of it out of your system." She's back to her calming technique, but it won't work. I don't have time for that shit, and the last thing I need is to get in a ring with Jase. I don't want to hurt my best friend. It's not that I'm a better fighter than him, because I'm not, but when I'm like this, no one can handle me. When I start hitting, I can't stop. I can't even see what's in front of my face. It's as if a thick fog takes over until I have nothing left.

"That's not a good idea right now. I gotta go," I say, snatching my arm from her grip. She looks hurt. I know I was overly harsh with her, and I'll apologize later, but not right now. Right now, I'm angry with her. It's not something I'm used to. Nikki has been a constant in my life. The only person I've ever trusted completely. She gets me because she's just like me. At least, I thought she did. I'd never have kept something like that from her. Never.

"Nick, please don't be mad at me," she says, but I don't respond. I don't look back as I pull myself out of her car and slam the door, walking the short distance to my house. I'm beyond mad right now. I've never wanted to kick my sister's ass more than I do right now.

CHAPTER TWO

O nce I'm inside, I close the door and fall back against it. Sliding to the floor, I rest my elbows on my knees, allowing my head to fall forward into the palms of my hands. If I could go back to that November day, I almost wish I had never laid eyes on Shannon. Not because I don't love her. I do. More than I ever imagined possible. But it's because of me there is so much darkness in her world.

I'd give anything to take that darkness away from her.

I sit here for several minutes, letting the guilt consume me. I don't know how to fix any of this. What I've done to her is unforgivable.

I take a deep breath and exhale with a loud scream. I then bang the back of my head against the solid wood door. My head is still pounding from the headache that hasn't stopped since last night.

Pulling myself up, an overwhelming pressure builds inside my head and throughout my body. I don't know how to get rid of it. So, I do the only thing that ever helps. I hit. I punch my fist straight through the wall next to my front door. Yet, it's all still there, front and center inside my skull. If anything, it intensifies, so I throw my left fist through the drywall and follow again with my right.

Nothing.

No relief.

I take a deep breath and force the air back out rapidly as I make my way into my kitchen. I head straight for the cabinet above my stove. I grab the half-empty seventeen-year-old bottle of Johnnie Walker. Moving a few cabinets down, I retrieve a small tumbler. At the island in my kitchen, I pour the liquid into the glass and down it like a shot. Placing the tumbler back on the counter, I run my right hand over my face. I can't recall the last time, if ever, I drank this early in the day.

Looking over at the clock on the microwave, I confirm just how early it is. It's not even ten in the morning. I look back down and repeat the process of pouring and slamming the drink. It burns, but it's a good burn. I need something to take the edge off and keep the beast inside at bay.

My mother.

My thoughts land on her and what she's done. I feel betrayed. She could have put an end to this last week. She could have told me. I grab the bottle from the counter and tip it up, take a swallow, then place it back on the countertop. Turning on my heel, I grab my keys lying on the countertop and head for the door. Time to pay Mommy dearest a little visit.

Once the door is locked, I make my way to my silver Audi parked in my driveway. After hitting the unlock button, I pull the door open and slide in. I crank my car and turn the stereo up as loud as it will go to drown out my thoughts. "Live This Down" plays, and I want to laugh as I put the car in reverse.

What's usually a forty-five-minute drive only takes me thirty minutes. Once I'm parked, I don't hesitate. I turn the engine off and get out. I slip my keys into my pocket as I reach the front door.

I don't bother to knock. Today, I don't care. I haven't entered my parents' house without knocking since I moved out right before my eighteenth birthday. Once I step into their foyer, I slam the door.

As I make my way to the kitchen, my phone vibrates inside my pocket. I ignore it. I don't have the time, nor do I want to talk to anyone right now.

As I enter, I notice my mother sitting at the table. She is dressed to perfection as usual, but she looks lost. Surely, she can't be sad my father is gone.

She turns her head in my direction.

"Nicholas," she huffs. Her voice is sad, confirming my thought.

Seriously?

She stands and walks toward me. "Son, please tell me it wasn't you. Please," she begs as tears prick her eyes.

"Mom," I begin. Obviously, I'm not going to tell her the truth, but I don't know what to say. I've been so consumed with what she kept from me that it didn't cross my mind that she would ask me if I killed him.

"Please, son." She pleads with me as two tears fall down her perfectly made-up face. Even sad, even with him gone, she dresses the part of what he considered the perfect little wife. Never let someone see you without makeup on or not in a dress. Women are supposed to wear dresses. I remember him telling her this when I was a child.

"No, Mother." I sigh in frustration. I haven't lied to her since I was a teenager, but I know I can make her believe anything. It's a skill I learned a long time ago.

"Oh, thank God." Relief crosses her eyes for a minute before sadness replaces it again. She wraps her arms around me, and I go stiff. I'm not here to be the consoling son. I'm not here to tell her it's going to be okay. I'm not here to take her sadness away.

Why is she sad in the first place?

"Mom?" I question, using somewhat of a harsh tone. She takes a step back when I don't return her hug. She looks hurt, and a question lies behind her eyes. I wonder what it is.

"I just can't believe someone would do that to your dad. He was such a respected man in our community. Everyone lov—"

"Are you kidding me?" I yell, cutting her off before she finishes. Surely, she can't be serious.

She takes another step back, stunned at my outburst. She looks even more hurt than when I wouldn't hug her.

"Nicholas," she says, taking a defensive tone, "your father was murdered last night. How can you act like you don't care?"

"Because I don't fucking care, Mother. I'm glad the bastard is dead. The person who did it deserves a medal of honor," I tell her. I don't really believe that. There's no honor in what I did. Justice, perhaps, but not honor.

"Don't you use foul language in my house," she hisses, and I want to shake my head. Authority has never been her strong trait.

"That fuck abused you for years. How can you feel sorry for him? How can you mourn him? Please tell me because I don't understand. Make me understand." There's nothing she can say that will make me understand, yet I beg anyway.

"He was my husband and your father. You will not talk about him that way. He's gone, Nicholas." More tears form in her eyes and spill over. "I loved him, and now he's gone," she whispers.

"My. God. I don't believe this. I can't believe I didn't see it before now," I say as I look up at the ceiling, shaking my head this time.

"Son . . ." she tries to interject when my eyes come back

down, meeting her blue ones. The same eyes that match Nikki's and mine.

"You're more fucked up than he was," I declare. I can't believe I never saw it. Her mind is warped or something. She probably believes she deserved everything he did to her.

Unbelievable.

"Nicholas Aaron Lockhart," she scolds as she places her hands on her hips. I almost want to laugh at the use of my full name as if it's going to change anything. As if she is trying to take charge.

"Enough!" I scream, and she takes a step away from me. A flash of fear crosses her face. I'm not the one who hit her. I'm not the one who told her she was stupid or ignorant or any of the other belittling terms my father called her on a weekly basis.

"I'm here because I want to know why my mother didn't tell me what my father did to the only woman I've ever loved." I pause, giving her a chance to speak, but she doesn't. She just stares like she can't believe I'm asking her this. "You knew how I felt about her, and you said nothing. Why would you protect him?" I yell.

"He's my husband. You're my son. Family, Nicholas. I'd do anything to protect my family from someone who could destroy us. Destroy you," she cries as anger floods my body. I can't believe her. I walk over, placing my palms on the island in the middle of the kitchen. I can't look at her. Hate and betrayal are all I feel at this moment.

"You had no right asking her not to tell me. You had no right asking her not to see me again," I say through clenched teeth.

"I had every right!" she yells at the back of my head, and I whip around to face her.

"Like hell you did!" I yell back. "I protected you from him, and this is what you do in return. You protect him?"

"I loved your father, Nicholas, but it was always about you. I had to protect you from yourself." Her voice is calm. She believes what she's saying, but the truth is, she protected the monster I watched hurt her too many times. Ultimately, this is my own fault, and I know that. If I had stood up to him a long time ago, Shannon would never have been hurt. I take a deep breath and push it out in one long exhale as I stare at my mother staring back at me. Without addressing her, I start to walk out of the kitchen.

"Where are you going?" she asks.

"We're done, Mom," I state and continue out of the room. I don't hate my mother like I hate my father. I want to, but I don't. I love her. She's my mom. But I don't have to see her, and frankly, I don't want anything to do with her. I'm angry over her part in this.

"Nicholas." I hear her call my name, but I don't acknowledge her. I make my way through the foyer and out the front door. After jogging down the steps, I head for my car. Once I'm inside, I crank it up and pull away, unsure if I'll ever step foot inside that house again.

CHAPTER THREE

"I need another drink," I say as I drive down Pacific Ave. I'm close to The Cove, and frankly, it's the best place to be if I'm going to drink myself into forgetting the jacked-up mess that is my life.

Once I pull up, I put the car in park and open the door to get out. Josh is rounding my car, so I toss him the keys. He's a nice kid, just out of high school. He works here during the day so he can play in his band most nights.

"When should I pull her back around, Mr. Lockhart?" he asks, gesturing to my car. Like a lot of guys, the kid always refers to vehicles as a "her." I never really understood that. My best friend does the same thing and has named every car and truck he's ever owned. To me, it's just a machine, a way to get from point A to point B and then back to A.

"Tomorrow. Maybe," I respond, thinking I may just drown myself in whiskey for the next few days and possibly straight through the weekend. It's a Thursday and the middle of the day, but what the hell? I'm the boss, aren't I? I can take off whenever I please.

Making my way inside, I head straight to the elevators, passing the receptionist's desk on the way. Jessica is helping an older gentleman when she catches my stare.

"Good afternoon, Mr. Lockhart." She beams.

Damn, my staff is way too cheerful sometimes. I try to smile back and nod but continue to the elevators. I'm not in the mood for chitchat, and that's exactly what Jessica is good at. She's perfect at her job and keeps my customers happy, so I can't really complain.

I feel dirty and need to take a hot shower. The elevator doors open after a few seconds of waiting, and when I look up, my eyes flash with more anger, as do the man's staring back at me. We don't speak as he exits, guiding a petite brunette. I enter the elevator, press the code for the penthouse floor, and as the doors close, I wonder why Jeffery Chaney is in my hotel. The last time I checked, it wasn't a pay-by-the-hour motel, so what the fuck?

My hatred for him may be misplaced, but I don't care at the moment. His hatred for me isn't, and really, can I blame him? Still, I never liked the prick in high school, and I certainly don't like him now. As long as he stays away from what belongs to me, we won't have a problem.

The ride up the elevator is short, and I'm lost in my thoughts. When the doors open, I exit, walking the distance to my room. Once the door is unlocked, I enter and slam it shut. I head to my kitchen first for that drink I'm so desperate for. Seeing the unopened bottle of The Famous Grouse Scottish Oak Finish sitting on the countertop, I walk straight over to it and open it as quickly as my fingers will twist off the cap. I toss the cap on the granite and retrieve a small tumbler from the cabinet above me.

After pouring a large amount in, I pick up the glass, tip it up to my lips, and toss it back, swallowing it in one gulp. Seems like such a waste of expensive scotch. It should be sipped, but that isn't my goal. Without setting the glass back down, I pour another large drink and throw it back like a shot. Setting the glass down, I place my palms down on the edge of the granite and close my eyes.

Opening them back up, I take a swig from the bottle. The alcohol hasn't started working yet, and I don't like the image staring back at me when I close my eyes. I see the lifeless body of my father lying beneath me. I take another swig. I put the bottle down when I feel the vibration of my phone in my pocket.

Why can't people just leave me alone? My cell has buzzed more than a dozen times since I shoved it in my pocket this morning. I should turn the damn thing off. Taking my right hand off the counter, I fumble into my pocket to retrieve my cell phone. With one smooth slide to the right, it opens, showing me about a dozen missed calls and more than three times that amount in text messages. Shit. Apparently, my father's death—murder—has broken. That's what it was, right? Might as well be honest with myself.

First, I clear all the calls, noting that most are from my sister, with a couple of others from Jase and one from Marcus. Clicking over to clear my texts, I see they range from Rachel and a few other staff members from LP, including Teresa. Most are from the few people in my life who I actually consider my friends: Jase, Nikki, Shane, and Matt. A couple of the messages are from numbers I don't recognize, and I have one from Shannon. I stare at her name the longest.

I should just turn the phone off. Easy, right? Just have to press one button and slide my thumb to the right on the screen to power off. So do it, Nicholas.

Finally, I click on the message she left.

Ah, hell.

Shannon: Happy Birthday.

It's her birthday.

It's my birthday.

A great birthday today is.

Without thinking, I toss my phone on the countertop. "Goddamn it," I spit, right before it hits the hard granite, making a cracking sound. I reach for it and turn it over as I pick it up. Sure enough, the glass screen is a shattered mess. "Fuck." Oh well, it's not like I planned on talking to anyone for the remainder of the day.

I set the phone back on the granite, then grab the bottle and push away from the counter, turning to leave the kitchen. I walk through the living area to the bedroom. Heading for the bathroom, I walk in and turn the light on. I take a swig of the alcohol and then turn the shower to hot.

Turning around and walking to the sink, I set the bottle down for a moment so I can shed my clothes. Once everything is kicked into the corner of the bathroom, I look into the mirror and stare at my reflection. The steam starts to filter out of the shower, telling me the water is perfect, but I keep looking at myself, seeing only a slate of inked emptiness looking back at me.

As I continue to look at myself, I pick the bottle back up, bringing it up to my lips, where I wrap them firmly around the opening and let the liquid burn down my throat. The pain feels good. I enjoy a similar pain when I'm fighting or getting work done on my body. People talk about tattoos like they're an addiction. Once you get one, you can't stop. Well, for me, it's not an addiction to the tattoo itself. It's the pain, the piercing of the needle I enjoy. The pain, the burn, the hitting, it all makes the mountain of shit processing in my head go away. If only for a few seconds or minutes, it's gone, and I feel free.

Until a week ago, I didn't need the pain any longer. When I had Shannon, I felt freedom like I had never felt before. I was happy for the first time in my life. I think that's why I lost it so easily when I thought she . . . with my dad. I can't even think it. I was stupid. There aren't many people I trust, and I trusted her completely from the beginning, but I let a split second of doubt fuck it all up.

I set the bottle back down to run my hand over my face, through my hair, and back down over my face again. Looking down at the soon-to-be half-empty bottle, I suck in air through my mouth and then exhale in a long, drawn-out breath. Quickly turning toward the shower, I take a step and almost lose my balance. I spring forward, grabbing the corner of the wall to catch myself. I stand still for a few seconds to gain my balance back. I shake my head from side to side and then continue forward, stepping under the hot spray.

I stand under the heat, letting the water fall onto my head and run down my achy body. I stare at the water pooling at my feet, waiting to go down the drain, washing away the dirt. If only everything jumbled in my head could wash away that easily. I'm going to be a father, and I don't know what to think. I really never thought I'd be here. It's not like I never wanted kids. I did . . . do . . . but I would never have considered bringing them into this world as long as that man was alive. No kid should be subjected to that evil bastard. If I'm really honest with myself, I never wanted to carry his genes further in this world. I wanted them to stop with Nikki and me.

What if I'm a shitty father? What if I'm worse than he was? What if I'm really just like him? Shannon would be better off without me, and certainly the kid would too. A pain shoots through my chest at the thought of living a life without her. I turn, grab the bottle of shampoo, and push all thoughts of her out of my mind. The more I think of Shannon, the guiltier I feel, but the more I try not to think of her, the more I do. It's a lose-lose situation no matter what I do.

I pop the top on the shampoo and squirt a small amount into my palm. Placing the bottle down, I lather the white, creamy liquid in my hands and then run them through the dark strands on my head. Once I've scrubbed my scalp, I do the same to every inch of my body. And I'm not gentle about it. I feel dirty, and no matter how rough I am, that clean feeling never comes.

After showering, I towel off and quickly dress.

Alcohol. I need more.

I decide to leave my hotel room. I could stay and finish off the scotch, but I'd rather be down at Quaint. At least I know Sam will keep my mind off things I don't want to think about. Looking at my watch, I see it's almost three in the afternoon. Perfect timing. Sam should be arriving soon.

I walk out the door, letting it slam shut behind me. I make my way to the elevator and press the down button.

Once on the ground level, I exit and head for my destination.

"Mr. Lockhart." I hear as I'm about to walk past Jessica. Her voice is stressed and packed full of concern.

Not now.

I stop and turn as she rounds the desk.

"I heard. I am so sorry to hear about your dad. Is there anything I can do, Mr. Lockhart?" For starters, you can just not give a shit like me, but I don't say that. No, I know I have to act like a man who actually cares that his father was killed.

"No, Jessica, but thank you," I tell her. She pauses right in front of me. She has a hesitant look in her baby-blue eyes. I think she wants to hug me but isn't sure if it's appropriate. In hopes of distracting her and getting her off the very topic I don't want to think about, I ask, "Is everything going well today? Is there anything I should know about?" I may employ people to ensure this place runs smoothly, but I'm still the owner, and I still feel the need to make sure I know about everything.

"Yes, sir," she responds. The expression on her youthful face is genuine sympathy, but she doesn't bring my father back up, and I'm grateful. "Everything is going great today."

"Good," I say and sidestep her at the same time. I continue to the bar. Quaint is everything a bar should be: small, dark, and quiet. It's a place to be alone where no one bothers you. Well, no one except the bartender. It's not a place to hang out with friends. At least for me, it's not.

Walking through the dark mahogany-framed entrance, I see Tabitha behind the bar. She is currently serving a drink to one of the retired regulars. I walk to the other end of the bar and round the corner on the right. I pull out a chair and take a seat in my usual spot. Tabitha turns her attention away from the man and notices me for the first time. She flashes her flirtatious grin my way as she strolls toward me. It's a smile that says, "Do me. Any way you like."

No thanks, honey.

Even before Shannon entered my messed-up world, I never would have considered bedding this one. It's not that she isn't pretty. She is, although a little too thin for my taste. Tabitha, or as everyone else calls her, Tabby, is petite at about 5'-3". She has a cute heart-shaped face with medium-length brown hair pulled up high on her head and secured with a hair tie. She is dressed in her uniform, a black button-up long-sleeve shirt, black straight pants—highlighting her narrow hips and flat ass—and a black apron tied around her waist.

She also has that "employee" status working against her. I've made that mistake before and won't be doing it again, no matter how drunk, alone, or miserable I am. It's not worth it, plus now there is Shannon. And I don't have the slightest clue what to do about her, or them, rather.

"Hey, Mr. Lockhart," she says as she reaches the end of the counter in front of me. "It must be my lucky day. You're never in this early," she beams. Her brown eyes sparkle as she pauses for a breath. "Do you want the usual?"

"Please." I respond, wondering how she knows what my

"usual is" before adding, "without the water." The light buzz I had going up in my room is melting away as thoughts of Shannon, my father, and the past fight to make their way back into my head. If only I could rewind a clock and go back to that day ten years ago. Knowing what I know now, I would have handled things differently. I would have made him pay instead of taking out my anger on another. But this is life, and there is no turning the hands of time back.

"Here you go, sir." Tabitha's warm words hit my ears, bringing me out of my thoughts as I look up to see her place a small, clear glass filled with Johnnie Walker in front of me.

"Thank you." I lace my hand around the glass holding the dark liquid and lift it off the bar. I decide to sip this time. I don't want it to be a long night, but I don't want to fall on my face either. Especially in a bar, a bar I own at that. The cold glass hits my bottom lip as I tilt it up and let a large sip flow into my mouth. The liquor's rich, bold flavor hits my palate as I swallow.

"Wait." I stop her as she turns to leave. Placing my glass down, I glance up.

"Yes?" She smiles as she turns back around and places her palms on the bartop to give me her full attention.

"Can you bring me a phone? Please," I add, knowing I don't use that word as often as I should.

"Sure thing." She turns on her heels. Within seconds, she's back, hand outstretched, offering me the phone.

I take it and nod. I quickly dial the phone number to my office.

"It's a beautiful day at Lockhart Publishing. This is Rachel. How can—?"

I stop her before she gets the rest of the spiel out of her mouth.

"It's me," I say, and I hear the shocked gasp in her voice.

"Nicholas. Oh my God, are you all right? I heard. What can I do? Seriously, boss, what do you need?" As usual, Rachel's mouth is running a mile. She talks fast, and if you aren't paying close attention, you'll miss everything. This annoys most, and normally would me too, but I have a soft spot for her. Her voice is always pleasant to my ears and seems to settle me, a lot like my sister's.

"A phone," I say. "I broke mine, and I need a new one." I can't stay out of contact forever. I do have two companies to run. I snort at that thought. Hell, maybe I don't. I could still go down for my father's death. The police aren't stupid. There will be an investigation. I could easily be accused.

"Okay." I hear Rachel say softly, like she wasn't expecting that to be what I needed. I know I need to play the part of the son whose father was just killed, but I can't. It's not in me. I'm not the loving son type. Never have been.

"And please reschedule my meetings," I tell her. Knowing Rachel, it's already done. She is smart and quick. I rarely have to give her direction, which I like.

"Everything through tomorrow is done, boss. I'm working on next week now." I can hear her pause. Her breath is loud and tells me she isn't done speaking. "Are you okay, Nicholas?"

No, I'm not. I'm far from okay. I don't even know what okay looks or feels like. "I will be," I tell her. Rachel also worries too much and is a people pleaser. That is probably the one thing that bothers me about her. I don't understand people pleasing. Who gives a fuck? "I'm at The Cove. Can you have a new phone delivered to me today?"

"Yes, of course. I'll have it to you within a few hours. Is there anything else?" She sounds hopeful.

"No, and Rachel"—I pause, looking for the right word— "thanks," I say, knowing I don't tell it to her enough or anyone else for that matter. Probably won't ever.

"Anytime, boss." Before I can end the call, she chimes in

again. "Um . . ." She's hesitant, which tells me she knows I don't want to hear what she's about to say, but she has to say it anyway. I roll my eyes as she says, "Teresa told me to put you through to her if you called today."

"Don't care. I don't want to talk to her today, and the last time I checked, you work for me, not her, so you don't take orders from her. Got it?" I huff out, irritated and sounding too harsh. That woman's name alone is starting to agitate me. I should have never promoted her, but I can't deny she's good at her job. Matt would have been a better choice for a vice president though. Why the hell he wouldn't take the job is beyond me.

"Yes, sir," she says, and I can hear the laughter behind it. Rachel isn't as easily offended by my tones or moods. "Expect a new phone shortly," she adds as I click off the phone and end the call.

Setting it down on the counter, I grab my glass and toss it back in one gulp. So much for the sipping method.

"Figured you could use another." I hear and look in front of me. Sam is standing with another glass, a bigger glass of whiskey than the one I just killed.

"Thanks," I say as I take it from him.

"Saw the news." He grabs the empty glass and puts it on the counter behind him. I take a large sip and then look up to meet his stare.

"And what did the news say?" I ask, partly because I need to know and partly because I know Sam isn't going to shut up. And maybe I don't want him to. It's the reason I came down here in the first place. Sam is chatty, a great distraction.

"That the good judge was found dead, washed up on a beach not far from a pretty little junior District Attorney's condo." He smirks.

"Is that an observation, or was Harper Douglas's name thrown out into the media?" She's been my father's mistress for

31

a long time. Since she was in law school, to be exact. I wonder what my mother now thinks about the man she loved and took abuse from. He didn't love her. He didn't love any of us. Not that he loved Harper, either. He only loved that she allowed him to hurt her physically. Whacked bitch.

"Not my observation. Some mousy reporter on Channel 5 put it together from what I heard," he offers. "So any ideas on who did it?"

Fucker. He's trying to goad me. He knows I hate my father. Hell, he's probably standing here wondering if I hate him so much to do something like that. Yes, apparently, I do. Serves me right for getting hammered in this bar on more than a few occasions

"No," I say and take another sip from my glass.

"Well, in that case, new topic. How much more do you need to drink before you agree to sell The Cove to me?" And here it is. Our typical conversation. He wants to own my hotel. If the old timer only knew, at this rate, I'd give the place to him so it was one thing off the list of endless shit on my plate.

"How much, and bring me a fresh one? This one's about to be gone," I say as I tip up the half glass of whiskey and swallow the contents down. I concentrate on the fire I feel from my neck down into my stomach. It quickly passes, but it feels good. So good I think I want to do it again.

"Why don't I leave the bottle here?" Sam says as he sets it next to my drink. Smart man, but at this rate, I'm not going to last more than a few hours. Perhaps that's best. If I'm passed out, I can't think about my father, Shannon, or the baby.

The baby. There's a kid inside her. My kid. How the hell am I supposed to be a dad? Let alone a good one.

I glance up, giving Sam a "well, I'm waiting" look.

"What?" he asks.

"How much?" I force out through clenched teeth. "You want

to buy my hotel, then how much are you willing to pay for the fucking place?" Sam may be a bartender, but it's not to make a living. He does this job for fun. I'd be willing to bet the old fuck has more money than I do. I'd be surprised if he didn't tip the scale at billionaire status.

"Nicholas, you're not serious, so who the fuck cares? If you're looking for a distraction, you have it in front of you." Sam glances down at the alcohol in front of me. I smirk as I pick the glass up and take a healthy sip.

"Perhaps, but who's to say I'm not being serious?" Am I being serious, or am I just jacking with the middle-aged man standing in front of me? At first, I think I was curious much he's willing to pay, but as I sit here eyeing him, I don't know anymore. Something feels right about this idea. Sam's been trying to get me to sell it to him for almost two years now. So why now do I want to do it?

Shannon?

The baby?

Maybe, but hell, it's not like I can run a business if I'm in prison. Selling is probably the best option. This place is more of a hobby anyway. Lockhart Publishing is my pride and joy. My dream after my first dream was cut short.

"Because you're not, and we both know it." Sam sighs, bringing me out of my thoughts. "This isn't some game for me, Nicholas. I do want this place." He gestures around the bar with his arm. Like I don't know he's serious. He's the only person I'd even consider selling to.

"Well then, let me put it this way, old man. It's the only time I'll ever entertain the idea. So if you do actually want this place," I say, emphasizing the last word and gesturing around the room as he did a moment ago, "then now is the time for you to speak. How much, Sam? I won't ask again."

He looks at me for a minute without speaking, like he's trying to gauge my reaction. His eyebrows pull together, and he briefly looks down. When he looks back up, he says, "Why now?"

"Why not now?" I counter, bringing my glass back up to my lips and tipping the liquid back, draining the last drops before going to pour myself another.

Before I can grab the bottle, Sam reaches for it and then takes my glass from me as he stares me in the eyes. I'm guessing he's trying to decide just how serious I am. If he knows me at all, he knows this is his only opportunity. After a beat, resolve shines through his brown eyes. He down-casts them, pours me a hefty drink, and slides it in front of me. I pick it up and take a sip. And I wait.

"Okay, then. What do you want?" he asks a few moments later.

"No. I asked you how much you were willing to pay. Now, I want to hear it." My voice is firm. It shouldn't be, considering everything I've drunk today, but it is and I'm rolling with it. This is keeping my mind off all the other shit. I need this. It's working better than the whiskey.

"So," he drags out, "you're actually serious?"

Christ, have mercy.

"Yes," I bark. "So your ass better throw out a fucking number sometime soon, or the offer is off the table. Is that serious enough for you?" I swallow down half the contents of my glass.

"Twenty-five."

"Do not insult me," I say harshly. Sam's smart. He knows to start low, but twenty-five million is way too low for this place. I'm a realistic man. I know I will never get the seventy million dollars it's worth, but I also know he wants The Cove, so he'll pay. I also know the set amount I'm willing to accept, but this back-and-forth is the distraction I desperately need.

"Fine. Forty. It's a good offer for all this," he says and gestures around the room again.

"Try again." I take another sip. He sighs heavily. More dramatically than necessary.

"Fifty," he spits out at me. He looks as though he's getting angry. I like angry.

"You're doing great. Keep going," I tell him in a condescending tone, purposely trying to push his buttons.

"I'm not paying more than fifty." He almost shouts it at me, causing a few heads to turn. I want to laugh for the first time today, but I don't. I keep my face hard.

"Sure you are. You're going to pay sixty and not a penny less."

"What the fuck?" he mumbles, almost to himself, and I know I have him. He'll pay it. If he wants it like he says he does, anyway. I stay silent. This is what I'm good at. I read people well. I know how to get them to do what I want because I know how and when to push.

I can see the wheels turning over in Sam's mind. He's weighing it out. Finally, his eyes snap to mine, and I smirk at the same time he says, "Deal."

I pick up my glass and swallow down the last half. "Have your lawyer draw up the contracts. Send them to Rachel, and she'll handle the rest."

A FEW HOURS LATER, SAM IS NOWHERE TO BE FOUND, AND I'M PAST drunk. I haven't eaten a thing all day, and I know at this rate, I'll put Shannon's little pass-out performance a few months ago to shame. I need to leave. I just don't know how the fuck to get off this stool and up to the top floor.

Some scrawny kid I've never seen before dropped off my new cell phone twenty minutes ago. At least I don't think I've ever seen him. Then again, it's been a while since I've been this wasted. I've been sitting here since the kid left, staring at

Shannon's name in my contact list. When I turned it on, everything was the same as the old one. Rachel is great like that. She always takes care of anything I ask of her and tends to go a step further.

It's Shannon's birthday. I need at least to acknowledge it. Show her I'm not a total dick. But I am, and I know it. I walked out. She tells me she's pregnant and I leave. I was already resolved in my decision. I was leaving. Not because I wanted to, but because I knew it was better. Better for her. Better for our baby. They deserve more. They deserve better than me. I close my eyes, picturing her face when she knew I was walking away. She looked crushed, shocked even. I'm glad I never turned around after she told me the news. I knew if I did, I'd fall. I'd have fallen at her feet and begged her to forgive me for everything. But I don't want her to know. She can't find out. Not ever.

Yes, I'm a coward—a guilty piece of shit coward—that's what I am.

Just before I open my eyes again, a strong, firm hand grips me lightly squeezing between my neck and shoulder on my right side. Normally, anyone who grabs me like that would be laid out on the floor by now. But I know Jase like I know myself. He's been like a brother since the first day of kindergarten. He knows how to handle me better than anyone. Better than my sister even.

"Took you long enough," I breathe out as he releases his grip and takes a seat next to me at the bar. He flags Tabitha, indicating he wants a drink.

I knew Jase would show eventually. He always does.

"You needed time to cool off. You needed time to drown." He eyes the half-empty bottle of liquor in front of me and then turns his face in my direction. "And it looks like you're there."

"What will it be tonight, love?" Tabitha asks Jase as she eyes him up and down hungrily. This is nothing unusual. Jase is hit on everywhere we go. He's often mistaken for a rock star rather than an MMA fighter with his tattoos poking out from his clothes. It's how he got his nickname, Rockstar, early in his fighting career. If the girls could only see all the ink underneath his clothes, they'd probably cream their panties. Girls like tattoos. Not sure why, but they do, and Jase is covered. His opponents often find themselves distracted by all the ink, me included, and I've been with him when he's received every ink mark on his flesh.

"I'll have whatever he's having, I guess," he tells her. Tabitha pulls out a clean tumbler and fills it. She smiles but doesn't wait for a thank you before she turns to leave. Good thing because getting a "thank you" from Jase is about as easy as getting one from me.

"Want to talk about it?" he asks, and I pull my head in his direction.

"What the fuck do you think?" I say flatly. "You take care of my dog?" I ask as an image of Niko lying in a pool of blood on Shannon's doorstep enters my mind.

The bastard killed my dog. I failed him too.

"I took care of it last night. He's buried in your backyard." That's what best friends do. They take care of your shit without you having to ask because they just know what to do. And they don't need a thank you for it either.

"You owe your sister a fucking apology," he starts, but I quickly cut him off.

"Leave it alone," I say through clenched teeth. "She's my sister. She fucked up, and she knows it."

"Maybe, but she didn't deserve the way you treated her."

"Drop it, Jase. I'm not going to ask again. Nikki and I will be fine. We always are. You also know I'll apologize when I'm damn good and ready, but that isn't today." And he knows this. But I know why he's pushing the issue. The same reason I'd be all over his ass if he had done what I did. She's his. She always has been.

And no one hurts what is yours. No one. Not even your best friend and brother.

He stares at me. I can see it in his eyes. He'd love nothing more than to beat the shit out of me right now. And he could if he wanted to. Not because I'm drunk as shit, but because he's the better fighter. I can beat Jase on a good day, but not if he puts his all into it. Not if it's a real fight. There's no one else I'd rather have at my back, even if we constantly want to kill each other over my sister. She is his, but she's mine too. And no one hurts my baby sister. The look in his eyes right now is the same one I've given him countless times.

He tips the contents of his drink back in one gulp, and he waves for another. Doesn't he see the bottle in front of him? He can fix his own glass.

I wave Tabitha off as she saunters over. Grabbing his glass from the counter, I pour the remainder of the liquid in the bottle into his tumbler and push it back in his direction, spilling a small amount in my jerky movements.

"Finish it quickly. I need to get out of here."

"Then let's go, brother," he says, and once again, turns it up and downs it like a shot. Hopping off the stool, he waits for me.

Yeah right. Like it's that easy. *I've been here for a while, dickhead.*

"Let's go, lush," he laughs as he grabs my arm and pulls me off, wrapping my arm around his neck for support. The look of wanting to see my face under his boot is forgotten.

Jase maneuvers us out of the bar and to the elevator with ease. He's done this on more than one occasion. He's done this a lot, actually, but rarely ever here. I don't like to get drunk in my own hotel.

Once in my penthouse, he pushes me onto the couch in the center of the room and starts to walk off. "Ass fuck," I mumble under my breath.

"Want another?" I know he's talking about alcohol.

"What the fuck do you think?" I say to him for a second time tonight as I try to right myself. The last thing I want is to sober up. The last thing I want to do is think. But that's exactly what I can't seem to stop doing. Except everything is jumbled and flying at me too fast.

Leaning my head back against the top of the couch cushion, I inhale deeply and close my eyes. *Shannon.* I can picture her beautiful face anytime I shut my eyes.

I left.

She told me she was pregnant, and like the asshole I am, I continued out the door.

I'm a dick.

No, I'm worse than that, but what else could I have done? She deserves more. She deserves better. I've done nothing except cause pain on top of pain. She just doesn't know to what degree. And I don't want her to. It's selfish, and I know I need to tell her everything, but I don't think I can. She already has too much to deal with.

A shadow passes over my face, so I open my eyes. Jase is standing in front of me, his hand outstretched, holding a small glass of dark amber liquid. I lean forward, and my head spins a little, but I grab the glass, bring it to my lips and tip it back. I only take a small sip. It won't take much more to push me over the edge and into oblivion. My goal.

Jase turns and sits in a chair next to the couch. He leans back and crosses one leg over his knee. He stares. He waits. He sips.

He's waiting for me to talk. He knows if he pushes, it'll only piss me off and unleash a whole lot of hell. Well, screw that. I don't need to talk. I want to forget. In reality, I realize I'm only ignoring things. But that's what I do. I thought if I ignored my father's ways long enough, it would go away.

It didn't.

It got Shannon hurt. No, it got my girl raped. Raped by my own father. Everything in life has consequences. The messed-up part is you never find out what they are until it's too late. You can't go back and change a damn thing. I wish the son of a bitch were still alive so I could beat the life out of him again.

"So," Jase starts, bringing me out of my thoughts. He sighs deeply and takes another sip. "What did it feel like?" he asks, and I know exactly what he means.

Fuck me.

Jase knows me better than anyone. I know he's often wanted to do the same thing to his dad. Not for the same reason, but he hates his dad just as I've always hated mine. He won't, though. He may hate the man, but he also loves him, and that's our difference. I didn't love my father. I don't remember ever loving him.

"How did what feel?" I huff out. I'm only prolonging the inevitable. I know I'm going to tell him. He knows I'm going to as well. I tell this motherfucker everything. I always have.

"Don't" is all he says. His voice is laced with irritation. Jase isn't one to walk around a subject. He's to the point. Straight forward. You always know where you stand with him.

I sit there for about a minute, simply eyeing my best friend. *Ah . . . fuck it.*

"It felt great. It was like all my anger, frustration, and hate poured out into every goddamn punch. I wish I could kill him again just so I could release it all over again. Afterward, I felt awful. I wish I could take it back. What do you want me to tell you, Jase? My head is beyond fucked up right now, man."

I silently scream inside my head as I yank on the strands of my hair.

"I don't regret it, but I do. He hurt her. What was I supposed to do?" I say, although it's more of a statement than a question. "You would have done the same thing if it had been Nikki."

"Yes, I would have," he tells me as a more serious expression crosses his face while his eyes lock on mine. His look tells me he still wants to beat the shit out of me for the way I spoke to my sister earlier today. I can't blame him. I'd do the same thing, and I have. But she betrayed me by keeping something that huge from me. I don't care what her reasons were. I don't care if she thought she was doing the right thing. Yeah, deep down I get it. I get why. I know it was Shannon's story to tell, but fuck that. If I had known, my father couldn't have hurt her a second time. And for that reason, I'm angry with my sister.

"Nikki had no right keeping that from me. She's my sister, goddamn it. She should have told me." I say as my body heats from within. My free hand balls into a fist automatically. I'm pissed. Don't get me wrong, I'd never hit Nikki or any woman, but that doesn't mean I don't want to hit something. It's the only way to release the anger, the pent-up frustration, all the hate inside me.

Trying to contain myself, I take a deep breath and down the contents of my glass. My fist releases, and I take another breath.

"I don't disagree with you," he sighs, but then his voice turns firm. "But goddammit, brother, she feels responsible. She thinks if she had told you, then James wouldn't have been able to . . ." He pauses and looks down. I know he doesn't want to say it. Probably because he knows there's a chance it will set me off. "Do what he did."

"Rape her," I bite out, saying the words he wouldn't. "That's what he did to her," I yell out as I jump off the couch. My intent is to get in his face. I just need a reason to hit him. I want to hit something. I need a release.

But that isn't what happens. As soon as I stand, I falter. Trying to catch myself before I fall, my glass slips out of my hands and lands all over Jase, who never flinched until the liquid hit his shirt.

"What the fuck?" he shouts and leaps out of his chair, only to push me back on the couch.

And I laugh. My rage settles and is replaced with a smile I'm failing to contain.

Jase stares down at me as he pulls his now-soaked shirt over his head. "Fuck you."

"Sorry, man."

"Like hell you are. Fuck off," he spits as he turns and heads for my bedroom. I hear the shower turn on a moment later, followed by the door slamming.

Looking over to the chair Jase was sitting in, I see there isn't a drop of liquid on the furniture. At least I managed to get it all on him and not the soft fabric of my chair. I chuckle for a moment before my thoughts filter back and a hard expression replaces that smile.

Shaking my head, I push myself off the couch. I stand there for a few seconds to make sure I'm able to walk. Once I feel sure, I set off on a slow path to my kitchen for another round.

Finally, I make my way there and go straight for the liquor cabinet; since I'm sure I left the good stuff in the bathroom earlier today. Knowing Jase, he probably found it with the bottle damn near empty. Opening the cabinet door, I eye an unopened bottle of Elijah Craig 18 year and smile. That's exactly what I want. I reach for it, pull it down, and quickly open it.

Taking a swig, I walk over and grab a tall, clean glass from the cabinet. Setting the bottle down, I walk over to the ice maker, quickly grabbing the refrigerator door handle so I don't fall. Standing there for a moment, I place my forehead on the cold metal of the stainless steel. Once I'm certain I can stand without needing something to brace myself against, I step back and place my glass up to get ice. I add a small amount of water to take the bite off the alcohol.

Walking back over to the counter, I grab the bottle and pour it in until it reaches the top rim of the glass. I sip and walk over to a barstool on the other side of the granite island.

Jase walks through the doorway freshly showered, barefoot, and wearing a pair of my blue jeans and one of my black T-shirts. As expected, he holds up a now-empty bottle of The Famous Grouse Scottish Oak Finish. I gesture with my eyes to the bottle of whiskey I just opened. Jase walks over and retrieves it before joining me. He slides onto a stool off to my side and takes a large sip. Jase rarely needs water or anything added to his whiskey. He likes it straight. When Jase wants to get wasted, he doesn't waste time. He goes all in, just like he does everything from his fights to trying to make my sister his wife. I just don't know if that will ever happen for them.

We sit in silence. Me sipping my drink and looking off into space, looking at nothing and thinking about everything, and Jase, well, he's more or less just chugging liquor.

I take another sip as he tosses something small onto the granite countertop. Once I realize what it is, I cut a hard look at him and grab the small velvet box. I don't open it. I don't have to. I already know what's inside. I've had it for the past six weeks. Well, Jase has had it for the past six weeks. If I had kept it, I would have asked her to marry me the afternoon I first walked into her gallery.

"Is there a reason you brought this tonight?" I ask, knowing damn well what point he's about to make. I know Jase as well—if not better—than I know myself.

"You know what your problem is?" It's more of a statement than a question. I train my eyes on the wall directly in front of me, waiting to hear the line of bullshit about to spill out of his mouth. "You don't appreciate all the good shit you have."

"The fuck!" I shout as I turn my heated eyes on him and slam the box on the hard surface of the island.

"You don't, and you know it, brother. You know I would kill

to be in your shoes right now." And here it goes. The reason my best friend is trying to get as drunk as I am right now. My sister. Everything always comes back to Nikki and her inability to commit. "If you'd ask her," he says, gesturing to the box clutched in my hand, referring to Shannon. "She'd say yes, and you'd have everything you want. Her. A kid. A happily ever fucking after." He spits the last sentence out, and I almost want to laugh at the ridiculousness of it.

There is no happily ever after for us. There never was. I just didn't know it until last night. I've messed everything up beyond repair. There's no undoing any of it. I've lived most of my life questioning if there was a God. I thought if there was, then a man like my father wouldn't have existed. But if the Devil exists, then there must be a God too. And if so, I have a lot of sins to pay for.

"Get rid of this. It isn't going to happen." I toss the box in his direction, hitting him in the chest with it, but Jase is quick. He scoops it up before it lands on the countertop.

"You're so stupid sometimes," Jase whispers as he slowly shakes his head from side to side.

"Fuck you!" I state as I toss the rest of my alcohol down my throat. The burning effect is long gone. Now there's only a dull, numb feeling in my head. This . . . this is the feeling I wanted.

I rip the bottle of whiskey from his hands, bringing it to my lips and downing the contents. As long as I have this, as long as I feel nothing, the guilt that consumes my every thought isn't there.

CHAPTER FOUR

A loud sound jars me awake. My eyes fly open, and the sunlight stings, causing me to shut them quickly. Opening my eyes slowly, I realize I'm in my bed at The Cove, lying on my stomach. As I rise to my forearms, I notice a wet spot on my pillow where I obviously drooled. *Nice.*

"Stop moving, fuck-head." I hear to my right as Jase's voice penetrates my now-pounding skull. Not that it matters. My head hasn't stopped hurting for two days now. The events of last night start to come back to me as the door to my bedroom swings open, hitting the wall behind it and making a loud thud. I look up to see my sister standing in the entryway with her hands on her hips. She looks pissed.

"Did you two ass-fucks have a fun fucking night?"

Great. This is exactly what I want to deal with this morning. At least I'm assuming it's morning, but who knows? I slowly push myself up and sit on the edge of the bed. Ignoring my sister, I look around, searching for my phone.

"Head's up," Nikki says, and as I turn to look at her, she is tossing something in my direction, but I'm not quick enough to reach out and grab it before it lands on the bed next to me. Looking down, it's my phone. "Try answering it once in a while, would ya?"

"I'll answer it when I'm good and ready," I say, pinning her with a stare and trying to remember why I ever gave her a key to this place, but then Nikki has a key to everything of mine. "And don't throw my phone. I just replaced the son of bitch yesterday." Picking it up, I see I have a heap of missed calls and text messages.

"Can't you people pipe the fuck down or go into another fucking room?"

I look behind me at Jase, who now has a pillow covering his head. I'd roll my eyes, but what's the point? He can't see me. The last time I checked, this was my bedroom.

Nikki pushes herself off the doorframe and walks over to Jase's side of the bed. "Get up, babe."

The second she gets it out of her mouth, Jase reaches out, pulling her onto the bed and rolling on top of her.

"Oh, come the fuck on," I say as I jump up. This is not what I need to see, and certainly not in my bed, either. "You two can take that shit the fuck home," I shout as I make my way to the bathroom for a quick shower.

Slamming the door behind me, I walk over and turn the shower faucet to hot. As I wait for it to heat, I discard my clothes and get in the shower. I stand there for a few minutes letting the hot water soak into my skin.

Once thoroughly clean and fresh, I head out of the bathroom. Jase is pulling a T-shirt over his head while my sister is walking back into the room.

"Mind telling me what this is about?" She walks up to me and hands me a thick manila envelope. I take it and toss it on the bed as I head into the closet to dress.

It's got to be the contract and check for the purchase of The Cove. Sam is quick. I'll give him that, and I didn't doubt for a second that he was serious. He wants all of this, and I don't anymore. At this point, I need to inform my staff before he does. It needs to come from me, not him. They are all loyal and deserve to know what's going on immediately.

Once I've dressed in a pair of jeans, a white T-shirt, and boots, I walk back out of the closet. My sister is eyeing me, clearly waiting for an explanation.

"Get off his ass, Nikki," Jase tells her. Then he turns his eyes on me. "Drag your ass to Knocked Out. You need a release. You need to pound that shit out."

"Give me an hour, and I'll be there." Walking over to my bed, I pick up the envelope and open it. I purposely don't look at my sister, although I feel her eyes on me. Jase walks out, and a few seconds later, I hear her let out a dramatic sigh, but she turns and follows him.

Picking up my phone, I open my contacts and scroll down until I find the number to my general manager's office. Once he answers, I request a meeting with as many people who can be pulled off their duty to be in the large community room on the second floor in thirty minutes.

Once I hang up, I sit on the bed and review the paperwork. As expected, my lawyer, along with Rachel, has indicated notes for me to read before signing. Once I have checked over everything, I sign the pages that require a signature. Mainly I want to make sure the amount of the check is right and the ownership of this penthouse remains mine. Both are here, so I'm satisfied.

Once I'm done, I look at my phone and see it's time to head for the meeting. I type out a quick text to Rachel as I walk out.

Me: Documents signed. I'll be at Knocked Out within an hour. Come get them. YOU. Not someone else.

I don't trust someone else with that amount of money. I'll be damned if I hand over a sixty-million dollar check to some random errand boy. My phone chimes seconds later.

Rachel: Sure, boss.

AN HOUR LATER, I PARK MY CAR IN FRONT OF KNOCKED OUT. REACHING behind my seat, I retrieve my gym bag from the floorboard along with the envelope holding the signed paperwork to give Rachel before climbing out of my silver Audi R8.

To say my staff was shocked is putting it mildly. No one was upset, but they were all comfortable with how I ran things. My employees are loyal and not used to change.

Making my way up the stairs, I take them two at a time until I reach the glass door. I enter and immediately see my assistant chatting with my sister off to the side of the steel cage that takes up a large space in the middle of the gym's first floor. My fists are itching to get inside there. There's nothing like the feel of pounding another person's flesh to relieve the tension stretched tight across my body.

My sister glances up when I walk behind Rachel, and I meet her blue stare briefly before she quickly looks back to my assistant. Rachel turns, her warm chocolate eyes connecting with mine.

"Hey, boss." She's the only person who calls me boss, and she uses it more often than she does Nicholas. It used to drive me crazy, and if it were anyone else, I'd have strangled them long ago, but like everything else with Rachel, the term has grown on me. Don't think I don't know why she does it. She fully knows it used to irritate the shit out of me.

"Everything is signed, including the check, so handle it," I tell her as I pass the manila envelope to her. She takes it and stuffs it into an enormous pink and purple purse. I swear I don't understand women. How much stuff does one person need to lug around with them on a daily basis? A man only needs keys, a phone, and a wallet to serve all our needs.

"Where's Jase?" I inquire as I turn to face Nikki, successfully dismissing Rachel. She quickly takes her cue and mumbles a "catch you later" to my sister right before she turns and leaves.

"Don't you think we should discuss what you just did?"

"No, I don't. So where is he? I need to hit something, and your man's face is just that something," I say, trying to get her off the subject. It's really none of my sister's concern what I do and don't do. It's about time she learned that, but I know that will never happen. Nikki will always insert herself into everything I do. She's been my shadow since the moment she learned to crawl, and the truth is, I like it that way.

"Nick," she sighs. "We need to talk. Can we go to my office?" She places her hands on her hips. "Please, it's important," she stresses, making me certain this is one conversation I do not want to have today.

"No," I roar a little too loudly, causing a few fighters' heads to turn in our direction. Great. A scene, just what I need right now. Can she not see that I need to be left alone?

Without waiting for her to say another word, I turn and head for the locker room to change clothes. As I make my way to the back, I pull my phone out of my pocket and shoot off a quick text to Jase.

Me: I'm here. Meet in 5.

Not more than a few seconds later comes his reply.

Jase: On my way down the stairs.

Entering the locker room, I set my bag on a wooden bench and quickly start changing. After placing my belongings inside my locker, I put on my signature black shorts and wrap athletic tape around my hands, then slide red gloves on. Now I just have to get my head on straight and in the zone.

"Hey, man." I hear and quickly turn to see Shane approaching the lockers, a white towel wrapped around his waist.

"Hey," I mumble as I shove my gym bag into my locker and close the door.

"I heard about your dad. I'd say I'm sorry, but I doubt you are, so no point, right?" he chuckles. He doesn't know much about my relationship with my father, only that I hated the man.

"Yeah," I reply and leave without another word. My father is the last person I want to think about right now. The thought of him will only make me angrier. That is the one emotion I can't seem to shed. I thought hurting him, ending him, would make all my feelings cease to exist, but they didn't. If anything, my hate and anger have intensified, and I'm at a loss as to what to do about it.

Once I'm back in the main room, I look over to the steel cage and see my friend already inside. He's waiting for me, but I can tell his mind is on something else, or someone else rather. If it were anyone else, I'd get involved, but it's my sister. It's always my sister, and that's where I have to draw the line. I can't take sides. Well, that's not true. Nikki will always come before my best friend. But I can't talk out his problems about her with him. I wish I could, but I can't. I can't even help myself with relationships. Which is why I never wanted one. Not until Shannon, that is.

God, I am a sorry bastard. Even she probably realizes that by now. Who walks out on their girl when she tells them she's pregnant?

Me, apparently.

Entering the ring, I take a deep breath. Every time I've ever entered an octagon cage, or hell, even a boxing ring, there is this moment, a split second of peace that washes over me—starting at my head and flowing all the way to my toes. I love this feeling. It's even better than all the adrenaline that follows seconds later.

The clang of the bell signals us to start. This isn't a real fight, but we spar as though it is.

I never rush. I'm never the one to throw the first punch, swing, or kick, but today isn't a normal day.

Jase isn't expecting it when I throw out the first swing, but he's good. I can see the surprise in his eyes as he pulls back and then shoots out a kick to my ribs that I successfully block.

"You can do better than that, Lockhart." Jase always wants to have a conversation. Anyone else, and he wouldn't be speaking until he wipes the floor with them, but with me, he always wants to chat. With me, he never wears a mouthguard, and neither do I.

"Shut the fuck up." And I take another swing and miss. Jase smiles. He does this because it will piss me off. Jase is a master at goading me.

"Well, that's not going to happen," he replies, and I try for another kick, but once again I'm blocked.

I charge him, pushing him back against the cage, and follow with a punch to his ribs. Jase pushes against me and counter-moves as he swipes his right calf behind me, knocking me to the ground. He's quick and on top of me a second later. Trying to go for a headlock, I twist, and I'm on top of him, wrapping my legs tight around his waist. I hit him on the side of the head as he flips me over. We tangle together on the ground for a few moments, then the sound of the bell has us both releasing immediately.

We both jump to our feet and take a breather. Closing my eyes briefly, I stretch my arms wide and crack my neck before rolling it from side to side. Thirty short seconds later comes another bell, and he and I are locked back up.

"You're going to need to do better than that, brother," rolls from Jase's lips. We both breathe shallowly now, but I manage to jab him a few times in the ribs.

"Are you planning on shutting that pretty little mouth of yours today?"

"Nope." And with that comes a swift kick to my ribs that sucks all the air out of my lungs momentarily. It's enough to make me charge my friend and lay him out on the ground with a punch to the jaw, followed by a knee to the gut. I continue to pound him until he manages to swing his legs up and push me off.

Once Jase is on his feet, he charges me, pushing me into the cage. I take a few knees to my gut, but I can't get a tight grip on him to push him off. The bell sounds, and he releases me and backs up. I push myself off the thin, hard steel behind me.

The tightness and tension in my body are lessening. I feel lighter already. This is what it always feels like. Fighting is the relief I need. It makes me forget, even if it's only for a few moments, but I feel free. I feel alive, along with a load of pain in my left rib cage. The pain is what makes me feel alive. I love it. Fucked up, I know, but it feels so good.

The bell sounds again, signaling the start of our last round. Jase comes at me hard, but I step and swing my right fist, successfully landing a blow under his jaw. He counters and lands the same punch on me, followed by a kick to my leg. Moments later, we are once again tied up on the ground, both trying to get a punch in.

Jase's grip slips, allowing me to take advantage by wrapping my arm around his neck. He strains and tries to buck, but I have him where I want him. I'm wrapped as tight around him as possible, and with my left fist, I lay into his left side a few times.

Sweat pours in rivers off both of us, and with that comes his chance to take advantage. He slips an arm out and flips over, forcing me on my back, where he gets in a few punches to each of my sides.

We are lost in each hit thrown. The last round ends with the ringing of the bell, and we both reluctantly stop. Jase rolls over on the mat on his back, breathing hard. We lie here, both coming down from our high, the adrenaline still running strong in both of us.

"You need to stop acting like a little bitch-ass pussy and go see your girl." Jase huffs out.

"Can you stay out of my shit for once?" I bite out.

"No, I can't. You need to fix that shit before it's too late."

"It's already too late. Don't you get that?" I say as I hop up on both feet. The calm I felt a moment ago is gone the second Jase opens his mouth.

"Since when are you a quitter?" he shouts back as he pulls himself to his feet. He's not standing long before I walk over and land a fist to his mouth, which knocks him on his ass.

"Fuck you," I spit before turning and leaving the cage. I make a beeline for the locker room before my sister has a chance to pounce. I need a cold shower to stop the smoke I'm sure is pouring off my body.

That motherfucker is always pushing me. I walk through the door and head straight to the showers. I turn on the water and quickly shed my clothes before entering the freezing water.

Sometimes, I question why I'm even friends with him. A day doesn't go by where we aren't arguing like two bitches. Why I ever entertained the idea of marriage when I've had a wife since kindergarten is beyond me. He's enough fucking drama in my life.

Turning off the water, I grab a clean towel and wrap it snug around my waist as I make it over to my locker to retrieve the clothes I had on earlier. Once I'm dry and dressed, I run my hands through my hair a few times. The technique Shannon uses seems to relieve the pressure in my head, but when I do it, nothing.

I miss holding my woman in my arms. The moment I found her lying on the floor in her closet and she jumped into my arms was like coming home for the first time. There's nothing like the feel of her against me. Too bad it was short-lived.

I make my way out to the main floor and walk over to where I see Nikki. As I get closer, I can hear her conversation with Shane. He's asking her about the pending funeral. I stop in front of Nikki and look down at the man staring holes into my head from the bench he's sitting on. Jase is pissed. I'd be pissed too if he sucker-punched me.

"Hello?" I turn away from Jase to see Shane looking at me like he's expecting something.

"What?" I demand.

"I asked if your woman was going to be back in time for your father's funeral." No way would Shannon get near that man again. Dead or alive I don't give a shit. No way in hell would I want her at his funeral. Not that she would mourn him, but still. It takes me a second, and then I realize he said something about her being back.

"What do you mean by 'if she's going to be back?'" I question and cut my eyes to my sister. Is that what she was trying to tell me? "Where is she?" I turn back to Shane, who obviously knows more about Shannon than I do right now, which doesn't sit well with me. The tension I finally released is starting to form again.

"Uh, Vegas is what Katie mentioned to me this morning," he says as he backs away as if he's expecting me to blow up. Maybe with the look I'm giving him, he should be worried.

"Why the fuck is she in Las Vegas?" I shout.

"Dude, maybe you need to ask her that," he tells me.

What the hell?

"Well, I'm asking you since you seem to know more than I

do." My voice is rising and we're getting a few looks in our direction.

"I'm sorry I said anything, okay?"

I take a deep breath and feel my sister place her palm on my forearm. Believe it or not, she does usually help calm me down this way. She's been doing it since we were kids, and even though I'm still pissed at Nikki, I can never stay mad at her for anything.

"Look, just tell me what you know." My voice is softer, well, as soft as I can force it to be when I want to strangle something.

"Katie said she was going there for a few days. Something about going to see a doctor. Seemed a bit weird, but whatever. Chicks do weird things."

A doctor? Why would she go to another state when every doctor imaginable can be found in Los Angeles? Unless . . . No, she wouldn't. Would she?

"What?" Nikki whispers. When I look at her, I can tell she's arrived at the same thought I have, but there's something else behind her eyes. I'm not certain I want to know from the look she's giving me. Her blue eyes widened as if she mentally said, *"Oh, shit."*

What now? I don't know if I can take more from her.

"Nikki," I say slowly, my voice stern. She releases my arm and takes off toward the stairs. "Come back here," I force out through clenched teeth as I follow her. She rounds the stairs and starts to run up them. When I finally make it up and into her office, she grabs her cell phone.

"Why did she go to Las Vegas?" My sister doesn't answer. Jase walks up behind her a few seconds later.

"Answer him, Nikki," Jase orders. She looks up and meets my eyes.

"I don't know." She tosses her phone onto her desk and falls into her chair.

"Mind telling me why you have a guilty look on your face right now?" I shout as I place my palms flat on her small wooden desk and train my eyes on hers.

She looks away, and I know she's holding something back. There's something she doesn't want to tell me, but she's going to one way or the other. This is the second time in the last twenty-four hours that I've wanted to kick my sister's ass.

"Nikki, don't make me tell you again," Jase says from behind me. His voice is laced with heat. If there were any other time he used that tone with her, I'd probably lay him out.

"I'm sorry, Nick." Every time she fucks up, she starts with "I'm sorry." I'm going to kill her. What did she do this time?

"Cut the 'I'm sorry' bullshit and tell me why Shannon went to Vegas, now!" I shout, and I'm sure everyone in the building can hear me.

"A few weeks ago, I may have told her you don't want kids. Ever."

Is she kidding me?

"What the fuck?" But it doesn't come from me. No, Jase can't even believe what just came out of Nikki's mouth. I close my eyes and try to calm down. I've really never wished harm on my sister before this moment. I grab the edge of her desk and grip it as tightly as possible. If anything happens to my kid because of my sister, I don't think I could ever forgive her. Why would she do that?

Jase places his hands on my shoulder and bicep. I can feel him shaking, but when I open my eyes, I realize it's my body that's trembling, not his.

"I'm sorry, Nick. I . . ." Her voice trails off as my eyes snap to her scared ones. Jase's grip tightens as he pulls me back off the desk and closer to him.

"Why?" I ask. "When have I ever given you that idea? Please fucking enlighten me."

"You told me a long time ago that you didn't," she whispers as tears pool in her eyes. I hate her tears. Even when I'm the one who causes them, I still can't stand seeing her cry. A small part of me wants to round the desk and pull her into my arms to stop them from spilling down her face.

"No, I did not. I told you I never wanted to bring a child into this world as long as our father was still breathing the same air. I never wanted another kid to be subjected to the same evil we were. Don't put me into the same category you do yourself. Just because you don't want kids doesn't mean I never do." And as I say that, I instantly regret it. Jase tenses and his fingers bite into my skin. The one subject he and my sister skate around I just brought home, but I can't think about that. I can't even wrap my head around what Nikki had admitted to.

Jase's grip loosens until I no longer feel his hands on me, then I hear his heavy body fall into the chair behind me.

"You need to find her right now. Don't call me until you have." And with that, I exit her office and practically run down the stairs and out the door. I have no idea where I'm going, but I have to find her. I have to stop her if . . . No, surely she wouldn't get an abortion, at least not without talking to me first.

You walked out, asshole.

You didn't give her a chance to talk, remember?

Pulling the keys out of my pocket, I press the button to unlock the door. I get in, start up the engine, and I speed off. I have no idea when she left. My phone. It dawns on me. *Call her.*

Lifting my right hand off the steering wheel, I reach down and squeeze my hand inside my pocket, pulling my phone out. I quickly find her name from my contacts and wait for her to answer. Luck isn't on my side today; it goes straight to voice mail.

"Fuck!" I shout as her voice tells me to leave a message. "Please call me," I say after waiting for the beep. Ending the call,

I quickly locate another name. Fuck driving to Vegas. I don't have a few hours. I need to find her now.

"Nicholas?" I hear on the other end of the phone. I'm sure Marcus never expected me to call him. He called twice yesterday, but if he knows me, he knows I wasn't planning on returning his call.

"I need to get to Las Vegas. I need your plane and pilot," I say, getting straight to the point.

"I'm sorry. Come again? I don't think I heard that right."

I don't have time for his shit.

"You heard correctly. Plane. Pilot. Now. And I need yours. I don't have time to schedule a flight. I need to get there now, five fucking minutes ago. Got it?" I stress.

"Why?" he questions. He's always challenging me. Why I haven't a clue, but I don't have time for this now. I need to get to Shannon. No one will stop me from finding her.

"Look, Marc . . ." I start out harsh but quickly ease up. Bullying him won't work. I know this. He's probably the only man on this earth I will bow down to. Mainly because he knows how to make me. Marc taught me everything I know about fighting, and I'm not dumb enough to think I could ever take him on. Not really, anyway. "I don't have time to explain. Shannon took off to Vegas. I need to find her. That's it, man." I pause and wait for him to respond. I can hear his breath on the other end of the line as I speed down the road. "Please," I force out, hoping that will get me what I want.

"Was 'please' that hard?"

"Fuck you."

He laughs, making me want to reach through the phone and wipe the smug smile I know he has off his face right now.

"Am I correct to assume you are already en route to the airport?" he asks, his tone more serious.

"Yes. I'll be there within twenty minutes."

"Make it ten, would you? I have a medical conference in Scottsdale in a little less than an hour. Hurry your ass up."

"Got it," I bite out and end the call. The motherfucker wants to give me a hard damn time when he's already on the plane leaving. I toss the phone on the passenger seat and accelerate hard.

CHAPTER FIVE

An hour and a half later, Marc's Citation XLS lands in Las Vegas, Nevada. You would think a thirty-minute flight from LA to Arizona wouldn't leave much room for conversation, but it did.

Marc is a talkative motherfucker. Went on and on about my father's "accident," as he called it. Then delayed his conference for another thirty minutes because he thinks I'm avoiding dealing with his death. No, I'm not. I'm the bastard who killed the man. I'm dealing with it all just peachy. Not that I can tell him that. Instead, I sat there with my tail tucked between my legs and listened. I hate listening to other people talk.

"Mr. Lockhart, would you like me to have a rental car brought here?" I look up after taking my seat belt off to see the pilot standing in front of me.

"No, but you can call a taxi," I say as I reach into my pocket to retrieve my cell phone. I quickly take it off airplane mode and call my sister. She answers on the second ring, but I don't give her a chance to speak.

"All I want to know is where she is." My tone is relatively calm considering how pissed off I am.

"Hard Rock, room 912." She sighs dramatically. And with that information, I end the call before she can start spouting off more "I'm sorry's." I'm curious how she found out so quickly, but I can't think about that. I need to get to that hotel as fast as possible.

I stand up, placing my phone into the pocket of my blue jeans as the pilot opens the door. The bright sun attacks my aching brain.

"A taxi should be here any minute, sir," he mumbles as he turns back to walk past me. I nod my head, thanking him without verbalizing it.

I exit the plane and head down the stairs just as a cab pulls up. Walking up to the taxi, I open the back door and throw myself down into the seat.

"Where to, sir?" the cab driver asks while looking at me through the rearview mirror.

"Hard Rock Hotel," I answer roughly as I realize I have no clue what I'm going to say to Shannon when I arrive. I don't have a plan. It's not like I can just knock on the door and when she opens it be like, "Hi, honey. I'm sorry I walked out on you again. I lost it, killed my father, and then at some point decided you were better off without me before you laid the mother of all bombs on me, and I freaked me the fuck out." Yeah, I'm sure that would go over well. Not with my fiery little redhead.

Within twenty or so minutes, I look out the window to see the driver turning on Paradise Road, then moments later pulling up right out front of the hotel lobby. I fumble in my back pocket for my wallet, pulling out enough bills to cover the fair and his tip, then I hand the cash over.

"Keep it," I tell him as I open the door and exit the car.

Taking a deep breath, followed by two more deep breaths that don't help, I stalk off inside the building. I've stayed at this hotel plenty of times. Vegas has always been my escape. As weird as it is, there's just something about Nevada that calms me. The air and the overall feel here are different. And this hotel, at least for the last five or six consecutive years, has been my choice to crash at.

Every single one of Jase's many tattoos was acquired in Vegas —mine too. I don't have nearly as many as he does, and I never will, but Jase leaves every trip with more. And lately, so does my sister.

Locating the elevator in the Paradise Tower, I enter and take the ride up to the ninth floor.

I still have no clue what I'm going to say.

Walking the distance to the end of the hall, I come face-to-face with a door embellished with the number 912. I want to knock. Hell, I really just want to burst right in. But I can't. Physically, I can't bring myself to knock. You would think it's such a simple movement, yet I can't do it.

Raising my arms above my head and clutching the sides of the doorframe, I lean my forehead against the door. It's cold. Not cool like you would expect, but cold. It makes my head hurt even more, but I don't care.

I don't know how long I stand here. A few seconds, maybe even a minute or two, but the door suddenly opens, and a gust of cool wind slaps me in the face as I look up to see a stunned Shannon.

"Nick." It's a disbelieving whisper. It's everything I can do to hold myself back. All I want to do is grab my girl by the waist and bury myself deep inside her. She is my home. She means everything to me. Seeing her in front of me has my breathing returning to normal again.

"We need to talk," I tell her.

"Talk?" she screeches but steps back allowing me to enter her room. I walk past her as I take in the space. It's a fairly large corner room with two of the four walls comprising floor-to-ceiling windows overlooking the pool area. I'm used to staying in one of the suites, but this is nice too.

"Now you want to talk? As soon as I leave LA, you conveniently want to talk to me? Well, you know what? Fuck you." And she walks out of the room, slamming the door.

Just great.

Perfect.

Where is she going?

I sit in a tall, plush chair next to one of the windows and wait.

And wait some more.

Hours later, I'm pacing the room. I've called her a dozen times, enough to be considered stalker crazy. Where is she? Her phone is turned off, and it's driving me mad.

Looking at the clock on the wall, I see it's nearly eight. My hands are twitchy. My damn arms and legs are twitchy. My whole body is twitchy.

Sitting forward with my elbows on my knees, I lean my throbbing head into my palms. I don't know where to go to look for her. I should've installed a GPS tracker on her phone. At least then I wouldn't be going insane wondering where she is and if she and the baby are okay. *The baby.*

God, please don't let her have done anything to the baby, thinking I didn't want the kid.

The sound of a door opening brings me out of my thoughts. In walks Shannon wearing the same black tank top, cut-off blue jean shorts, and sandals. Her eyes look worn and tired. She looks stressed, and her eyes are full of sadness. I want to go to her and take it all away.

"You're still here," she states, acting as if she is surprised. She knows damn well that if I came, I wouldn't leave until we spoke.

"Yeah. I said we needed to talk. Remember?" I know I sound annoyed and pissed and you know what? I am. Why did she take off?

At this, she laughs out loud. It's one of those bitchy laughs that chicks do.

The hell.

"Yes, Nicholas." She turns, her voice serious. She has never called me Nicholas. Not one damn time. I don't like my full name rolling off her lips. I'm not Nicholas to her. I'm Nick, damn it. "I remember. I also remember you walking out on me. Twice," she adds sarcastically.

And what do I do? I ignore it. I don't know what to say. Maybe I do, but I'm not going to. She has enough to deal with. Besides, I never want her to know. I couldn't bear it if she looked at me like she knew I could have prevented it. But I could have, and I didn't.

"Where did you go? Where have you been for the last seven hours?" I rush out as I stand up, crossing my arms over my chest and staring at her. She crosses the room, closing the distance between us. I can see as she gets closer that she is fuming mad. The fair skin on her delicate cheeks is flushed a bright red.

"Where have I been?" she mocks as she gestures to herself with her thumb.

Yeah, this isn't going to go smoothly.

"I don't see how that is any of your business anymore," she barks out. Her voice tells me she's more hurt than angry. But I stand here, not saying anything, waiting for her to tell me something.

"I had an appointment somewhere, okay? It's nothing you

need to concern yourself with," she finally tells me. As she turns away, I hold her arm softly as panic washes over me at the same time nausea engulfs me. I'm pretty sure I'm going to be sick.

"Please tell me where you went, Shannon," I beg. I've never begged a soul for anything in my life. But I've never felt the kind of fear I do at this very moment. I have to know.

I release my hold on her as I fall back into the chair I'd been sitting in for hours. Leaning forward, I place my head into my right palm and look down.

"Please," I whisper. There's silence for a few moments before I look up to see Shannon kneeling in front of me. She places her palms down on my knees. The small amount of contact shoots currents through my body, and it's the feeling, the connection I get every time we touch. I love it.

Her eyes roam all over my face before landing on my eyes. She's searching for something. What, I don't know, but the waiting, the silence, the not knowing is killing me slowly. Maybe this is the kind of death I deserve.

It's not like I ever thought much about having kids. I never dated girls in school. Sure, I fucked them. I've been having sex since I figured out why my dick got hard. But I never wanted to get close to anyone enough to want more. I never wanted to love one. Then Shannon just sort of happened out of the blue.

And love. Love doesn't even come close to describing the way I feel about Shannon. She's it. The other part of me. I didn't know what it meant to breathe or live until the day I saw her.

"Why do you need to know so badly? Why is it important?" Her voice is soft, and even though she probably still hates me, she's now more concerned about me. That's Shannon. She is too worried about everyone else and tries to please other people before she pleases herself. It's the only thing about her that bothers me. "But first, why are you staring down at my stomach?"

I glance back, meeting her eyes. I hadn't realized I was looking at anything other than her face.

"The baby. Is he? I mean . . ." Fuck. I can't make a full sentence. This is difficult. I don't even know how to ask.

"He?" she questions as she scrunches her eyebrows together. "Whoever said this thing is a he?" she asks me as she places her hand over her stomach and my face lifts.

"He's still in there?" I ask, pointing to her tank-covered belly. The hopefulness in my voice is obvious. She didn't? But then, she didn't exactly say she didn't.

"Well, they don't just go away, Nick," Shannon deadpans.

"So you didn't get rid of him?"

"I'm sorry?" she questions. Her green eyes widen as realization sets in. "You thought I . . ." She stops mid-sentence, not able to finish. "What gave you that idea? Is that what you were hoping I was doing?"

"No," I quickly state as I stand abruptly, causing Shannon to fall backward, landing on her butt.

Shit.

"Sorry," I mumble as I reach down. She takes both of my hands, lifting her to her feet and bringing her flush with my body.

"I'm fi . . ." She trails off as her eyes lift to meet mine, and her breath catches. The moment only lasts for a few seconds before she releases my hands and takes a step backward. "You thought I came here to have an abortion?"

"No. Yes. Maybe . . . Hell, I don't know. The thought crossed my mind, okay?" I hammer out. I mean, what other reason would she go out of state to see a physician? Hell, California is a big state, and she still left to come here.

"How did you know I was here? I didn't tell anyone where I was staying." She places her hands on her hips, waiting for my reply. Not that I have a good answer. Certainly, my stalker tendencies with her are showing.

"I was at the gym this morning. Shane was there. He mentioned it, and your friend told him about your planned doctor's visit. When he told me, I guess my mind went a little wild. Nothing else made sense. Why would you leave town to see a doctor unless you were, you know, and then my sister . . ." I trail off as I think of Nikki. The last person on Earth I would ever think would make me fighting mad is her. It still pisses me off. What's up with her lately?

"What about Nikki?" she questions, bringing my attention back to her.

"She said she told you I didn't want kids, and I flipped out on her again," I rush out.

"What do you mean by *again*?"

"Enough with the twenty questions. Please tell me you didn't. I need to hear you say it." Fuck me; I'm back to begging again. God, I sound like a little bitch.

"No, Nick, I did not have an abortion. I didn't even come here to see a baby doctor." She says it like it should have been obvious, and yeah, maybe it was, but I still needed to hear the words. And relief. I let myself drown in it. I haven't felt this amount of relief in days. But I still don't know why she is here.

"Then what kind of doctor did you go see? Why did you come to Las Vegas?"

"Uh-uh. First, you answer my questions, starting with the last one. Why did you lose your cool with your sister multiple times?"

For the love. I don't want to get into this. My head can't take anymore.

"Lots of reasons. Lots of reasons I don't want to get into right now. It's been a long, fucked-up and miserable couple of days for me." And I instantly regret the words that just came out of my mouth. Shit. I have a lot of damn nerve for saying that after everything she has been through. "Fuck, Shan—" But she quickly cuts me off.

"Seriously? And you think it's been peachy perfect for me?"

"I know." Wow. I can't stop myself. I should not have just said that.

"No, you don't know. You don't know what anything has been like for me. You left. You walked out of the door like it didn't matter. Like I didn't matter. Like we didn't matter to you one bit," she says the last part while placing her hand over her stomach once again.

No. That is the last thing I want to hear coming out of her mouth.

"Don't say that. I'm sorry, okay? But don't think for a minute that you don't matter to me. You matter more than anyone ever has or ever will."

"Then why did you leave me?" And right there she loses it. "You just walked out. After everything we said and everything I told you, you left. You left me. Why? From the moment I woke up that morning, I knew. I just knew. I saw you pulling away. What was it, Nick? Why did you leave me when I needed you the most?" That question guts me more than anything else in my life ever has. "You're a bastard for doing that to me, and I hate you. And the kicker to this whole mess is I hate that I hate you because I love you. Right now, I don't want to love you, but I do. I don't know how to stop loving you because you have penetrated my soul."

"You should hate me," I say as defeat takes over. She needs to hate me, but I don't want her to. Not ever. "I'll never deserve you. Not even a little bit. You deserve someone who can protect you, but that isn't me. I didn't protect you." She takes a moment, soaking my words in. Hopefully realizing I'm right. I should have prevented what happened, but I didn't. I should have protected her. I should have ended his life sooner, a long time ago.

"So you're feeling guilty. Is that it? Is that what you're trying to tell me?" Her voice is somber, and I don't want it to be. I want her to be mad. Maybe even hit me. Lord knows I deserve it.

Guilt.

Yeah, I feel guilty.

"Babe," I start as I sit back down in the chair behind me. I run my thumb and index fingers back and forth across my eyebrows, trying to iron out the headache that won't ease up on the full-out attack it's doing inside my head. I deserve it too.

"I don't feel guilty. I am guilty." I'm guilty of a lot of things. Things I don't have the balls to tell you. I should own up to my mistakes right here and now. She deserves to know the whole story, but I'm a coward. I don't want her to truly hate me. I don't want her to know it all.

Guilt. It's a real fucking bitch.

"Nick, it still hurts that you didn't give me the benefit of the doubt when you left the first time, but I get it. Really, I do." She kneels in front of me just like she did a few minutes ago, then she continues, placing her palms on my knees. "But there was nothing you could have done. Maybe there could have been if I had told you sooner, but I didn't. I thought silence was my protection, but it wasn't. Silence was my hindrance. You shouldn't blame yourself for something someone else did. You had no control over it."

"But I did, and I should have made a different choice." I stop myself before I say too much.

"Stop this, please. What happened isn't your fault, damn it," she says with force. I look down into her beautiful, pale green eyes. They remind me of a bright spring day. I love those eyes. I lift a hand and bring it across her cheek and into her hair. God, I love her hair. Just looking at it makes my dick swell, but she doesn't need that right now. Maybe not ever. This certainly isn't the time or place, even though I'd love nothing more than to bury my face in the hot, wet heat of her pussy.

"I wish I could. I wish it were that simple," I sigh as I drop my hand to my side. She drops her face for a second or two before bringing her wide eyes back to mine.

Great. She caught sight of my hard-on at the worst possible time. But hell, it's nearly impossible not to get hard when I'm near her. And when she's touching me, well, I just can't control it.

"You could try." Her tone is sad but with a hint of hope. "You could try for us?" she finishes, her eyes filled with lust.

"Is there an us?" I want there to be an *us*, but I just don't know. Even if we both want there to be an us. Sometimes, the damage is too great to be fixed. Pieces don't always go back together like they once were, no matter how hard you try. Glue doesn't really fix anything. Sure, it can mend things, but it's never going to look like it once did. I want the us we had weeks ago.

Her eyes cast down between my legs once again. It's enough to bring my cock fully alive and rock solid.

"Shannon?" I question as her hands start to move upward on my thighs. I close my eyes and lean against the soft back of the chair. I know she doesn't need this after everything she's been through, but I don't know if I can stop it. My dick would hate me for the rest of my life. Well, fuck him. If it wasn't for him, I might not have pursued her to begin with, and she would never have known me. She would never have had to face her past. She never would've had to face my father.

"Babe, you don't have to do this." She lifts my shirt to reach the belt buckle on my jeans and pulls it loose. "Shannon, you shouldn't want to do this." And it pains me to say that. If my dick had a fist, he would have just knocked me out.

"Nick, I'll never do anything I don't want to do, not ever. At least not willingly anyway," she tells me as she pops the button on my pants and then pulls down the zipper. I open my eyes to peer down at her to see if what she is saying's true. I know it is. Shannon is strong. Shannon is defiant. She marches to her own drum.

"There's still a lot we need to talk about, and I mean a lot, but I want this." She looks up at me. "I don't know yet about sex, regular sex, but I know I need this. I need you. And right now, I need you in my mouth."

No sane or crazy man would ever say no to that. As she grips the waistband of my jeans, I lift to allow her to pull them down. She doesn't stop there. She proceeds to take off my boots too.

"I want it all off." She gestures to my shirt, and I thought only men thought this way. I quickly grab the hem of my T-shirt and pull it over my head before tossing it to the floor.

I sit naked in front of Shannon, and she stares at my package like it's a chocolate sundae she wants to devour. She's staring at my junk the same way I look at her pretty little wet pussy before I suck her dry.

She glances up at me as she reaches forward, taking my dick and wrapping her warm palm around my shaft. She licks her lips as she's getting ready to move south, but I lean forward, grabbing the back of her neck, just under her hair, as I lower my lips to hers. Running my palm up into her hair, I grip it softly, just the way she likes it. Just the way I know makes her wet. Her lips part, allowing me access to her hot, wet mouth. Our tongues meet and dance together before I latch on and suck. I love to suck on every inch of Shannon. If it were possible to overdose on her skin, her warm juices, it would be the most satisfying death I could ever imagine.

I run the back of my free hand down her neck and over her covered tits, down to the hem of her tank. I lift, indicating I want to remove it. She pulls back, breaking our kiss as I remove her shirt, tossing it to the side.

"Nick," she says, breathless. "I want you, please."

At this rate, with her hand slowly working me up and down, if she keeps begging, I'm going to blow before her mouth consumes me.

"Patience, baby," I say as I bring her lips back to meet mine. Quickly removing her bra, I skim over her nipple with my thumb, using feather-like precision. Releasing her hair, I move my other thumb over her other nipple and do the same thing. I know what this does to her, and I love teasing my girl.

When I know I can't take any more of just her hand on my cock, I pull back, breaking our kiss once more. Leaning back into the chair, I cast my eyes down to my dick and then roll them back up to meet her eyes again. My cocky smile flashes.

Shannon doesn't go for my length right off, though. No, first she pushes my thighs farther apart, and then she runs her left hand slowly up my leg. Bending forward, she places a soft kiss on my inner leg. She continues up, and her kisses change into licks as her tongue runs across the length of my lower abs. She traces each tattooed star before running her lips across the other side of my inner leg.

Women might not think a man wants or needs to be teased, and truthfully, we don't need it, but we sure as fuck love it. At least I do, as long as it's Shannon laying on the slow, torturous build-up.

Before her, I fucked, fast and hard, with quick and instant gratification. I didn't want this. Ever. This is how a woman can drive a man crazy with emotions.

Finally, her lips meet the head of my dick. Her hot, wet mouth makes me tense. I know I'm not going to last long, but I'm sure as hell going to enjoy every second of her lips wrapped around me.

"Fuck, baby. That feels so good. God, it feels so good."

Her lips make a popping sound as she releases me, and I'm pretty sure I just whined like a little bitch as I open my eyes.

"That's not God, baby. That's me." And that, my friend, is Shannon making me eat the words I once said to her. If we were in any other situation, I might laugh, but my dick is in need. In need of her mouth sucking me off.

"Mouth. Now." I manage to force out, knowing I'm about to blow my load. I reach up, pulling her head back down. She quickly takes me back into her hot mouth and starts to suck vigorously.

"Oh, fucking shit," I shout as she pulls me down her throat. My release comes quick and hard. She sucks me dry and swallows me down.

Opening my eyes, I see Shannon sitting back on her heels. Without wasting a second, I quickly lean up and reach to scoop her up by the back of her thighs as I stand. She doesn't have time to react or wrap her legs around me before I toss her onto the bed. She lands on a soft, all-white down comforter on the king-sized bed. I'm on top of her, covering her with my body and smiling down at the beautiful woman lying under me.

"Nick, please," she says softly, but it's not a begging kind of please. It's the kind of please that makes my smile fade. It's the kind of please that says no. It's the kind of please that makes my heart want to stop beating so I never have to hear those words from her lips again.

Dropping my head into the crook of her neck, I place a soft kiss on her skin. It's my favorite spot to kiss her, just above her collarbone on her throat.

I typically go with my instincts when I'm at a crossroads, and I rarely choose the obvious path. Usually, it works out in my favor. Other times, I end up losing my cool and going ape-shit crazy. Luckily, it's been a long time since I've lost it. Killing my father excluded. So now, when I know I shouldn't push Shannon, that's exactly what I plan to do. This is not for me, and I hope she doesn't see it that way. This is for her because I want to take away her hurt. I want to take away all her pain and replace it with something good—or at least better.

"Babe," I whisper against her skin. "I know everything is still fresh and old wounds were slashed open, but if you'll let me, I'll make you forget he was ever there." She tenses underneath me at the mention of my father. I don't want him to be on her mind, but I need her to know what I want to do, and I need it to be her decision.

"I don't—" I stop her before she gets everything out.

"Don't think about it. Just let me help." I don't know if it will work, but I want to try. I don't want her to remember him.

"Okay."

Moving to the side of the bed next to her, I place most of my weight on the bed. Taking my hand, I slowly skim down her belly until I reach her shorts. As I pop the button open and pull down the zipper, I kiss her neck, working my way up to her mouth. She opens, accepting my tongue that I so freely offer her. And as I kiss her ever so slowly, I remove her shorts and toss them off the bed.

Bringing my hand back down on her leg, I slowly work my way up to her breasts. Shannon loves to be teased even more than I do, and barely touching them will make her wet, and I need her wet for what I'm planning. With my thumb, I skim the tip of her nipple.

"Ahh," she moans, breaking our kiss, which gives me an opportunity to go down to her other breast. Just as I'm touching her nipple softly with my thumb, I do the same with my tongue. I swirl it around clockwise, wetting it before I pull back and blow cool air onto it. This causes her to take in a quick breath of air and arch her back. She is trying to push it up to my mouth, but I won't take it fully, not yet.

I continue my slow feather-like skims with my tongue and thumb for a few seconds longer before switching it up and moving my body across hers to her other side so I'll have better access to her other nipple with my tongue. After going around and around slowly over her nipple with my thumb, I move my arm down to her stomach and her hip. She lifts her ass, indicating she wants me to take off her panties, but I'm not ready. Close, but not just yet.

Adding a small amount of pressure, I get her to drop her ass back down on the bed. She sighs in frustration.

"Easy, baby," I say to her through my licks. "Patience. I want to do this right."

"Please, Nick. Please," she pants as I move my hand over her center. Cupping her, I run my palm softly, slowing my hand over her panty-covered pussy. I can already feel the moisture through the silky material. I love silk. The feel of it turns me on. I could stare at Shannon dressed in nothing but silk panties for hours.

Finally, I tap the side of her hip, letting her know I'm ready to remove them. She lifts up quickly, and I ease them down her legs.

Pulling her nipple into my mouth, I suck slowly as I bring my hand back down to her leg. Moving up to her thigh, I part her legs and open her up as far as I can. I release her nipple and skim down her body ever so slowly, my mouth barely touching her skin until I know she is hot.

"Please, fuck me already. I can't take it anymore."

Her words have me smiling like a fool. This is what my girl needs. Rising above her, I kiss her fast on the lips and then make my descent south. "As you wish."

I do plan on fucking her, but not with my dick. He will have to get over himself tonight. I'm going to devour her pussy and fuck her with my tongue.

Inching closer down, I kiss her stomach and linger for just a moment. There's a human growing in there. I still can hardly believe it. The thought fills me with unexpected pleasure. We will have to discuss him more, but later.

I move farther down, and when I reach my destination, I lick from the bottom to the top of her slick folds. Closing my eyes, I take in her taste. A taste I've missed. This is my Heaven on Earth. There's no place on Earth more beautiful than being up close and personal with Shannon's pussy.

"I'm starved for your pussy, baby," I tell her before returning to my little bit of Heaven. I'm not even sure Heaven could match this, let alone be better.

"Oh, Nick. Oh, please," she begs as I feel the sheet tighten, letting me know she has them in a death grip. I plunge my tongue inside her as far as possible and lick every drop of her juices. Twirling my tongue around, I coat it with all her delicious goodness. Coming back up, I latch onto her clit, and at first, I suck slow and steady.

"Faster, baby," she demands, and who am I to deny my woman a fast and hard mouth-to-pussy fuck? My sucking turns vigorous, and she moans loudly. I'd love to plunge my finger deep inside her, but I don't. That would be too much for her to handle at this point. Working her clit, I can feel her body shake, and I know she's about to come. I increase my speed just as she screams and comes all over my chin.

When I release her pussy, after the last of Shannon's shudders stop, I slowly move back up her body until I reach her beautiful face. Shannon grabs me by the cheeks, pulling my mouth down onto hers. She devours me, tasting every bit of herself lingering on my tongue. My dick gets hard every time she does this. What is it about a woman tasting herself?

Once she's had enough, she releases me, opening her eyes to stare into mine. Her eyes aren't sad or pained. They are happy, and I know I made the right decision. At least, this time I did.

Rolling onto my back, I take a deep, calming breath, finally feeling somewhat relaxed after the past three days of pure hell. Shannon turns and snuggles close to me, so I wrap my arm around her back and pull her flush against my skin.

"I'm hungry," she announces moments later.

"I could eat." It's the first time in days that I want something solid. "Go shower. I'll order something from room service. Any idea on what you want?"

"A fried chicken salad with honey mustard," she says with enthusiasm as she rolls out of bed and walks her naked ass to the bathroom.

Reaching up, I grab the phone as I hear the water from the shower turn on. While I'm waiting for someone to answer, I look up to see Shannon poking her head out of the bathroom.

"Get extra dressing for my salad, please." I nod in her direction as a woman asks me how she can assist. I quickly reply with our food order and hang up after she repeats what I've told her.

Getting out of bed, I hear the chime from my cell phone telling me I have a text message. Walking the short distance to where my blue jeans are lying on the floor, I pull my boxers and jeans on at the same time. I don't bother with my shirt as I pull my phone out of my front pocket.

It's a message from Marcus.

Marcus: About to head back to LA. Need a lift, or staying in Vegas?

Me: No, I'm staying. And thanks, man.

A reply quickly follows before I have time to check my other message.

Marcus: You know I'm here if you need me.

And I do. Marc has been somewhat of a big brother since I was a teenager. He took Jase and me under his wing when we were sixteen and doing anything and everything to cause trouble. He's Shane's older brother, which was how we met him.

He introduced all three of us to mixed martial arts and taught us a lot. Not just the fighting skills we each have today but about life and making better choices.

Marc's a good guy. Always has been and always will be. He likes to take care of people and fix everyone else's problems. Guess that's why he became a surgeon.

I decide not to respond to his last text. It's nothing I don't already know.

My next message is from Nikki. She can't stand it when we are at odds or when I'm mad at her.

Nikki: I'm sorry. I really am. I know I fucked up, but I also did what I thought was right at the time. I'm sorry, Nick.

Nikki: Please talk to me.

She did fuck up, and I'm beyond mad at her, but now that I've cooled off a little, I also know Nikki did what she thought was best. Nikki always has the best of intentions, even if they are wrong. My sister would never do anything to hurt me or deliberately withhold information unless she thought she had no choice. And knowing my sister as well as I do, I know it killed her not to come to me with everything she discovered.

I may not like it, but I know I have to get over my hang-up with what Nikki did or chose not to do.

CHAPTER SIX

I type out a message to my sister as I hear the shower cut off, so I know Shannon will be out here any moment. She is never one to linger in a bathroom long, doing whatever it is that chicks do.

Me: We'll talk when I get back.

I'm not going to apologize in a damn text message. I'm at least man enough to do it face-to-face. I know I was too harsh with Nikki. It's not like I'm sorry for what I said to her or how I spoke. I meant every word, but my little sister is my other half, and I won't let this come between us. I won't let anything come between us.

There's a hard knock on the door as I sit my cell on the nightstand next to the bed. Turning, I head toward the door. That was relatively quick for room service. I didn't expect them for at least another half an hour.

When I swing the door open, I'm unpleasantly surprised by who stands opposite me. I'm pretty sure by the look on his face he wasn't expecting me either. I still want to pound his fucking face in for hurting Shannon.

Her ex-fiancé.

"You just don't know how to go the fuck away and stay away, do you?" I question, surprising myself at the calmness of my tone. It's only an illusion, though. My body started to heat the moment we locked eyes, and if he gives me the slightest reason, I will lose my shit on this motherfucker.

"That's funny because I heard that's exactly what you did." His face is smug like he thinks he just one-upped me. *Not even close, douchebag.* Even if I hadn't come looking for Shannon, he's a dumb fuck to believe she would ever take his sorry ass back.

"Nick, the shower is—" She stops mid-sentence, and I turn to see her shocked face. She's wrapped in only a white towel, her wet hair hanging down the front on one side. A lot of men might freak out at another man seeing his half-naked woman. I'm not one of those men.

"What the hell are you doing here?" she barks out as she storms over. She's quick, and before I realize it, she ducked her head underneath my arm and is now standing in front of me. I pull her back by wrapping one arm across her chest and pulling her protectively against mine. To my surprise, she doesn't resist. "More importantly, how did you know where I was, Luke?"

This is something I'd like to know too.

"Can we talk, please?" he asks Shannon. His voice has turned soft. He's pleading with her. "Alone."

Like I'll let that happen.

"You can answer my question," she demands, making me smile proudly. She isn't taking his shit, and that makes me happy. Shannon is a lot stronger than most would think. After everything that has happened, she doesn't seem to be broken, and I'm not sure who I need to thank for that. Maybe there is a God after all.

"Shannon," he coos like a fucking baby. Hearing her name rolling off his tongue disgusts me. "Please, give me—"

"Answer me," she demands, successfully cutting him off.

"I still have access to your credit card. Allison heard from Stacy that he," he says as he gestures to me with the same look of disgust I'm sure I showed a moment earlier, "left you, so when I saw activity here, I came to find you. We belong together, baby. I know I messed up, but we can get back what we had."

Yeah, that one is going to sting for a while. I did walk out, and I did fuck up, but I didn't leave because I don't love Shannon or because I don't want her or the baby. Shoving all that shit to the back of my mind, I harden my expression as I tighten my hold around Shannon.

"You know there's a word for people like you. I think it's called stalker," I grit out, furious he's been watching her. I don't trust him not to hurt her. He's done it twice before; he'll do it again. They always do it again. And if I have to listen to him call her baby once more, I'm going to smash his head through a wall. And I'll love every minute of doing so.

Shannon bursts out with a quick laugh before replying, "Honestly, I can't believe you right now. Wow. Umm . . . really? I don't think so, short dick." And she slams the door right in his face. Not even I saw that one coming.

"I can feel the steam rolling off your skin. Go take a shower. The food will be here soon, right?"

"Yes," I respond. A shower isn't what I want right now. I want to beat the shit out of that punk. He deserves it. "It should be here any minute. I'll shower later."

"Take one now. You need it." I'm pretty sure I've just been issued orders from a girl. Luckily for her, I'm smart enough to know she's right. If I stand here any longer, I'll bolt out the door and hunt that dickfuck down.

"Fine," I bite out. As I release my hold on her, I realize I was gripping her too tightly. I turn and head for the bathroom. "Don't open that door for anyone other than room service."

Without waiting for her reply—that's sure to be some sort of smartass remark—I enter the bathroom, walking directly to the shower and turning the water on to hot. I may need a cold shower to cool down, but my body is strung too tight right now, and I need the heat to relax me.

When I walk back into the room after my shower, I see Shannon talking on the phone. She is already dressed in a purple tank top and black cloth shorts. The look marring her face is one of annoyance. Once she sees me, she wraps up her call and tells her mom she has to go.

I make my way to a small table big enough for two people. It's just off to the side of the floor-to-ceiling windows. The curtains are open, and all the lights of Vegas light the town up beautifully. This is what I love. I don't know why, but I do. I take a seat so I'm able to look out the window.

Shannon has already laid out the food, so once I'm seated comfortably, I take my first bite. I might have gone overboard with the order, but I'm starving. Other than a nibble here and there, I haven't eaten in a few days.

"Hungry much?" she asks in a playful tone as she comes over to sit across from me.

"A little," I mumble through a mouthful of burger. I practically inhale the damn thing. It's delicious. I watch as Shannon piles two containers of thick honey mustard onto her salad. I don't want to watch, but I can't look away either. That shit is nasty.

"Oh my gawd," she drawls her words out as she takes her first bite. I'm happy to see the effect of our playing around hasn't had negative results. Her happiness makes me smile. "This is so good. I can't remember the last time I enjoyed a meal."

"Good," I say as I finish off the last of my burger and move on to my french fries.

"Do you want a beer or anything? I'm going to get a Coke out of the mini-fridge." She gets up to walk the distance across the room.

"A water will do fine." I don't think my body could handle another ounce of alcohol right now. I move on to my fried chicken salad before I ask, "I thought pregnant chicks weren't supposed to drink soda?" I pour ranch on top of the salad and mix it around the bowl before taking a bite. She is right. It's mouthwatering. At least mine is with the correct dressing.

"Are you a doctor now?" she spits, and it's laced with a hint of sarcasm.

Touché, baby. Tou-fucking-ché.

"No, but I'm pretty certain it's a known fact." I match her tone. I look up as she places my water in front of me. She holds a can of caffeine-free Sprite out for me to see as she takes a seat. I set my fork down and take a large sip of my water as she moves to open her can and takes a small sip.

"So are you ready to tell me why you came to see a physician here in Vegas?" I really want to know because, for the life of me, I can't think of a possible reason. If she didn't want people to know, they wouldn't. It's not exactly a small city by any means. LA is fucking huge.

"Not yet. I want to know why you're mad at Nikki. When I saw her yesterday, she said you weren't talking to her." She takes another bite of her salad. With the facial expressions I'm seeing after every bite she takes, you would think she was making love to her damn food.

She may have successfully steered the conversation away from her, but I won't be dropping this. I will find out, but as I think of my sister, I can't help but get a little angry again. Nikki could have taken a knife and stabbed me through the chest, and it wouldn't have hurt as badly as her keeping things from me.

Important things that could have prevented Shannon from getting hurt again.

"Nikki should have told me. If she had told me what she knew, I could have prevented what happened. You wouldn't have been hurt again." My appetite leaves me, and I place my utensils down and put my head into my hands. My light mood and relief at seeing Shannon is now broken as the guilt filters back in. I'll never get past this. It's too much. I know I could have stopped this.

I should have known my father was bullshitting me when he came to see me a few weeks back. I know better. I've never trusted or believed a word he's ever spoken. What the hell was I thinking? I'd beat the shit out of myself if I could. I messed up big time.

Why I let Teresa convince me otherwise, I'll never know, and I'll never forgive myself for either.

"Don't do that," she chimes in as she also stops eating her salad to reach across the table to squeeze my forearm with her small, soft hand. "Stop feeling bad or guilty for something you didn't do. What happened, happened, Nick. There's no changing it, and it wasn't your fault."

That just isn't going to happen, but I don't want to bring her down with my shit, so I try to change the subject. It's something we need to discuss anyhow.

"So when is . . .?" I pause, searching for what I'm trying to ask. I have no idea how to approach this subject. "When is he coming?" I force the words out as I eye down past the table to where I know her belly is.

"Why do you keep calling it a he? It could very well be a she instead of a he, you know."

Well, yeah. Obviously, it could.

"Yeah, I know that, but what am I supposed to call him? I'm not calling him an it. What are you calling him?"

"Oh, well, I've settled on *my minion*, but that's my word. You can't use it." She's smiling at this like it's funny.

"I'm not calling our baby a minion, and neither are you, damn it." My baby is not a fucking minion. *Our baby*, those words feel strange rolling off my tongue. Honestly, I never thought I'd be saying them. I hate to admit it, but it feels weird. Not weird in a bad way, just weird; odd I guess.

"I'll call my baby anything I want. Get over it, Nick."

"He's not a fucking minion."

"He's probably not a he either," she throws back at me. I'm being an ass. I know this, but I am an ass.

"Woman," I say with a softer tone. I don't say anything else afterward. She is strong-headed and stubborn. Going down this road will only lead to an argument and I don't want that.

"So you're okay with this?" she asks as she places her hands over her stomach.

"I don't know. I mean, I haven't really given it much thought. I've thought about it, sure, but I haven't, not really, if that makes any sense. I don't know how I feel about it. I know I don't want anything bad to happen to the baby. I don't want it to go away. I think my brain just hasn't fully wrapped around it yet."

"It makes perfect sense, actually. I was in shock myself. Maybe I still am. I know I need to make an appointment with my gynecologist, but I haven't yet. I think I feel the same. I don't want anything bad to happen to it, and not even for a second did I consider getting rid of it. I wouldn't do that. Catholic or not, I still wouldn't."

"I'm not sure if knowing you feel the same makes me feel better or worse." I don't have my shit together. I certainly don't have a clear head right now, but I think one of us needs to.

"I know this isn't an ideal situation, but it is what it is, and we'll deal with it, okay?" she asks before adding, "And I'd like to deal with it together."

I sit back in my chair, pulling my arm free of her hold before standing and walking over to the window overlooking a beautiful pool and Sin City.

Leaning forward, I press my forehead against the cold glass. It feels nice against my heated skin. Moments later, I feel Shannon standing directly behind me. She mimics my stance by placing her forehead on my back and her hands on my towel-covered hips. Only her thumbs and forehead are touching my skin, but it's enough to cause small tingles to shoot up my back and make me forget what we were talking about.

All I want to do is get lost inside her hot, wet heat, but I know she isn't ready for that. I'd be a bastard to push her, but damn it, I feel like it's been forever since my aching cock has been inside her body instead of the nearly two weeks it's been.

I instantly feel the warmth of her hot breath wash over my skin, making me shiver all over when she parts her lips to speak. My dick grows hard underneath my towel, but no sound comes out of her mouth. I know she has something to say, but she is hesitant.

I suck in a steady breath of air through my mouth, trying to calm my growing hard-on. The air that I exhale is shaky as Shannon moves her hands over the towel and onto more of my exposed skin. My erection is getting stiffer by the second. What is she doing to me? I bring my palms up and press them flat against the window to steady myself. This woman will have me dropping to my knees like a whipped, submissive little pussy any moment now.

God, what's happened to me? I'm certain my man card expired the moment I laid my eyes on her all those months ago. I'm also pretty sure my brain has gone to mush because I can't think past the feel of her warm hands and the hot breath coating my skin like the thick, humid heat you only find in the South.

As I'm calming my breathing, she kisses the center of my back. Damn, a man only has so much willpower, but when it comes to her, I have zero, nada, zip.

Yeah, I'm definitely pussy whipped.

But fuck me, her lips feel good. My straining cock is starting to scream. My balls are aching for her to touch them too, and just as I'm about to remove my palm from the window to place my hand underneath the towel before it falls to the floor, she stills. No more kissing or caressing my skin. Just hot breath on my back and delicious heat. Something changed. As I'm about to twist around to find out what's wrong, Shannon bolts.

I've never seen another person run that fast in my life. One minute she's behind me, and seconds later, she's in the bathroom. I'm not far behind, and when I enter, she already has her head hovering over the toilet.

I walk over, gather her hair, and pull it out of the line of fire. I hold it in one hand while I lean over the sink and grab a clean washcloth. After running cool water over it, I squeeze out the excess.

I'm not new to this. I've taken care of Nikki plenty of times when she's been sick or when she's been plastered, but this is different. This . . . this is gross. The massive hard-on I was sporting only moments ago is gone. No guy wants to watch shit come back up the sexy little mouth they kiss, suck, bite, and devour.

"Babe, you okay?" I ask. She seems to be done. But no, I'm wrong. She is far from done. She starts again. How on earth does she have that much in her stomach? She didn't even eat much. She ate a salad, just a salad. That's a fuck-load more than just a salad. Why am I even looking in the toilet?

"Are you sick?" I ask when she sits back on her heels. *Please, God, let her be done.*

"Just morning sickness." She reaches up for the washcloth and runs it over her face and mouth. When she's done, she hands it back to me.

Yeah, this is gross too, but not nearly as bad as watching your girl worship the porcelain god.

"It's night," I deadpan, and she looks up at me with a glare like I'm stupid. What? It is. How can she have morning sickness at night?

"It's only called morning sickness. It can occur any time of the day." That makes no sense, but I'm not going to say that. Not after the look she gave me.

"So you're okay, though, right?"

She stands, flushes the toilet then walks over to the sink.

"Yeah, I'm fine. That was nothing compared to earlier today." She grabs her toothbrush and toothpaste. Moments later, her mouth is clean, and I walk out of the bathroom behind her.

Shannon walks over to the bed and climbs in. I remove the leftover food and containers and put them in the trash. Once I'm done and the table is clean, I turn and face her. Her eyes lock on mine. I'm not sure I want to find out my fate. Does she want me to stay or go get another room to stay in?

"Am I sleeping in that bed with you?"

She just stares at me. Seconds tick by like hours while I wait on her response.

"You're here, but your clothes aren't. I don't think it would be fair of me to kick you out with only a towel." At that, I smirk. Yeah, I know I shouldn't, but I'm going to sleep next to my girl again. "Get in. I'm tired."

Shannon cuts off the lamp as I make my way around to the other side of the bed. Before climbing in, I drop the towel onto the floor.

The sheets are cool against my skin as I sink into the plush bed. Without asking, I pull Shannon to my chest and plunge my nose into her hair. Call me fucking weird, but I love the smell of her, and I haven't had this in what feels like forever. She doesn't try to stop me, which I'm grateful for as my head and body settle down, and I finally doze off, relaxed for the first time in days, hell, weeks.

CHAPTER SEVEN

Why didn't I have enough sense to pull the curtains closed last night? It's bright as hell in here, and I haven't even opened my eyes.

Shannon, that's why. I can't think clearly when I'm near her. She allowed me to stay in her bed, and I practically jumped in it with her.

She's still curled up against my chest in the exact spot we went to sleep. It's taking every last bit of restraint I have not to tighten my hold on her and pull her farther into my body. I can never get her close enough. I know I don't deserve to be here right now, and I certainly don't have a right to hold on to her like she's my last breath. But hell, I love this woman, and I'm a selfish son of a bitch. I've always gone after what I wanted. Well, for the most part, anyway. When I was a boy, I wished my mother would have taken Nikki and me away and never returned. When I got old enough to understand more, I told myself once I got old enough and strong enough, I would stand up to my father. I'd take my mother and sister away from him and never return.

I didn't, though. Sure, the day I turned twenty-one, I made

sure my father never laid a hand on my mother again. I don't think he ever touched her after that day. If he did, I never found out about it. And I'm certain my father believed every word I told him that day, but he's not a man who would bow down to anyone. Especially not his own son. No, he decided if he couldn't hurt his wife, he would find someone else. I just thought they had been willing women. Women who got off on pain. Masochists who welcomed the suffering and bruises he offered.

I screwed up that day in more ways than one. Had I gone after my father that morning after seeing what he did to my mom, two people would not have been brutally hurt at my hands. Sure, only one of them suffered physical injuries from me personally, but Shannon suffered the most damage. Damage I caused because I didn't stand up to my father the way a man should.

"You're thinking too hard."

At the sound of Shannon's voice, I snap my eyes open. She's awake, and she pulls lightly on my wrist, where I have my arm wrapped around her. Realization dawns on me, and I immediately release my hold on her, pulling my arm away.

I didn't even realize I was squeezing the shit out of her side. No matter what I do, I can't seem to not cause her pain. I'm an asshole. She stops me before I'm out of reach and brings my arm back around her waist.

"I'm not ready to get out of bed. Stay, please," she pleads as she scoots farther into me. Moving the arm I have behind me, I slide it under her head and wrap it around her shoulders, successfully bringing her as close as I can. Taking a deep breath, I inhale the sweet, light scent of her hair. It always has a faint scent of something tropical and I love it. It's not overpowering. It's mellow, but it's just enough that it makes me wish we were lying wrapped up in each other on a beach.

"I saw a therapist yesterday." My body stills and I stop breathing.

"Come again?" I ask, clearly not understanding.

"A psychiatrist, a shrink, a head doctor, that kind of therapist." She rushes it out like she doesn't even want to be having this conversation.

"Oh" is all I manage to say. I'm not sure what she is trying to get at, but I'm listening. At least she's telling me where she went yesterday. When she doesn't elaborate, I ask, "So, why did you need to see a voodoo brain doctor?"

I can almost feel the steam coming off her body. And even though I can't see her beautiful green eyes, I know she is rolling them right now.

"Not funny, Nick." But she can't hide the smile from her voice. I wasn't trying to be funny, but I'll take it. I can't figure out why she would need to see a psychiatrist, but she doesn't leave me to my thoughts for long.

"Because I never dealt with what that man did all those years ago." Oh. The blond "duh" moments just went off inside my brain. "And after what happened a few days ago, I thought it might be best to talk to a professional."

At the mention of my father and what he did, mental flashes of pictures of him rush through me. I want them to go away. Yet I wish I had killed him slower, made him suffer more for what he did to her. I know my body has tightened, but I'm trying hard to watch myself so I don't hurt her again this morning. I take a calming breath, trying to control the powerful need to smash my fist through something hard.

"Makes sense, I guess," I finally say. "Did it . . .? I mean, do you . . .? Fuck, I don't know what I'm trying to ask here. Baby, I'm so sorry." I bury my face in her hair. I could happily get lost in all of it.

"Stop, Nick. Stop apologizing."

Shannon turns, rolls on her back, and looks up at me. I don't want to look into her eyes. What if she can see the truth? I don't want her to know the truth. Well, I do, but I don't.

"I'm not sure if it helped. I only met with him for about an hour, and I didn't go into many details."

"But you were gone for hours."

"Yeah, well . . . I needed to be alone. Working actually helps the most, and I got a lot of great shots taken in the city and out in the desert."

"Photos? You came here to take photographs?"

"Partly, yes. Well, mostly yes. Las Vegas is the setting for my third book. I needed to get out of LA too. I was coming here, so I found a physician to see me while I'm in town."

"You said you're not sure if it helped."

"Right. It was only an hour. I can see how talking things out might help in the long run, but I didn't want to say too much."

"Why?" I can't help but ask. If talking could help her cope and recover from this, then that's what she should do.

"Why don't you tell me what happened to your dad?"

Hell no.

And "Dad" isn't the word for that man. Sure, he's my father, and there isn't anything I can do to change that, but he isn't a dad.

I can't tell her what happened to him without telling her what I did to him. If I can't tell her the other shit, I certainly don't want her to know I'm a murderer too. Sure, she might agree that I did it for the right reason, but if I'm capable of that—which I am—then she might wonder what else I'm capable of doing. Before I have to respond, I'm saved by a light knock on the door.

Rolling out of bed, I scoop up the towel I left on the floor up and wrap it around me. Shannon is up, out of bed, and walking toward the door before I'm covered. Immediately, I'm on alert. What if her jerkoff of an ex is back? Dealing with him isn't what I want to do right now, but maybe it could be for the best. If he thinks I'm going to let him near her and my baby again, he's got another think coming.

Shannon glides the door open partially without looking through the peephole to see who it is. What is wrong with her? Doesn't she know how dangerous that can be?

As she closes the door, she thanks the person on the other side, then turns around with my freshly laundered clothes. We meet halfway, and she hands them to me. I take them, discarding my towel by tossing it to the floor. As I dress, I notice the look in her eyes. She wants answers.

"I want to know what happened." Her voice is firm. I don't look at her as I pull on my black boxers.

"What's the point? I don't want to upset you," I tell her as I button and zip my jeans. I don't want to lie to her. I'm not even convinced I could tell the woman I love a lie straight to her face. Honestly, I don't want to find out if I can.

"Because I need to know. I need closure, I guess. That man killed our dog."

Our dog? I like the sound of that. "I meant your dog. Sorry, I just miss him. I got really used to him being around and . . ." She starts to sob, so I pull her to my chest just as I get my T-shirt over my head.

"Baby, don't cry," I say in what I hope is a soothing voice.

"I'm sorry he killed Niko over me. I'm sorry, Nick."

"No, Shannon, it's not your fault. That sick fuck did that to prove a point to me. It wasn't you. I swear."

"What do you mean?" She sniffs as she pulls away from me to wipe her face with the back of her hands. I take a deep breath, knowing if she asks me, I'll be honest. I don't want to, but I'm going to.

"He wanted me to know he was in control and he could and would do whatever he pleased, and there would never be anything I could do to stop him." But I did stop him, and I'd do it again in a heartbeat. I would never let him touch my girl again.

"I don't understand."

"Everyone bowed down to my father in one way or another. My mother, literally. She would never talk back to him or stand up to him. She tried a few times and was quickly reminded who was in charge, who was in control. People who worked for him weren't scared of him physically, but they were afraid to question him. He made people believe he knew what was best. They all knew he held the power. They, too, bowed down to him."

"Okay, but what happened the night he got killed? The night you and I were asleep in my bed?" She emphasizes the word "asleep" a little too much, causing me to briefly stop and think. Does she think I did it? She would come out and tell me or just ask me if she thought that. Right?

"I don't know much more than what my sister told us a few days ago. I haven't exactly spent the last few days sober." That's not too much of a stretch; I know it was all over the news. Not that I saw any of that, but I know it was. I know they haven't found who did it, or I'd be in jail right now. I know I'm going to have to deal with it all once I get back to LA. But I don't want to go back home. Maybe we can just stay here and forget about all the baggage that is my life. Start fresh. Isn't that what people talk about? A fresh start is what Shannon and I need—what we deserve. Well, it's what she deserves. What I deserve doesn't include happiness and her or our kid.

"Yesterday was the first time since leaving your house that I wasn't drunk, and trust me, that would not have lasted longer had I not found out you came to Nevada."

"I'm hungry." She changes the subject as if sensing I don't want to discuss my father any longer. She really is too good for me.

"Get dressed. I'll grab some food." I place a chaste kiss on her lips before she turns and heads into the bathroom. I sit on the bed and pull on my socks and boots.

Shannon walks out of the bathroom with a toothbrush in her mouth and only wearing a silky black thong. The loose-fitting jeans I'm wearing tighten as my growing dick takes up all the excess room.

Damn, she's beautiful. She doesn't even realize how hot she is. When she bends over, grabbing clothes from a small suitcase, I have to fist the material in the comforter so I don't pounce on the sexy little ass taunting me.

"Baby, you need to hurry up and put your clothes on or walk back into the bathroom."

"Huh?" she says through a mouthful of toothpaste as she glances up. She sees the look on my face as she spits and rinses her mouth. Without saying another word, she saunters back into the bathroom and shuts the door, but not before I see the smirk that crosses her face.

Down boy, down, I attempt to tell my throbbing cock.

CHAPTER EIGHT

By the time Tuesday morning rolls around and our plane lands in LA, I'm feeling edgy. The calmness I sported through breakfast yesterday and while I tagged along with Shannon to shoot some great photos along the strip last night is gone. I don't know if it's being back home or the fact that I'm about to have to face the shit storm that is my father's death that has my body stiff.

I'm certain Shannon can tell something is up with me. Ever since we left LAX to retrieve my car, she's glancing my way, her eyebrows pulled in tight.

"What's wrong?" she finally asks as I throw her Porsche into park next to mine.

"Just have a lot on my mind." I don't give her a chance to question me further because if I do, she will. "You going straight home?"

"I suppose. Are you?" She removes her safety belt and turns in her seat, slightly facing me, waiting for an answer. I'm unsure if she's asking if I'm going to my house or hers. Normally, I'm not a pussy and would come right out and ask her to clarify, but a part of me wants her to say she wants me with her, while the other part is wondering why she's still allowing me to be in her presence. She shouldn't want me around her or our baby.

"I have an apology to issue my sister first."

"Yes, you do. Nick, she didn't do anything wrong."

For the motherfucking love . . . If I have to hear her say that again, I may just lose my shit altogether. Yes, I admit I was too hard on Nikki, but the hell she didn't do anything wrong.

"Plus, it's the only way to get my dog back. Apologize, or Jase will hold Charmin hostage." I'm trying to lighten the mood, but it's not exactly a lie. Jase called me yesterday and all but said if I didn't make up with Nikki, I could kiss my dog goodbye.

"Oh, okay. Yeah, um . . ." She pauses and looks down while chewing her bottom lip.

"Do you want me to bring Charmin home?" She looks up with hope in her eyes. "To your house, that is." Her eyes light up.

"Yes, please. I miss her."

"Okay, babe, I'll bring her home shortly." I keep using the word, *home* when referring to Shannon's house. I like my house; don't get me wrong. It was perfect. It was me until Shannon moved into her house. Then her house sort of became my home. At least that's what it feels like. It's the only place I ever want to be. It's like walking into a peaceful sanctuary. Then the disturbing image of my father with Shannon enters my head, and I can't help but wonder if she still wants to be there.

"Shannon?" I question, looking at her, not knowing if I'm about to ask the right question. "Do you . . .? I mean, are you okay with going back to your house after what . . .?" I can't even bring myself to finish. Just the mere thought of what happened makes my vision cloud with red. My body heats. I hate when I get like this. I can't seem to ever control myself. My temper always seems to blow up when I feel this intense. I need to get out of her car, but I need the answer I seek more.

"I . . ." She looks down. "It's my home. I don't want to leave if that's what you're asking." She pauses, but I can tell she isn't finished. "I'm . . ." She stops again, closes her eyes, and takes a deep breath. Watching her struggle with her words has me tightening my grip on the steering wheel. "When I'm there, I see it all over again, but at the same time, I'm not scared. Maybe it's because he's gone. I don't know."

"Would you rather stay at my house?" What if she doesn't? I don't want to assume she wants me with her. "I mean, you're more than welcome to stay in the penthouse if you prefer." *Please don't prefer.*

"I . . ." There's doubt in her voice. I'd do anything to never hear it again. "Nick, I . . ." Again she pauses, and I swear if my skin tightens anymore, the flesh is going to rip apart.

"Shannon, I wasn't trying . . ."

She doesn't let me finish. "No, don't. Let me get this out." She looks up and sucks in a quick breath of air. "I don't just want you in our little minion's life." She smiles at that word knowing I hate it, but I don't hate it anymore. It's kind of growing on me, but she successfully makes me feel a fraction lighter. "I want you in mine too. I want you. I want us. I love you. That hasn't changed. I don't think that could ever change. I also want to be in my home. I had started to think of it as our home. God knows you and I have moved fast. Faster than I thought we should, but . . ." She pauses, and hell, I think I would have needed a breath sooner than that. "It's like we're inevitable. God, I sound like a girl right now." She puffs air out of her mouth, causing her hair to fly around her face. Before it lands back in place, I reach over and yank her into my lap, bringing my lips down on hers.

"Does that mean you want me at home with you?" I ask once I release her from our kiss. She blushes. I've missed that.

"Yes."

"Okay. Then I'll go see my sister tomorrow."

"No," she immediately fires back. "Go see her now. Bring my dog home."

"Yes, ma'am." I open the driver's door and maneuver my way out from under her, which lands her in the driver's seat. I'm not sure how I did all that, considering how damn small that car is. And that leads me to something else entirely. She needs a bigger car—for her and the baby. "On second thought, you take my car."

I pull her out of her car as I dig my car keys from my jean pocket. Once I have them in her hands, I sink back into her Porche. Yeah, this is definitely too small.

"Nick, what the—" But I don't give her a chance to finish.

"No time, babe. I have to go get our dog." And with that, I slam the door shut and put the car in drive.

Pulling up outside Jase and Nikki's condo, I park and turn off the ignition. Both of their vehicles are here, I notice as I look around. With the way my mind is running in different directions, I didn't even think to call first. Nikki is usually at Knocked Out by this time of the morning. Odd, but whatever, I don't think about that for long.

I trudge up the steps to their second-floor apartment. A large part of me dreads coming face-to-face with my sister; the other part just wants to get this over with.

Coming to a stop in front of their door, I raise my hand to knock, but before I can, the door swings open and Jase nearly barrels into me before realizing I'm standing there.

"What the . . .?" He stops inches before me. I have to take a step back, and he does the same. His face is heated, and his eyes are a shade darker than his normal blue eyes.

Looking past Jase, I see my sister sitting on their couch. Her face is red and blotchy. She's been crying. Immediately, my fists ball and I turn back to Jase. Only two people in this world can make her cry, and we're staring at each other. I don't have a right to judge. Not really, not when I'm here to apologize for the ass I was to her. But all the same, she is still my little sister, and no one is going to hurt her.

"Problem?" I ask, pinning Jase with my you're-a-fucking-dead-man look.

"Leave it, Lockhart," he forces out through clenched teeth as he shoves past me and jogs down the steps.

Looking back inside, I eye my sister before walking in and shutting the door. She's sitting on the couch, barefoot, with her knees pulled to her chest and arms wrapped around her legs.

Ah, fuck.

"Want to talk about it, sis?" I sigh as I walk the short distance and sit beside her. Before my back hits the soft leather behind me, she leans over and places her head on my chest. My arms automatically go around her shoulders, pulling her closer.

"No." She's forcing back a sob.

Hell, how am I supposed to stay mad? I can't.

"Then we'll start with me and come back to you. I'm sorry." Nikki lifts her head and looks at me like she can't believe that word came out of my mouth. "I am, okay?"

"Yeah, okay." She doesn't sound convinced.

Great.

"Look, I'm mad. I am, and there is nothing I can do to change that. But I shouldn't have blown up on you." I pause, taking in air through my mouth. "And for that, I'm sorry."

"Hmph," she puffs out as she lifts her head off my chest and then leans her back against the couch. She takes a deep breath and glances up at me. I can see she is sorry. She has a hard time saying it, although she's much better at it than me.

"You're my sister. The fact that you didn't come to me

immediately burns. It really fucking burns, Nikki, but I'll get over it. You know I will, but right now, I can't stop myself from being angry."

"I know, Nick. God." She pauses as she tries to reel in her emotions. "Fuck, I'm sorry. Okay? I am. I know I should have come to you. It's not like I didn't consider it. My head told me to tell you, but I couldn't. It went against my gut."

"Come here, brat," I sigh.

She places her head back on my chest. Nikki loses the battle over control of her emotions, and a sob breaks out.

"Shannon is the last person I'd ever want to hurt. I'm sorry she got hurt because of me."

"Stop right the fuck now." Nikki peers up at me with glassy blue eyes. The sadness behind them guts me. I'm an asshole. I never stopped to think Nikki would blame herself too. This isn't her fault. No matter what she kept from me, she isn't at fault. "You didn't cause him to hurt her. Don't for a second think you had any part in it. I'm sorry. I should have never made you think that. I was pissed, okay? But I never blamed you, and I shouldn't have said what I did."

"No, I deserved it. I knew better. Something inside me said to tell you first, but I didn't follow my instincts. I can't even tell you why I didn't. I'm sorry."

"Then it's done. You're sorry. I'm sorry. It's over, and we're okay." I pull her to me and kiss the top of her head.

"Okay," is all she says as she wipes the last of her tears away with the back of her hand. She forces a small smile and stands. "I need to get dressed and head to work. I know I don't need to say this, but this shit never happened."

I laugh at her as she points to her red, blotchy face. "Yeah, sure, Ms. Tough-Ass. I got it, but we aren't done."

"Yeah, we are, big brother," she says, giving me a pointed

look that says, "what you walked in on earlier isn't up for discussion."

Too fucking bad.

"I don't think so. Spill it. What did Jase do?" I say this knowing damn well it isn't something he did. It's something my sister did. It's always her in some way, but I can't say that. It would be like taking his side, and I won't take sides when it comes to them.

"No," she says with more force. "There are some things a brother just shouldn't know, so please drop it."

The way she says it makes me stop and think that maybe she has a point. Doesn't matter. I already know too much about my sister and best friend's relationship. Much more than a brother should. I can also tell when my sister isn't going to budge. If I want to find out what happened this morning, I'll have to get it out of Jase.

"Fine. It's dropped for now." I decide to switch topics. I can see it in her eyes; she's about to get pissed. "How's Mom?"

I was pretty hard on her too, but unlike my sister, she won't get an apology from me. Nikki's heart was in the right place. It always is. She was trying to give Shannon time to tell me. My mother, on the other hand, tried to persuade Shannon not to tell me, to let me go. She knew what that sick fuck did to her for weeks, and she chose not to tell me. She chose to protect the same worthless piece of shit who hurt her for as long as I can remember.

"She actually misses him." Nikki's expression changes and her eyes grow dark. They always do when the topic of our father comes up. If I didn't know any better, I'd think she hates him more than I do, but that's impossible. She's the one person I tried to shield from him when we were kids. If something happened, if she got in trouble or did something I knew he wouldn't like, I always found a way to take the blame. There was no way in hell I would have allowed him to touch her like he did our mother.

Nikki throws her hands up. "Can you fucking believe it? I just don't get it. How can she miss him? How can she love him after everything?"

"I wish I knew. I don't understand it myself." I don't. It makes no sense to me. He not only beat her more times than I care to remember, but he emotionally abused her, calling her every nasty word in the English dictionary.

"Um, Nick?"

"Yeah?" I look up at her.

"The funeral." She pauses, as if searching for the right thing to say.

"What about it? I'm not going, if that's what you're about to ask me."

"No, that's not it. It was supposed to be tomorrow, but it's been postponed until Friday. There's an extensive autopsy and investigation. Mom says the cops are working the case pretty hard to find who did it." Nikki's eyebrows pull in tightly, and her blue eyes are scared. She has an alibi. I wonder if she thinks I had something to do with it.

"Okay. I'd expect nothing less, so what's that look for?" I gesture at her face.

"It's just . . ." She pauses again and takes a deep breath before continuing. "If what happened to Shannon, if what he did to her gets out, all eyes will fall on you. People will think you did it. There's motive if that comes out."

She's right, but I'm not about to ask Shannon to keep what he did a secret. She's held on to that for too long. She needs to get it out so she can move past it.

"So what? Just chill, okay? Let the chips land where they may."

"How can you say that?" Her voice is high. "Nick, this is your life on the line. You're about to be a father. Can't you just ask her to stay quiet about it?"

"Nikki," I say with a firm voice. "You and I just moved past a lot of shit. Do not go there. Do not even think of asking Shannon to do that. This is where you need to drop it, right the fuck now. Just don't."

"But—"

"No," I practically yell, cutting her off. "Leave it. This is the end of this discussion. Shannon is off-limits. Do not even bring our father up in front of her. Ever. Are we clear?"

"Okay, Nick. I'm sorry. I shouldn't have mentioned it."

"You shouldn't have thought it." She rolls her eyes at me, but I let it go. "Aren't you going to ask about Shannon?"

"Why would I need to?" She looks at me like I'm stupid making me think I've missed something. "We've been texting since Sunday. I know you two are back together. Now leave. I have to get dressed for work." She doesn't give me a chance to respond. She turns on her heel and walks down the hall, slamming her bedroom door behind her.

I take that as my cue and leave.

As I'm jogging down the steps, I realize I forgot my dog.

"Dammit," I mumble as I reach for my cell phone tucked inside my pocket. I send a quick text message to Nikki.

Me: My dog. Take her to Shannon's. And tell your newly acquired BFF I'll be a few more hours. I'm going to find Jase.

CHAPTER NINE

Walking in the door at Quaint, I stop momentarily, taking everything in and realizing the hotel is no longer mine. Maybe that should pain me, and perhaps it does a little, but I know deep down I've grown bored. This was my first success. I bought this place nine years ago and grew this company to what it is today. I'm proud of what I've accomplished, but I'm not sad to see it go. Plus, I know I handed it over to someone who will only grow it further. Sam is a good man. Lockhart Publishing is my pride. It's my passion. It's where my heart is.

It's still early afternoon, so there aren't many people drinking, but the one person I am looking for is. I look over to the far right of the bar and see him sitting there with a drink in hand and his head down as if in thought. Jase looks defeated. What the hell did my sister do this time?

Scanning the room, I see Tabitha behind the bar once again. She's flirting with an old man at the other end. He throws his head back and laughs. As I make my way over to Jase, I nod in her direction as she looks over at me. She flashes her eyes from me to the left side of the room, causing me to look in that direction. When our eyes meet, I stop dead in my tracks.

Jeffery Chaney.

Twice in less than a week. I could go without seeing his face for the rest of my life. He smirks and then turns back to the woman sitting in a booth across from him. It's dark in here, and I can't see her face, but I can tell she has long dark hair. Jeffery is an average-sized guy, about my height but not as built. Still, he's much larger than the woman in front of him.

I shake my head and continue. There isn't anything I can do about Jeffery anyway. Not my bar, I remind myself.

I pull out the stool and sit down. Jase doesn't look up. He doesn't have to. He knows it's me. I'm certain he knows I'd find him eventually. It's what we do.

"Hey, you." Tabitha beams as she walks over. "What's my ex-boss up to today, and, furthermore, what can I get you?"

"Just a glass of water," I tell her flatly, not bothering to answer her first question. She's sweet and all, but I'm not here to converse with her, and I really don't want to deal with the flirting that comes with Tabitha.

Tabitha catches on that I don't want to talk. Once she places my water down on a white napkin, she smiles warmly and then walks back to the other side of the bar.

"Is this what reverse déjà vu feels like?" I laugh, but my hopes of lightening the mood die out like I knew it would when Jase turns, pinning me with a glare that says, "Fuck off."

"Not in the mood." Turning his attention back to his drink, he lifts it and tosses it back in one shot. He looks at Tabitha, holding his glass in the air and shaking the empty cup.

Great. How many of those has he had?

"That was only my first."

Did I say that aloud? I don't think I did.

"You got that judgmental look on your face, asshole," he follows, as if reading my thoughts.

"You know I'm the last person who's ever judged you, so don't give me that shit." The asshole might be able to read my thoughts, but he isn't going to sit here and spit bullshit because he wants to piss me off. When Jase is mad or upset, it's what he does. He wants everyone else to be as miserable as he is. He goes out of his way to pick fights.

"What do you want, Lockhart?"

"Motherfucker, don't start shit you can't finish." And this is what I do. I goad him. I fuel his anger because it's what he needs. Fucked up I know, but it's the only thing that works for us. Fighting out our pent-up frustration, anger, stress . . . It's the only way to get rid of it. If only it worked for my guilt too, but it doesn't.

"That pansy-ass mouth of yours needs to shut up before I shove my dick down your pretty little throat, showing every motherfucker in this place what a little bitch you really are." His voice may have been harsh, but the slight upward turn of his lips tells me he's not thinking about his and my sister's shit any longer.

Tabitha sets my glass of water down in front of me and then eyes Jase and me back and forth. She can't tell that this is just fucked-up friendly banter. I wave her off as I lift the tall glass to my lips and take a hefty sip.

"Drink this and let's get out of here," I tell him as I slide my nearly full glass of water in front of him. "You need to punch that shit out. I'll even let you use my face to do it."

My chuckle dies out when Jase whips his head over in my direction. "Kiss the fuck off, asshole."

I'm about to say something when Jase's eyes look past me. His expression hardens, and I witness his body go rigid as he sits up straighter. I feel someone walk up to the bar. They're standing next to me on the left.

"Are you leaving so soon, Mr. Chaney?" Tabitha asks as I look over to see Jeffery toss a credit card on the counter. She scoops it up and turns to head over to the machine to run it through. Jeffery turns his head and eyes us both before looking directly at me.

"I'd offer my condolences, but we both know I wouldn't mean it, and well, it's not like you're the least bit sad over his death now, are you?"

"Fuck off, Chaney," I spit out before turning back to face Jase. He dislikes the fucker just as much as I do. Mainly because he will always have my back, and any enemy of mine is an enemy of his.

"Gladly." But as he walks off, he says something that nearly has me flying out of my seat. "But before I go, I was wondering . . . Did my favorite little photographer get any great shots for me while she was in Vegas?"

What the mother . . . ?

Before I can stand, Jase grabs my arm and pulls me back. How the hell did he know she was in Las Vegas? A better question is, why was she taking photos for him?

"No worries, Lockhart. I have a meeting with her next week. I'll find out what she has for me then." With a smirk, he turns and leaves.

"Don't," Jase says.

"Let go," I demand.

"Not a chance, brother. That fucker is trying to get a rise out of you. He knows Shannon is his ticket to set you off. He'll use anything he can, and you know it. Don't jump to conclusions before you ask her." His voice is stern, and I know he's right, but I also can't help myself. Like hell she is going to meet with him. Over my dead body will she ever do any work for him.

"Then let me go so I can do just that."

I go to walk out as he throws cash down on the counter to follow me. Seconds later, he's by my side as I exit the bar.

"She's at Knocked Out."

"Excuse me?"

"Nikki sent me a text before you came in. She mentioned Shannon was there."

WHEN I ENTER THE GYM, IT TAKES SECONDS FOR ME TO SCAN THE FLOOR. My eyes land on Shannon in the far back corner. She's throwing kicks and punches into a red punching bag Nikki is standing behind. My sister is moving it from side to side, forward and backward, to throw her off, trying to make her miss her targets.

The only other time I've witnessed Shannon throw a punch was when she and Nikki sparred weeks back. I stop dead in my tracks. I'm a little stunned. She's good. Sure, she put Nikki on her ass, but I thought that was pure luck. The woman has strength and skill. I'll give her that.

No matter where Nikki swings the bag, Shannon doesn't miss it. Each hit and kick are dead-on, and shit, it's hot. Her long, makes-my-dick-hard-every-time red hair is pulled back into a high ponytail. She's wearing a black sports bra and a pair of black loose-fitting shorts with "Knocked Out" spelled out across the rear in white letters. Her hands are clad in black gloves that have the fingers cut out. Her feet are bare, making her look sexy as fuck.

Talk about a turn-on.

My sister is also dressed in similar attire, except she's wearing her signature Knocked Out red tank top.

"You planning on staring like the rest of the motherfuckers in this place all day, or are you going to walk over there? You sure flew out of the bar like you were planning to rip off her head."

I pin Jase with a kiss the fuck off look. He smiles.

When I pull my head back around, I notice damn near every man in the place is looking, no staring, at Shannon and Nikki. They're all pussyfooting around with the weights, barely lifting anything.

I take a deep breath that does nothing to calm the storm sitting just below the surface.

"Come find me when you're done. You promised me I could use that ugly mug of yours as a punching bag." He pushes past me as he makes his way to the locker room.

Asshole.

I stalk my way over. Nikki sees me coming but does nothing to warn Shannon. I know she can tell I'm pissed. As I get closer, I watch Shannon land kick after hard kick into that bag, and a thought enters my head. Should she be doing that? Is it safe since she's pregnant?

You really need to research baby shit, Lockhart.

"Get lost," I bark as I wave Nikki out of the way and take her place behind the hanging bag. My sister rolls her eyes and then mumbles a "later" to Shannon before she walks off.

"What's up with you?" Her eyes are full of concern, yet I ignore her question. Sure, I know I'm starting this conversation off by being an ass, but guess what? I am a fucking ass.

"No more leg kicks, but continue to jab the bag." My tone is harsh and full of heated emotions. I've always let my feelings fuel my temper. It's probably my biggest downfall. Shannon looks at me, her eyes full of questions. She just stands there. "Today, please."

"What's your problem?" she fires back. Her eyes flash, showing me she'll give back every bit of what I'm about to lay on her. This really is one of the many things I love about her. She fights. She's so defiant. She doesn't take my shit.

"Just punch the bag," I grit out as I try to control my dick from getting any harder so I can remember why I was so angry when I walked in here. Ah, yes. Jeffery Chaney. "I'll ask the questions here."

I'm a dick. I know I should give her the benefit of the doubt for once. I almost ended us and, in the process, got her hurt—again—because I let my anger control me.

Guilt. It's always there, but I'm here for a reason, so I shove that pussy shit back inside.

"I'm waiting," she almost shouts. I continue to stare at her. I'm not ready to bring Chaney up yet. My temper needs another minute or twelve to cool down. Plus, I'm pissing her off, so telling her she isn't allowed to work for that shit fuck wouldn't go over very well.

"Is it safe for the kid for you to be doing this?" I ask as I motion between her and the punching bag in front of me.

"Huh?"

"Is it safe for the baby?"

"Why wouldn't it be?" she counters, like I'm asking the dumbest question she has ever heard.

"Well, have you seen a doctor yet? Made sure the baby is okay? Especially after what . . ." I stop mid-sentence, not wanting to finish. Why didn't I take her to the hospital? Fuck. That's what I should have done. Why the hell didn't I get her checked out? I close my eyes as I pull in a breath of air and push it back out.

Opening my eyes again, I look down at the gray carpeted floor, and I want to punch myself. No, I want to do a lot worse than that. I was so angry and hurt and only thinking about my own guilt that I let him inside my head again. He consumed my every thought, and I had to get it out. I had to hurt him. I had to kill him.

I cast my eyes back to hers and finish where I was going a moment ago. "What my father did to you."

Shannon stills at the mention of him and looks down. Her slender arms are hanging by her side.

"Um, no." Her voice is a whisper. Surely, she knows she should have gotten checked out too. A second later, she glances back at me, and those green eyes shred me. All I want to do is close the distance between us and take her in my arms. I want to grab her, scoop her up, and take it all away. Her eyes have so much lingering pain behind them. "I did make an appointment, though for later this week. Happy now?" she finishes as she places her hands on her hips.

"Good. Now hit." I place my hand on the bag, moving it so it swings to my right. She simply stands, eyeing me with suspicion.

"Nick, that's not the reason you're here in one of your pissy moods. So, what's crawled up your ass in the last few hours?"

"Hit the goddamn bag, Shannon." I really should shut up. We had two perfect days in Las Vegas. I'm ruining it. I know that, but hell, I can't help myself. Really, this is her fault. She brings out the fire in me. She challenges me. Who the fuck challenges me? No one. So why does she have to do it all the damn time?

"No."

Goddamn female. I hold the bag back in front of us and let go. She is going to be the death of me.

"Woman, don't start this with me. Hit. The. Mother. Fucking. Bag." Yeah, that's not going to go over well. *You're an idiot, Lockhart.*

"Fuck off." I'm staring at her with blazing fire behind my eyes, yet I don't anticipate her move. She raises her left leg and kicks the bag dead-on, sending it directly at me, or my balls, more accurately.

My eyes grow wide, and even though they momentarily cloud with moisture—yeah, that's right, moisture—I'm not a pussy. I don't cry. I see the shock on her face before her mouth drops, and I drop to my knees in pain.

Why the hell do women always have to go for a man's nuts? Fuck, that hurts.

"Shit. Fucking hell," I yell. Does it help? No, it does not. My palms land on the carpet, and now I'm on all fours. *Fuck.*

"I didn't mean to do that, Nick." I can tell by the soft tone of her voice that she didn't. She was irritated. I pissed her off, and she was just shoving the bag at me. Not that I'd admit it, but I deserved that.

"Damn." I hear Jase jogging over in our direction. "That was a nice hit, girl." I look up to see his arm draped over her shoulders while looking down at me with a mile-wide smile on his face.

That's Jase. One minute, he's pissed at the world, or rather Nikki, and thinks his heart is breaking. The next he's back to laughing and brushing it off like it never happened. I should have found out what was really bothering him. I'll never get it out of him now. For him, it's over. Never to be spoken of again.

"Piss off," I choke out. Shaking my head from side to side, I try to gain control again and push myself off the ground.

I knew this conversation would go badly, but I never anticipated my dick being rendered inoperable.

"Go easy on him, will ya? He's still got an ass-kicking coming from me, and I like my opponents to be able to fight back. That way I don't feel so bad when they get hurt."

I growl in his direction. "Yeah, we'll see who ends up on their ass."

"Yeah, we will, fuckhead." Jase releases Shannon and walks off, with me glaring at the back of his skull.

Motherfucker.

"I'm sorry about your junk, but you shouldn't have tried to

order me around. Not happening. Not today, not ever. Try asking next time."

Now that the blood flow to my cock is back, the pain has eased considerably.

"Shannon, will you hit the goddamn bag? Please," I add in a sarcastic tone. I'm certainly not helping myself with that one.

"Sure," she replies, mocking my sarcasm as she throws a punch with her right fist. I swing the bag slightly, and she follows with a left jab.

"Pull your elbows in."

"I don't need a coach. You wanted me to hit, so I did. Now if there's something else on your mind, please, by all means, let's hear it." Again, her tone is packed full of sarcasm.

"Maybe you do need a coach. You're leaving yourself open."

"Oh, for the love, Nick. You're not here to talk about my form. I've been boxing for years. I'm not some little first-timer, okay? You can't possibly judge me after seeing two punches, so what's this really about? You were fine a few hours ago."

"Hit again, please." Shannon rolls her eyes but complies. This time her arms are pulled in just as they should be. The woman actually has good form. It could be better, but it's not bad. And yes, I can judge based on two throws. Not going to say that to her, though.

"I'm still waiting, by the way." I'm trying here. She could at least drop the attitude. The mere thought of her doing any kind of work for Jeffery Chaney makes my blood run cold. I might be a loose cannon when it comes to my temper, but that motherfucker is as controlling, conniving, and vindictive as they come. He's waited a long time to get back at me. I know he will use anything and anyone to bring me to my knees. I know in my gut that Shannon is his ticket to do just that.

"Fine," I bark as she throws another punch, but misses because I purposely swing the bag out too far and step up in front of her, getting right in her personal space. She has to step back because I'm so far forward the bag won't hit me when it swings back.

"What the . . . ?" But I don't give her a chance to finish. I move closer looking down into her eyes, closing any distance between us.

"Were you in Vegas taking photographs for your next project, or were you there because you went behind my back and took Jeffery Chaney on as a client?"

"Excuse me?"

"Answer me, Shannon. Are you doing a job for him?"

"First of all," she states as she straightens her back to try to match my height, knowing damn well she can't. "I did not go behind your back on anything. You broke up with me. You recall that, right?"

Yep, still stings.

I remain silent, but not giving up an inch on my stance. Damn her for trying to turn this around on me.

"Thought so. Secondly, who I take on as a client, who I contract with for a job, is my business, not yours."

"Wrong, baby, because it is my business. You are my business. Every motherfucking inch of this," I tell her as I grab her waist and the top of her arm, bringing her flush with my own body, "is my business and no one else's."

"Back off," she shouts as she tries to push me back. I allow her because I don't want her to get hurt trying to move me. I'm a dick, just not that kind of a dick.

"Watch it."

"No, you watch it. I asked you weeks ago what your problem with him was. You wouldn't tell me. You only said he's a lunatic. Well, that tells me nothing, so unless you have something else to add to that, then we're done. I don't tell you how to run your publishing company, so don't tell me who I can and can't take on as a client."

"Woman, I swear to God."

"Well, do you?" Her eyes are dark and heated. She's pissed. Good, so am I. Why can't she just listen to me?

"No," I yell as I storm past her. No way in hell I want her to know that mess.

CHAPTER TEN

I yank on the waistband of my shorts, pulling them up, and then slam the door to my locker closed. The urge to punch something is growing strong.

Why can't that woman listen? I'm only concerned with her well-being. But she can't see that. No, she has to argue and challenge me on everything.

Women.

My cell phone rings behind the closed door, but I don't bother. Whoever it is can fuck off. I'm done dealing with people for the day.

I turn and head out, pushing the door to the locker room open, causing it to slam into the concrete wall.

Not that I care. I'm fairly certain everyone heard my heated conversation with Shannon and knows by now this is not the time to mess with me.

I scan the room, purposely avoiding the area I left Shannon in. When I see Jase sitting crosslegged on one of the mats, I head over. I know I shouldn't be this upset and it's not her fault when I won't even tell her why I don't want her around Jeffery Chaney.

I can't.

I don't want her to know. She just can't find out.

"You and the missus done?"

"Stay out of it," I tell him as I lean my head from side to side, cracking the bones in my neck. Jase laughs as he jumps to his feet.

"Whatever, time for me to make that face of yours not so pretty anymore." He's still chuckling when I rush forward, catching him off guard as I hook my ankle behind his, forcing him to the ground.

"You can sure try, friend," I calmly say as I get mere inches from his face, hovering above him. "But I think I'm going to have fun showing your Judo students over there"—I gesture and nod to my left side—"what a pussy-boy bitch you really are."

Jase rolls his head over toward the two young boys eagerly watching the two of us before looking back up at me.

"We'll see who leaves here crying with a bloody twat, you little fucking girl."

He has me in a double wrist-lock before I realize it. My head is bent over to the side of his body; Jase's legs are wrapped around my torso as he pulls my wrist back behind me. I have no choice but to tap the mat.

He releases.

"Tapped out after a few seconds?" He smirks as I lean back up, coming to rest on my knees.

"Shut up."

Bringing his right leg up, he wraps it around my neck, forcing me to fall forward as he also grabs my arm, securing me to his body. With my free hand and legs, I push off the mat, and I'm able to turn us, but Jase lands on top of me, nailing me in the jaw with his fist.

And like that, all the shit clouding my mind is gone. All the stress over Shannon and the baby, my guilt, my father, it's no longer pounding away inside my head.

I'm free, and in this moment, there's no one to judge me, not even me; I'm simply free.

Maneuvering my hand around his ankle, I twist my right leg, forcing him to the ground as I go for a kneebar. It takes a few seconds, and after applying more pressure, Jase submits. I release him, but he's quickly coming at me again.

Standing in front of me, he goes for a right straight, which I duck, but he catches my jaw with a left hook.

I welcome the pain, absorbing it into my body like oxygen, like a breath of fresh air.

"Come on, Lockhart. You can do better than that. Hell, your sister can do better than that."

"Fuckstick," I mutter before taking a step in his direction. The feel of the plastic mat against my bare feet is cool, welcoming.

Jase charges me and tries to hook his ankle around mine to take me down to the mat, but I manage to sidestep him and land a kick to his hip. He quickly turns, facing me again, and begins a slow stalk, causing me to move backward.

As he nears, Jase throws out a punch, which I easily block, but he follows with another hit, which lands against my jaw on my right side. I stumble momentarily before recovering my footing.

"Why don't you just tell her your issues with Chaney? Or, rather, his issues with you?"

"Did I not tell you to leave it alone?"

"Sure you did, but you know I'm not going to."

"You're pissing me off."

"I've already pissed you off, and you've pissed me off too, so bring it, bitch. Show me what you really got. Show me all that shit you don't want to release."

I stare at my friend for a moment.

Fuck it.

It's on.

I rush him, and Jase smiles, wanting this as much as I do. I know he's still pissed over how hard I came down on my sister. This is his way of taking out his own built-up frustration.

Bringing my knee up, I slam it into his gut. This is no longer two trained fighters caring about rules or a code of honor. This is two men throwing hit after hit into flesh and bone, not caring where our fists land.

He needs this just as much as I do.

I couldn't tell you how long we give it our all. Time doesn't matter; the need to release the shit inside our heads is much greater. The feel of the blood running down my chin is a mere tickle, a minor irritation, and I want more. I need more.

With my elbow, I swing as hard as I can, nailing him in his upper arm, but I receive a punch to the rib, followed by Jase's foot into the back of my knee, taking me to the ground.

Our brawl doesn't last too much longer before we're both on our backs on the mat, breathing heavily.

"Had enough yet?" His words come out rushed but with no heat behind them. He's done, at least with his aggression toward me.

I roll my head to the side. "For now."

"Boys, note that's what not to do." Jase and I glance up to see my sister standing at the edge of the mat with her arms crossed over her chest. The two teenagers from Jase's Judo class are standing behind her.

Shit.

No doubt we just made fools of ourselves in front of impressionable kids. And Nikki's right. This isn't an appropriate form of training. At least not one those two should witness.

Jase simply snickers, which pisses my sister off even more.

"Clean my goddamn mat up. You two are un-fucking-believable." Shaking her head, she turns and walks off.

"Hey," I call out, and she halts. "Where's Shannon and did you take the dog to her like I asked?"

Looking over her shoulder, she trains her eyes on me. Eyes that tell me I've fucked up once again. But I know that already. I can't seem to do anything or say the right things around my woman.

"Did you really expect her to stick around after your little scene?"

Bitch.

Not that I'm going to call my sister that to her face. Jase would murder my ass and rightfully so.

"And you asked me to take Charmin to Shannon's house. I did that before coming here."

Nikki doesn't bother to tell me where she went, but I have a feeling she went home. It's either that or work.

I get off my ass and stand as I wipe the blood off the back of my hand and onto my shorts. Looking around, I take in the ground as Jase jumps to his feet.

Blood, small amounts of it, is all over the mat.

Nice.

Oh, well, I can't say I'm sorry. We both needed that. It's been too long since he and I had it out for real. And here is the best place. It's what keeps us friends.

"You two," Jase calls out to the kids. "You both wanted to watch. Well, now you both get to clean it up. Hurry up. Class starts in ten."

I laugh, remembering being their age and having to do the same.

"Really?"

"What?" Jase walks off, following him to the locker room to get cleaned up.

"You don't remember Marcus making us do that same thing when we were teenagers?"

"Sure I do, and ever since, I've wanted to do it to another punk kid."

"You're an asshole." I shake my head. If I were in his shoes, I'd probably have done the same thing.

I push the door to the locker room open and head straight to the showers.

By the time evening rolls around and the sun goes down, I'm no closer to making myself drive to Shannon's house than I was when I left Knocked Out. I tried, twice actually, but when I got to the turnoff to Malibu, I couldn't take it. So here I am, driving around West Hollywood. Why I ended up in this part of town, I'm not sure. It's heavily infested with tourists and places to shop, two things I hate. They both involve people and lots of them.

My cell phone rings, so I exit the road, pulling into a parking lot off to my right. It's summer, and apparently kids have nothing better to do than hang out at the mall. After maneuvering through pedestrians walking to and from the stores, I locate an empty parking spot close to the end of the strip and park.

Unbuckling myself, I lift my ass off my seat to pull the phone out of my pocket. Just as I look to see whose call I missed, it pings, telling me I have a voice message waiting. I don't recognize the phone number, but I do remember it's a number that's called a few times over the last few days.

Pressing a button, I bring it to my ear and listen to the message play.

Mr. Lockhart, this is Detective Mike Manning with the Los

Angeles Police Department. I need to speak to you regarding your father. Please call me at . . .

I stop listening and toss the phone in the passenger's seat before the man starts rambling off his number.

A feeling of dread washes over me as I look out the window. I'm parked in front of Shannon's shop or gallery, as she refers to it. I hadn't realized I had pulled into the Gateway shopping center until now. Looking around me, I see my Audi R8 parked a few spots down from my parking spot.

Shit.

At least I can switch cars with her and stop driving this tiny shitbox. This car might be fast, but it isn't meant for men my size. Hell, it can't be safe for a kid either, which reminds me why I took it this morning in the first place.

I quickly lean over, grab my cell phone and open the driver's side door. Getting out, I stretch my legs. Whose stupid idea was it to drive around in that thing for hours?

Oh, yeah, mine.

Dumbass.

Shutting the door, I lean back as I locate a contact in my phone. A few seconds later, Rob's voice comes through the speaker.

"Hey, man. How are you?"

"Good. Need a favor." I tell him.

"Sure."

"Need a Panamera, 4-door, in white. By tomorrow." I laugh.

"Shit. You aren't asking for much are you?" He chuckles too. "Let me see what I can do. You aren't getting rid of the R8 are you?"

"Fuck no. It's for my girl." I wait for the shock that's coming.

"So let me get this straight. Nicholas never-does-a-chick-twice Lockhart is buying a car for a woman?"

"Yeah, what of it?" I know this isn't my normal, but Shannon isn't normal in the sense previous women I've been with are. She's different.

"Nothing, man. Just not sure who the fuck I'm talking to right now." Rob lets out another laugh.

"Need me to remind you?"

"No man, I'm good. I'll call you when I got something. Later."

I end the call and look at the entrance of Art through a Lens. Pushing my ass off the car, I head in that direction. When I get to the door, I hesitate for a second but find the courage to pull the door open. It's unlocked.

Does this woman not know how to lock a damn door? It is well after closing, and anyone could walk in, just as I'm doing now. There's no one out front, so I head toward her office.

As I close the distance to the back, I hear a sound I've missed and see a flash of white fur skidding to a stop on the stained concrete floor. I bend down and scoop Charmin into my arms just as Shannon comes to see what's going on.

"How did you find me?" she questions.

"Coincidence."

She glares at me as if she doesn't buy it.

"Really, it was." Before she can challenge me further, I gesture to the unlocked door. "Reason it's unlocked while you're here alone this late?"

"I'm a big girl," she says condescendingly. "Are you looking for round two with me tonight?"

She places her hands on her hips, and I release the dog onto the floor.

Don't do it, Lockhart. Just keep your mouth shut. You don't always have to have the last word.

Oh, but I do. Except with her, that's not so easy.

"No, babe, I'm not. What are you doing here?"

She sighs, then turns away from me and walks to her office. I follow.

125

"I didn't want to stay at home alone. I brought Charmin with me, worked a couple of hours at the animal shelter around the block, and then came here. Thought I could do some work and get my mind off things."

The way she says *things* makes the pressure in my chest build.

Shannon comes to a stop inside her office, and I come up behind her, my body flush with her back as I wrap one arm around her chest and the other around her belly, around our kid. I pull her farther into my body.

"I'm sorry," I whisper into her ear. Shannon's body tightens in my arms. She closes her eyes as her lips part, pulling in one long breath of air before exhaling and leaning her head back onto my chest.

Seeing what I can do to her with the simplest of touches brings a smile to my face, but I release her as my dick grows hard.

Fuck, I want inside her so damn much, but not here and not now. I can't take the chance of her not being ready after what happened.

My need to keep Shannon and my kid safe and her head clear of him is more important than the need my cock has to get lost inside her heavenly pussy.

"I didn't take any shots for him when we were in Las Vegas. I haven't signed a contract with him either. He wants me to do a collection of photographs for his office, but I haven't said yes . . ." She turns to face me. "Yet."

By him, I know she's referring to Jeffery. Maybe she thinks verbalizing his name will make me angry.

Perhaps it will.

"Why can't you tell me what your problem with him is? What did he do to you?"

"Why can't you trust me?" I counter.

"I do trust you, Nick, but you need to trust me too. Trust me enough to tell me whatever it is you think you can't."

She's right, and there's nothing I can think of that would convince me otherwise. But it's not about that. I can't force the words out. The mouth only speaks when the brain is ready to tell the story.

She turns to face me and looks up as she wraps her hands around my waist.

"I told you what happened with your father. I told you the truth, the whole ugly truth of what happened. Now I'm asking you to do the same."

"That's not fair, Shannon."

I train hard eyes down on her. She can't pull that card every time she wants something out of me. It doesn't work that way.

"You're right. It's not, but I don't know another way to get you to open up to me"

I place my own hands on her arms, gliding them up to her shoulders and pull her closer to me. I place a kiss on her forehead.

There's no way in hell I can tell her everything right now, if ever.

"A long time ago, years, in fact, Jeffery made a promise to me. That promise, or threat because that's what it actually was, was that he would make me pay for something I did. He would take something away from me like I did to him."

Shannon pulls back to peer up at me.

"What does that mean?"

"You and that little shit growing inside you . . ." Her eyebrows turn in as I say that referring to our child. Like that's any worse than her referring to the kid as a minion. "Are the only two things in this world he could ever take from me that would destroy me."

"Why would he want to destroy you?" She pulls away from me but continues to look up.

"That's the part I can't tell you right now. I'm not saying I won't ever tell you, but I can't right now."

"But you will? I need to know that you will."

I turn around, unsure if I ever will. I want to, but sometimes wanting to and being able to are two different things. So I lie. I hate myself for it. I hate liars.

"I will, but it won't be today. It won't be tomorrow, and I doubt it will be next week."

"Then I'll accept that for now, and I'll tell him I can't work for him, not now, not ever." A relaxing exhale of relief flows out of my body at her words. She walks up behind me and leans her forehead into the center of my back.

I move away from her touch, still unable to face her as I bend down and gather Charmin into my arms.

"Let's go home. I'm starving," I tell her as I walk out of her office.

"Then you might want to pick up takeout on the way. My cooking skills are limited."

"Trust me, baby, I know this already."

She turns off the lights, and we switch keys as we walk out the door. Shannon locks up, and then we make our way to the parking lot.

"Your house or mine?" she asks in a nearly whispered tone. Had she not been standing next to me, I wouldn't have heard her.

"Yours. Do you not want to go home?" I stop in front of her car and pull her toward me.

"Yes, but . . ." She sighs.

"Baby, don't let what happened stop you from enjoying your home. He wins if you let it affect you like this. Don't let him win."

I know I can only do so much for her. If I could take away all the pain, all the memories that sorry piece of shit left her, I would. But I can't. This is something only she can get past.

"I know. Let's go home. I'll be fine."

"Are you sure?"

"Yeah, I am. Dog rides with me."

"Yes, ma'am." I hand over Charmin and pull Shannon into a kiss before getting into my car and following her home.

CHAPTER ELEVEN

I wake to a heel slamming into my hip bone. Not enough strength to cause pain, but more than enough to wake my sorry ass up from my worst nightmare come true. Blowing out air from my mouth, I try to shake the images from my head.

"Your phone. Make it stop. Sleeping."

I lift my head off the pillow to look over, seeing Shannon's face buried into the mattress with her pillow covering her head. I throw the comforter off and sit up, allowing my feet to fall to the floor. When I grab my cell phone lying on the nightstand next to me, I see I have two text messages from Rob.

Rob: I can have it here by Friday.

The message is followed by a picture of a Porsche Panamera GTS in white with what looks to be red rims. This car looks sweet, and I can't wait to see her in it.

I smile as I thumb a quick reply to him.

Me: That works. Thanks, man. Call Rachel for payment.

Tossing my phone back on the table, I get out of bed and make my way into the bathroom for a shower. After the beating

Jase laid on me, I need steaming hot water to loosen my stiff muscles.

I turn the faucet to the shower on, making sure it's hot before shucking my boxers to the floor and stepping inside.

As I turn the water off and open the door to grab a towel, Shannon walks in buck-naked. I wrap the towel around my waist to hide my hardening cock as I step out.

"Your phone rang while you were in the shower," she tells me as she turns the water back on.

"All right. What are your plans today?"

"Work," she replies as she walks into the shower and shuts the door. "Jenny is off, and I need the distraction."

Walking out of the bathroom, I retrieve my phone to see a missed call from my mother. I hesitate over her name before shaking my head and dropping the phone on the bed.

Honestly, she is still the last person on Earth I want to speak to right now. I've never been mad at my mom, so I don't know how to handle it, much less how to fix it.

I walk into the closet and pull a pair of clean boxers from the top drawer. Once I have them on, I grab a pair of jeans and a T-shirt, quickly putting both on, followed by my socks and sneakers.

Exiting, I walk out of the bedroom to see Charmin rolling around on the hardwood floor in the living room, playing with a tennis ball. Looking a little closer, I see the tennis ball is merely half a tennis ball, and I don't see the other half in sight.

"Give me that," I say as I grab the shredded ball from her mouth and take it to the trash can in the kitchen.

After tossing the half-eaten ball in the trash, I locate a racquetball from one of the drawers in the kitchen and toss it to her. She goes back to chewing.

Shannon walks out dressed in a white tank top, loose gray capri pants, and a pair of flip-flops.

"Let's go, TP." She giggles as she grabs her bag from the couch.

"TP? Really?"

She smirks in my direction before opening the door. "You named her after ass paper, not me." I walk over, giving her a kiss on the lips before she slips out of the door.

I'M FINISHING UP MY LAST REPS ON THE FREE WEIGHTS AT KNOCKED OUT when Jase walks over, covered in sweat.

"What's the matter, buttercup? Afraid I'll hand your ass to you again? You're over here pussyfooting around with a few hand weights now?"

"Dude." I set the fifty-pound weight down and look at him. "My jaw hurts. I have fat lips and a goddamn black eye. Do you know how long it's been since I've sported a black eye?"

"Probably since the last time I gave you one."

"Go the hell away." Fuckhead. I don't see him mentioning the faint black mark under his right eye or the cut across his left eyebrow.

"No can do, friend. Your sister asked me to meet her at Mint for lunch and to bring you. So go clean up and let's go. Can't walk in such a posh hotel sweaty and nasty now, can we?"

"Kiss off, asshole. Do I look like I do what Nikki says now?" Posh fucking hotel my ass. Sure, it's got that warm, luxurious feel that I created. Funny, he never called it a posh hotel when I owned it.

"Look, I have a fight Friday night. Mint is one of the few places I actually like that also serves food I can eat. I would like to sit down and eat a fucking meal with my best friend and my girl without all the drama of the last few weeks interfering and fucking my head up. Okay?"

"All right, let's go."

He's right. He needs a clear head. And it would be nice to hang out with my two best friends for a change. It's been too long since we just chilled.

———

An hour later, we walk into the restaurant. I shoot Shannon a text asking if she wants me to bring her lunch while Jase scans the crowd, looking for my sister.

"Son of a bitch."

"What?" I look up as I stick my phone inside the pocket of my blue jeans. I look in the direction of Jase's now pissed-off gaze.

"I swear I had no idea she would be here."

My eyes land on a woman with blonde hair sitting across from Nikki in a booth.

My mother.

"What the hell is my sister doing?" She turns her head in my direction, and I glare at her. Did she and I not just get over our shit yesterday? Yet here she is, thinking she's going to fix my relationship with our mother, I guess.

"No idea, but I'll handle Nikki. I assure you of that." I look over at a furious expression across Jase's face. He mouths a word to my sister, and she dashes our way.

"You're becoming an annoying little bitch, you know that?" I bark in a low tone, trying to keep my cool in the restaurant and not cause a scene.

"Hey." She starts to defend herself, but Jase cuts her off just as quickly as the word came from her mouth.

"Save it, Nikki." He grabs her by the wrist, then turns to leave. As they are walking off, he turns back to me. "I'm sorry, brother."

I wave him off. It isn't his fault. Then I make my way over to my mother and sit opposite her.

"So now you're using my sister to get me to speak to you?"

"You left me no choice, Nicholas. You won't answer or return any of my calls."

"Your point, Mother?"

Yes, I'm being an ass to my mom, but hell, she deserves it. She played a part in all this shit too. Should I be blaming my mom? Probably not.

"I know you are angry with me, son, but I'm not sorry for trying to protect my family."

"You're really going to start with that again? Mom, I don't want to hear it."

A waiter comes by, and I look up.

"Is there anything I can get you, Mr. Lockhart?"

He's one of the college students who started a few months ago.

"No, Jordan, I'm fine."

He nods and walks off. My mother picks up a coffee cup and takes a small sip before placing it back on the table. She sighs and looks at me with sad eyes.

I can't stay here much longer. Those eyes hurt my heart. I love my mother; I do, but yes, I'm mad. If she had told me . . . hell, if she would have left that monster years ago, what happened to Shannon might not have happened. I might not be responsible for a man's death.

"Very well then, Nicholas. I'll drop it. It's not what I wanted to discuss anyway. What I called you about this morning . . ." She pauses and sits up, making herself appear taller in her seat before leaning in. Her voice drops a little, not to a whisper, but you would have to be seated at our table to hear her words. "I've decided to have a memorial service for your father, open to the public tomorrow as I'm having his body cremated today."

The way she tells me this seems like she's hiding something, but I'm not sure what. Guess I'll have to bite.

"And you couldn't tell me that in a text message?"

Even I want to laugh at myself for that one. My mother, texting? Never.

She gives me a pointed look, making me feel stupid for even suggesting such a thing.

"Well, you could have left a voice message."

"And you, my son, could have answered your mother's call."

My patience is running thin. This better get somewhere soon.

"I needed to speak to you in person."

"And why is that, Mom?" I check the time on my watch. It's way past lunchtime, and I'm starving, but like hell I'm going to sit here and share a meal with the woman who helped put Shannon and my baby in danger.

I wonder if Nikki told her the news.

No. I don't believe she did. My sister isn't a blabbermouth. She can keep secrets like no one else, even when they shouldn't be kept. I know there's something going on with Nikki. She's been off, so to speak, over the last few weeks. I don't think Jase or anyone else has noticed, but I can see it. It's in the way she looks at me, or not, rather. She has been avoiding my eyes. She is hiding something else, but right now, I just don't have it in me to find out. And Jase, well, he's too occupied with self-pity to see a bigger reason behind Nikki's inability to commit to him fully.

"I spoke to the detective handling your dad's investigation. He told me nothing concrete came back from the autopsy. There wasn't much in the way of trace evidence, as he put it. So after a lot of thought, I decided to have his body"—she pauses and looks down, but I see the emotion in her eyes as she blinks back a tear—"burned, cremated."

Lifting her coffee, she takes a sip as I sit back against the soft, plush fabric of the booth.

She thinks I did it. It's obvious she suspects I killed my father and she is doing this for me. Despite the so-called love she thinks she has for that sick bastard, she still wants to protect me. How do I stay mad, angry, when all I want to do is wrap my arms around the woman I've loved my entire life?

Sure she has her faults, but don't we all? Only her faults don't make her evil like him. It just makes her human.

Still, I don't need her thinking I had something to do with it. That would only lead to the truth coming out, and that truth needs to stay between Jase and me. I know he would never tell another person, not even my sister.

"Mom." I soften my voice. I know I have been rather short and harsh with her this morning. "If you're doing this because you think you know something or you're trying to protect someone, then think again. Look at me, please."

She lifts her face, looking into the same eyes I share with her, and I lie—again.

"It wasn't me. I didn't have anything to do with your husband's death."

I'm so sick of calling that man my father.

"Your father," she states firmly.

"Whatever, Mom." And like that, the tension between us is back. She is never going to see that man for who he really was.

She's delusional. Why the hell I didn't see that sooner, I don't know. Maybe I've always known and simply didn't want to admit it to myself.

"I would like you there."

"Excuse me?"

"The memorial service for your father. I would like you present, please."

She can't be serious, but I know she is.

"After everything he's done to Shannon . . ." I look away briefly, trying to calm the heat within me that borders on scorching. "You expect me to show him respect? To mingle with hundreds of people and pretend he was father of the goddamn year?"

"Yes, that is exactly what I want you to do, son. And you will," she adds.

"Good luck with that. It's a little too late to assert any authority over me."

I exit the booth before she's able to say another word. As I walk through the restaurant, I pull my wallet out of my back pocket, retrieving three twenty-dollar bills. As I pass the kid who was serving my mother, I tap him on the shoulder. He turns around, facing me.

"See that my mother is taken care of, please. Whatever she wants can be charged to my account."

After handing the money over, I leave the restaurant but not the hotel. I realize it's early in the afternoon, but I'm in need of a drink, so I head over to Quaint, hoping chatty Cathy isn't serving today. Tabitha is sweet, but I'm not in the mood for her right now.

Walking in, I spot Sam behind the bar. Figures.

"Shouldn't you be running my former business instead of hanging out behind a bar?"

Sam pivots, smirking at me as he pulls a glass tumbler from underneath the counter and sits it in front of me.

"And why would I put on a suit and tie when I have people to do that shit for me? No, this is exactly where I want to be. Owning all this is just a perk."

He pulls out the whiskey, and I hold up my hand.

"It's too early for the dark stuff. Bombay with lemon, please."

Sam pours my gin and tonic, and as I drink, I begin to relax again.

Fuck.

Even I know I'm going to go, just like my mother knows I'll be there—fake fucking smile and all.

My phone chimes indicating someone sent me a text. When I glance at the screen, I see it's a message from Shannon.

Shannon: We already ate, but thanks.

CHAPTER TWELVE

I've been sitting and staring at my computer screen for at least half an hour, getting nothing accomplished. I have hundreds of emails to weed through, not to mention all the phone messages Rachel placed on my desk right after I arrived this morning. Missing a week of work was not ideal.

I flick my wrist and glance down at my Rolex to confirm I'm dead on the money. It's nearly nine o'clock, yet I walked into the building a little after eight.

I thought getting back into my normal routine would relax and center my mind. It hasn't. Sparring with Jase for an hour this morning only distracted me for a short time. At least this time, I didn't walk away with another swollen cheek to match the one Jase placed on the left side of my face on Tuesday.

My head has been a mess since the brief conversation with Detective Manning following my father's memorial service yesterday afternoon. I'd been avoiding his calls. Honestly, I hadn't realized I was avoiding his calls until he left me a voice message earlier this week. My phone has been blowing up since word of my father's death hit the local news. If a phone number wasn't attached to a name in my contacts, then I didn't feel the need to return their call or message them. Not that I returned any that were because I didn't.

A meeting.

He wanted to discuss the investigation of my father's murder. Yes, murder. That's what it is. I'm not living in a fantasy where I'm pretending I didn't kill him. I did, and I'm not sorry. Well, not really. I get a ping in my chest every time I think about it, but it's always followed by visions of what he did to Shannon —what I allowed him to do—and the guilt, the sorrow, goes away only to be replaced with anger.

Anger toward myself. I fucked up, and Shannon doesn't know it. I heave out a breath. What the hell am I going to do now?

"Nicholas, you're here."

My eyes glide over to the entrance to my office to see a stunned expression on Teresa's face.

Great.

I should've known leaving the door to my office open would be a bad idea. But I've been gone so long. I missed my weekly meetings with my staff who report directly to me last Friday.

"Why wouldn't I be here, Teresa?"

"Maybe because your father was killed a week ago and was only buried yesterday. That's why you shouldn't be here. You should be with your family."

So what?

She pushes off the doorframe, sashaying toward me. I've seen Teresa when she doesn't know I'm watching. She walks completely different than she is now. Who the fuck walks while swaying their hips from side to side? Do chicks really think that's attractive? Maybe it is to some. But to me, it looks dumb. I'm not stupid. I know she's trying to get my attention.

As she nears, I have no choice but to take in her

appearance. Her blonde hair is hanging in loose waves just above her shoulders. She's wearing a sleeveless black, A-line dress that hits a few inches above her knees. The dress fits her perfectly.

"Yes, well, that doesn't mean I can stop running my company now, does it?"

"Of course not, Nicholas. That's not what I meant." She rounds my desk and props herself against the corner of it, causing me to rotate my body and chair so I can look her in the eye.

"You know you bypassed two perfectly good chairs, right? I don't need you sitting on top of my desk. If there's something you need, then spit it out. If not, then please leave. I have work to get done and a pending meeting on my agenda." I know I'm being rude, but she's the one making herself comfortable on the edge of my desk.

Fucking inappropriate.

Fucking Teresa.

"Well, you don't have to be nasty. I've been concerned about you, Nicholas. You haven't returned any of my calls." She crosses her arm across her chest and gives me a slight pout.

"If there was a problem, you could have left a voice message or sent me a text, which you did not."

"There was no work problem. I had everything under control here. I always do. You know that."

I wish she would leave me the hell alone. I feel a migraine coming on, and having her in here will only make it worse.

She smiles at me and scoots off my desk. I think she got the message and is about to turn to walk out, but no, she moves closer.

What the fuck?

"You look so tense, Nicholas," she says as she bends at the waist and moves her hands to my shoulder.

141

"What the hell are you doing?" I question as I place my hands on her hips, halting her advancement.

"What does it look like?" Her eyes are coy, and her lips are turned up.

"For one, the goddamn door is wide the fuck open. Anyone could walk in right now. And—"

"So what?" the bitch states as she rudely interrupts me.

"And," I emphasize the word strongly, "what do you think it would look like?" I push her away and cross my arms over my chest.

"Um, two adults, one massaging and taking care of the needs of the other. Really, Nicholas, what is the big deal? There's no policy against you and I being intimate."

Fucking Christ.

"Okay, here's the deal. We're going to forget you just said that and move on. What happened between the two of us was a mistake, and I take full responsibility. We were both intoxicated, and it should never have happened. You work for me. You're my employee. That's all. Its ends there. We aren't friends, Teresa, or anything else, for that matter. Do you understand?"

"Nicholas," she forces out. I hate the way my name rolls off her tongue. It rubs me the wrong way. "If you would just stop for a minute, you'd see we could be good together. This company is great. We did that. We are two strong people, and together would be even better."

What is this bitch smoking?

"Stop right now, Teresa. This, whatever it is you think could happen between us, isn't going to happen. I have a girlfriend, and she isn't you. She won't ever be you. So you can stop now, and we can forget it. If not, then you will be looking for another job. Now, do you understand that?"

"What?" She places her hands on her hips. "You're back with her, that bitch who screwed your own father? Are you serious?"

Breathe, Lockhart. Just breathe.

The mention of my father and Shannon has my body screaming to hit something. I can't do that in here. This is not the place for me to show emotions. Showing them would make me look weak, and I'm not weak.

Uncrossing my arms, I place them on the armrests of my chair and push myself into a standing position, making Teresa take a step back.

"This conversation is over. I won't say it again, and if you value your job here, then I suggest you leave my office. Now." My voice is firm as I train my eyes on her brown ones. I can tell she wants to fight me on this. I can see it in her eyes, in her body language. But she doesn't. She is smart enough to know I'm not calling her bluff.

Without another word, she turns and exits the room. Before I can move to close my door, the desk phone rings.

"What?" I demand, even before the receiver touches my ear.

The nerve of that woman. I've always known she had a thing for me, but she took things too far today. It's one thing to flaunt her tits in front of me. It's another to touch me. There's only one woman I want touching me. Teresa Matthews certainly isn't that woman.

"You have a Detective Manning here, claiming to have a meeting with you," Rachel says calmly.

"Right. I didn't think to mention it when I walked in."

"It's okay, boss. Should I show him in now?"

No, I'd rather you not, I think to myself. I'd rather not have to talk to him at all, but I know I'm not getting out of it. Besides, I know it's best to know how the investigation is going and what leads, if any, they have. As well as find out if they suspect me?

What if the police do have me as a person of interest? What then?

"Yes, please do," I finally instruct Rachel.

Within a few seconds, Rachel enters my office, followed by the man I met yesterday. He is dressed in a black suit, with a dark gray shirt and black tie, similar to the attire he wore to my father's funeral. He's younger than my father but older than me. If I had to guess, I'd say he's in his early to mid-forties.

"Come in," I say, trying to plaster on a fake smile as I round my desk and move in his direction. When he's close enough, I extend my hand, which he accepts.

"Why don't we sit over there?" I say, pointing to the couch and chair on the other side of my office after he draws his right hand back.

"Certainly, Mr. Lockhart. I appreciate you meeting with me this morning."

I nod and turn my attention to Rachel.

"Will you bring us a couple of bottles of water?"

"Yes, of course."

"Nothing for me," the detective interjects. "I don't see this taking up too much of your time." I'm not exactly sure if that's a good sign or a bad one. Guess I'll find out soon enough.

"All right then, let's take a seat."

I follow him over. He takes a seat in one of the two chairs, and I proceed to the couch so I'm facing him.

"What is it I can help you with, Detective Manning?" I ask as Rachel hands me a small bottle of water before turning and leaving my office. She gently pulls the door closed as she leaves.

"I'm sorry for your loss. I don't like this part of my job, but it has to be done. I'm sure you can understand that, and please do not think I'm being insensitive to your family. I'm here to solve a crime and bring a criminal to justice. In doing so, I often have to ask questions and gather information that may upset you or even your family."

"No apology needed. You can be frank and to the point with me, Detective."

"Good. That will make this easier. First, can you tell me where you were the night your father was killed?"

"I stayed the night at my girlfriend's house. What does that have to do with my father's death?"

"Hopefully nothing, but in order for me to do my job and find the person who killed Judge Lewis, I have to know all the facts. Did someone have a grudge against him and hate him enough to take his life? Was it a random act and just being in the wrong place at the wrong time? In order to get all the facts, I have to know the people closest to him and their whereabouts the night of his murder."

Well, I did ask the man to be frank, didn't I?

"Of course."

"Thank you, and your girlfriend's name?"

"Shannon Taylor." I won't have her involved in this.

"Can anyone besides Miss Taylor verify you were there the full night?"

"No," I respond as I twist the cap off my water and take a small sip.

"Fair enough. Now, can you recount the events of that night? What time you went to bed, and what time you woke up?"

I never went to sleep. Not that I can say that. I take another swallow of water, trying to buy myself time and hoping I appear to be thinking about his questions.

"My sister and a close friend were over with us earlier in the night. They left, and I guess we went to bed maybe around eleven," I answer him as I remember Shannon falling asleep on top of me and me holding her for a long time before I placed her in bed. "I'm not sure what time we got up. My sister arrived around seven the next morning, I think. Shannon was sick a few minutes prior, so maybe a quarter to seven."

"Miss Taylor was sick on Friday, you say?" He removes a

small notebook from his jacket pocket and jots something down. The way he questions that seems a bit odd.

"Morning sickness. She's pregnant."

"Ah, a baby. Well, congratulations then." For some reason, this makes me smile. He's the first person to tell me that, and I might just like hearing it.

"Thank you."

"Yes, well, she did seem upset when I spoke to her last week."

"Excuse me?" Why the hell don't I know this already?

"Last week, Friday afternoon, actually. I was looking for you, and I couldn't reach you by phone. Your mother told me you may be at her home."

"I apologize. I wasn't aware you were looking for me. It's been a long and rough week. Shannon must have forgotten to tell me."

"Understandable. Tell me, did you know your sister, Nicolette, got into an argument and hit your father the day before his death?" The detective's face is unreadable and something I'm not used to. I like to think I read people well. Paying attention to your surroundings is really all that it comes down to, but this detective doesn't give an inch away.

"I heard. Nikki and my father didn't have that daddy's-little-girl, father-daughter type relationship. She is independent, strong-willed, and hardheaded, but I can assure you, my sister would never kill someone. She was at a mixed martial arts fight that night. She manages a fighter, Jason Teller. From what I've been told, she was there late and then celebrated at a local club until early the next morning."

"Yes, that was her statement as well." He pauses and makes another annoying note on his pad. "And several people have backed that up. Your family has been very cooperative, and the police department appreciates that. I appreciate that. I'm looking into Judge Lewis's past cases to see if I can find a link there. So far this week, I haven't found any leads. I know that isn't something you want to hear, but it's the facts."

"Okay." Keeping my response simple seems the best as I drain the rest of the water from the bottle. He isn't giving anything away and neither will I. At least I feel somewhat at ease. My sister doesn't seem to be a suspect.

"Is there anyone you can think of who would want to harm the judge?"

Lots.

"No, I cannot. I've racked my brain over the last week and still can't think of one person. He was well respected in the community, in the courtroom,"—I lean forward on the couch—"and at home," I lie.

Respect is earned, never given freely. My father never earned that from his family. He never wanted to.

"I spoke to Mrs. Lewis earlier this week about the investigation. I assume she has filled you in?"

"Somewhat. We spoke briefly, but my father's death has been hard on her."

"Certainly understandable. My team has hit a standstill. That doesn't mean our investigation is over, but currently, I don't have much. Evidence was lacking to link anything. The parking lot where the judge's car was found didn't have a working video camera, and none of the residents in the community saw or heard anything. I'm sorry I don't have more to offer, but like I said, the investigation is ongoing."

I nod my head, not exactly knowing how to respond.

"Well, I don't want to keep you any longer, Mr. Lockhart. You've answered all my questions. Thank you, and I'll be in touch as the investigation progresses." He stands, and I follow.

"I'll show you out."

"That won't be necessary. I'm sure I have taken up enough of your time this morning."

"Thank you," I finish as I extend my hand again. The detective shakes it as he stares back at me. He is slightly shorter than I am, so he casts his eyes up to meet mine before letting go and walking out of my office.

Sitting back on the couch, I lean my head back to relax. Exhaling, I let out a deep breath. That was one of the most nerve-racking meetings I've ever been in.

"Boss?"

"Yeah?" I look up to see Rachel standing just inside my office.

"Everything okay?"

"Everything is fine," I lie. I seem to be making a habit of that lately. "What do you need?"

"I was wondering if it was okay if I took an extra thirty minutes to an hour for lunch."

"Yes, that's fine. Is there anything else?"

"No, that's it. Want me to bring you something back?"

"Sure, doesn't matter what. You can decide. I need to get some work done here. Thanks, Rachel."

She looks at me with an odd expression, making me wonder if I really am such a dick that I don't thank her enough.

Reaching for my phone, I shoot Rob a message asking about the car I bought Shannon.

Me: Has it arrived?

Rob: Yes. Delivery still at 7, right?

Me: Correct. You have the address?

Rob: Yes.

Finally, something to be excited about. I smile and move to my chair, rolling forward in front of my computer.

I hate emails, and right now, I'm in email hell.

CHAPTER THIRTEEN

I ended up leaving the office much later than I anticipated. I wanted to make it to Shannon's by six, but as I pull into the driveway, it's a quarter to seven.

Shit, Rob will be here with the delivery, and I need to distract her.

As I climb out of the Audi, I see Jase's Jeep parked along the curb in front of Shannon's house. That means my sister's here, and she owes me.

Making my way up to the front door, I turn the knob, open the door and walk inside. Immediately, I'm greeted by Charmin jumping up and down. I toss my keys into the basket next to the door and bend down, scooping her into my arms.

Closing the door, I look around and see Shannon, Nikki, and Jase on the back deck. Nikki turns her head and sees me. I make a come-here gesture with my finger. She hesitates as I watch her but eventually comes inside.

"Want a beer?" she asks as she tosses her empty one into the trashcan. I follow her into the kitchen.

"Sure," I respond as I place the dog back onto the floor.

Charmin quickly runs to the doggy door, going through to the backyard.

After she hands me a cold bottle of beer, I take the cap off and then toss it onto the counter as my sister does the same.

"Reason you avoided me during the entire service yesterday?" she calmly asks, knowing she already knows why.

"You know why. Let's not play stupid on that one."

Tipping the bottle back, I let the icy cold liquid drain into my mouth and down my throat, damn near emptying the contents in one swallow. It's been a long day between dealing with that cop and Teresa pulling her bullshit games.

"Fine. I'm sorry. It won't happen again." Not accepting her sorry-ass apology, I lightly grab her by the wrist as she tries to walk past me, heading back outside.

"I'm tired of you doing shit, fucking up, and then wanting back into my good graces after the fact. I don't play that, the 'do it and then ask for forgiveness later' shit. What's up with you? This, what you have been doing, isn't like you. You've been off lately, so let's hear it."

"Not now, Nick." Her eyes are everywhere but on me. She's hiding something. I thought it a few days ago, but now I know it.

"Whatever is bothering you has that thing fucked up," I tell her as I point to her head. "You can tell me. No matter what you do or don't do, I'm here, behind you, in your corner always, little sister. You know that, right?"

"Yes, Nick, I do." She sighs and wraps her arms around my waist. "I'm fine. Just some things I need to work out on my own. I shouldn't have helped Mom ambush you. I'm sorry."

"Fine. I'll accept that for now." I pull her closer to me and kiss the side of her head, against the dark strands of her hair.

Releasing her, I down the rest of my beer and walk around Nikki to toss the empty glass bottle into the trashcan.

"I need a favor, and you actually do need to get back into my good graces."

She eyes me with suspicion as I pull another beer out of the refrigerator.

"So I need you to distract Shannon and not let her near the front until we leave. Speaking of which, where are we going before the fight?"

"To grab a bite to eat and have a few drinks with Shannon's friends. They're all coming to the fight tonight too. I'm pretty sure they are all coming, Ben, Kyle, Katelyn, and Stacy. You'll have to get Shannon to tell you where we're going to dinner. She told me earlier, but I forgot. So why do I need to distract her?"

"Rob."

Nikki throws up her hands dramatically. "You bought her a car?"

"Hush. Damn it, girl. If I wanted her to know, I'd walk out there and tell her myself. It's a fucking surprise, Miss Loud Mouth."

"Did you ask her, or did she give you any indication she wanted a new car? She"—Nikki points through the window to Shannon, who is outside talking with Jase—"seems to be happy with the one she has."

"Don't be so negative She'll love the new one, but to answer your question, no, I did not," I tell her as she opens her mouth. "Where do you suppose she will put a kid in the nine-eleven? Groceries don't even fit."

"I wouldn't start with that thought when you spring this on her. I mean, you have a point about the kid, but it isn't like your girl does much grocery shopping."

We both laugh at that. So true. My woman can't cook for shit. She can even fuck up breakfast, and what's easier to cook than eggs?

"Look, can you keep her busy for me? I need to shower and

change. Rob should be here any minute. I don't want her to see it until we leave."

"Yeah, I'll do my best. I'll just tie her up to a lawn chair if I have to."

"I bet your kinky ass would love to do just that too."

"You do know me." She smirks, and I walk off to get cleaned up.

As I'm sliding my watch onto my wrist, I hear my cell phone ding with an alert. Grabbing it, I read the text message from Rob.

Rob: All good, Nicholas. It's in the driveway now. I have the 911 on the trailer heading back. Let me know what you want to do with it.

Me: Good deal.

Making my way out of the room, I walk through the kitchen to grab a fresh beer and then head out the back door.

"You guys ready to roll?"

"We. Are. Starving," Shannon greets me.

"Then let's go." Untwisting the cap, I take a long swallow of beer as I start to feel a little nervous. What if Nikki is right? Maybe I should have asked Shannon first. She isn't the 'bow down and do as I say' type. And surprisingly, I love that about her. "You're the designated driver tonight, babe."

"Oh, am I?" she challenges me.

Walking to the front door, I swing it open and pull her outside while I still have the nerve to go through with this.

"Nick, I didn't get my keys." I laugh a huge belly laugh at that statement.

"Yeah, like the four of us would fit into that thing you drive."

As we exit the house, I feel resistance from Shannon as I try to pull her down the walkway. Stopping, I turn and face her.

She sees it.

"Where is my car, and where did that one come from?" She points to the white, sleek Panamera GTS that is parked next to mine.

I look at my sister, her arms crossed over her chest as she prepares for this show.

"That baby is your new ride."

Please love it.

"I had a ride," she replies as she uses air quotes when saying *ride*.

"And now you have a new one, a better one."

"Who's to say it's better? I had a sweet ride." Again with the air quote. "Speaking of which, where is it?"

"Not here. Now let's go."

"Let's not. Where is my car, Nick, and why did you buy me another one? Did you think to ask me if I wanted a new one?"

"It was a surprise."

Damn, surely she doesn't hate it. She hasn't even looked at it. It's a hot ride. It's not like I bought her a damn minivan.

She crosses her arms and looks at me.

"Oh, come on. Give it a chance, will you? Besides, you were going to have to eventually get something else for that little shit right there," I tell her, pointing to her belly.

"Stop calling it a little shit, fucker."

"Stop teaching it bad language."

"Oh, fuck off." She throws her hands up in a dramatic gesture as she walks toward the car, but doesn't manage to hide the smile that formed on her lips when her eyes landed on the machine parked in her driveway. Score!

CHAPTER FOURTEEN

Tonight is a good night. It's been weeks since Shannon's been out with her friends. Dinner at Hatfield's came and went all too soon. I have to admit, I actually like Shannon's array of friends. They mix well with the short list of people I consider my own close friends. Even that little sassy weather girl is growing on me. I can tell she's trying hard to act like she is still pissed over some comment I made the first night I met her.

Walking through the doors of the large warehouse housing the fights tonight, I feel lighter. Despite the musky smell of people and the crowd, I'm not agitated. There's no volcanic anger about to boil over. The only heat coursing through my body is from the lack of air conditioning inside this building.

Gliding my palm down the center of Shannon's back, settling on the lower portion, I continue lightly pushing her through the aisle and down the steps, passing men and women screaming and yelling down to the cage positioned in the center of a spacious area.

Two men I don't recognize are fighting in the steel cage. Both

154

look worn down, lightweights, and probably weighing a buck seventy-five soaking wet. The one with a shaved head has blood running down his neck from a gash on his left eyebrow. The other man with a tight military-style haircut isn't as beat up as his opponent. I can see his stamina returning; adrenaline is surely running through his body, kicking in as his pace picks up. In the blink of an eye, the fight ends by way of a kick to the jaw, knocking the guy out for a few seconds, but long enough for the referee to call the fight a KO.

"This is us." I lean forward, whispering in Shannon's ear as I motion for her to enter an aisle in the second row. Nikki has a few chairs in the first and second rows reserved for our crew. The first of the fights started well over an hour ago, but neither of us is too concerned with seeing a bunch of relatively new fighters simply working up a sweat. We have been there and seen it all before.

We're here for Jase's fight. He'll be making an appearance within half an hour to square off against Nathan Jareau.

"When does Jase come out?"

Shannon sits in an empty plastic chair, and I follow as I glance at my watch, checking the time to confirm I'm right. It's just past ten o'clock now.

"Around 10:30," I tell her as Shane takes a seat beside me, along with who I'm assuming is his new girlfriend. Shannon's friend Katelyn, who looks giddy, stares ahead as the fighters, commentators, and other people shuffle out of the cage. Two chicks, clad in small bikinis, walk in wearing clear stripper heels. They have every eye in the place on them, entertaining the crowd as the next two fighters get ready to come out.

Shannon's other friends, Ben, Kyle, and Little Miss is-it-going-to-rain-today, Stacy, take their seats in the front row.

Yeah, I'm not planning on leaving that one alone. Now that I know she doesn't like to be called a weather girl, I plan to use that to my advantage.

"What's with your friend?" I lean over so Shannon can hear me through the noise of all the people around and behind us. "She's been wearing a disgusted look since we walked through the doors."

Shannon snorts a laugh. "This isn't exactly her deal, you know what I mean?"

"So why did she come?" I breathe out as I drape my left arm over the back of Shannon's chair and around her shoulder, urging her closer to me.

Shannon shrugs as she glances over in the direction Stacy is seated; Stacy's arms are crossed as she looks into the cage at the women walking out.

"Everyone else was going. She didn't want to be left out, I guess."

Putting her friends out of my mind, I lean in closer. "So about that surprise earlier. How did you like driving it?"

Without looking at me, she once again shrugs. "Eh, it was okay. Drove well, I guess."

"You guess?" I question. I can see the strain she has placed on her face, although she tries to hide it. She likes the car. She wants to smile but is forcing herself to remain unfazed.

"Baby," I say, dropping my voice somewhat and leaning in farther, as close to her ear without touching, "you can like it, you know, and I can think of a nice way for you to thank me later."

She pulls back and away from me. "Thank you?" It's almost a laugh, and a forced one at that.

"Nick, you're lucky your balls are still intact right now. I wouldn't push your luck here, buddy."

Turning her face forward and looking at the cage, she leans back into her seat, folding her arms across her chest as she focuses hard on the two opponents inside the cage as the first bell sounds.

Leaving her alone, I turn and nudge Shane, who rolls his head in my direction.

"Who do you think is going to win tonight between Regg and Calvin?"

"Reggie, but I don't think he has it in the bag yet. He's going to have to bring it tonight to stand a chance. Calvin's beefed up his training quite a lot in the last month."

"You think Reggie wants it more?"

"I know he does. Marc's been training him hard too. Poor bastard hasn't gotten laid in weeks. He's too afraid my brother will make him kiss the concrete floor if he loses tonight."

"Guess we've all been there, huh?" Marcus is a fine coach. He's hardcore through and through. It's hard not to want to impress him and make him proud. He is the very reason Shane, Jase, and I, even Daniel, got into mixed martial arts in the first place back in high school.

My thoughts roll over Daniel briefly before shoving that shit back inside. No need to ruin what's been a pretty decent night so far.

"Yeah, we have, haven't we?"

We both laugh. Shane turns his attention back to his girl, and I glance over to Shannon, who's got the back of her hand covering her mouth, hiding a yawn.

"You good, babe?"

She nods her head as another yawn follows. Dropping her hand down to her lap, she looks over at me. "Just a bit tired. I seem to be feeling that way more often lately."

"You want me to take you home?"

"No way. I want to see Jase's fight. It's all Nikki's been talking about this week. That and, well, she's probably trying to put yesterday behind her."

By yesterday, I know she means my father's memorial service. Guess I am too. I'd rather forget that bastard even existed, if possible.

The bell sounds loudly just as I'm about to ask her again if she would rather go home. But I can see the excitement behind her tired eyes. She wants to see Jase's match, so I keep my mouth shut as I pull my head to the center of the room. The fight ended, and the referee is holding up the wrist of the winning fighter.

Jase is up next, and I'd like to stay through the end and see if Reggie can pull a win home. I check my watch again and see it's just under the half-hour mark.

I glance back at Shannon. I never imagined this, not really. Sure, I wanted a woman and a family, but I never believed it was possible. In the back of my head, I still don't. I keep waiting for the other shoe to drop, wondering when I'll lose her and my unborn kid too. I doubt I could survive without her. That week or so apart just about killed me.

It was his doing, his fault. He knew exactly what I'd do, and I played right into his hand like the stupid motherfucker I am. Clenching my fists together and letting my mind drift, I think about that afternoon.

"Your new little pet's picture book is complete."

"Excuse me?" I look up, staring at the woman sitting across from my desk. "What did you just say, Teresa? I don't think I heard you correctly."

She rolls her eyes as she crosses something off the notepad sitting on her lap.

"That collection of photos made into another book for Shana Taylor is complete, finished, and ready for you to sign off on publication."

Fucking bitch is getting on my last damn nerve.

"Shannon," I grit out, correcting her and knowing she did that on

purpose. *Teresa has never forgotten nor pronounced a client's name wrong, ever.*

"*Right, sorry.*"

"*A jealous, pretentious bitch doesn't have a place in this office. Ever speak about my girlfriend like—*"

The phone to my left rings, interrupting me, followed by a banging on my office door. I pin Teresa with a firm look, telling her to cut her shit as I pick up the receiver.

"*What and who's at my door, Rachel?*"

"*Sorry, boss. It's your father. He wouldn't wait out here.*"

Not the person I care to deal with today; I slam the phone down and press the unlock button on my desk, allowing the man on the other side to enter.

Teresa turns in her seat to see who's entering my office. He walks in, trying to act like he's someone, thinking he has some authority here. The fuck he does.

"*Can I help you with something?*"

"*No, son, but there is something I can help you with.*"

"*A phone call would have been nice. You can see I'm in a meeting.*" *I wave my hand in Teresa's direction.*

"*Well, what I have to tell you isn't something I wanted to do over the phone. I won't take up too much of your time, Nicholas.*"

He comes to a stop and takes a seat in the chair opposite me, the chair next to Teresa. She doesn't bother to leave, and frankly, I'm glad. I'd rather not have to deal with this fuck alone.

"*Please, have a seat.*" *I sound sarcastic, but that is the point.*

"*Son,*" *he states and then pulls his head up, looking me dead in the eyes, his lawyer pose I've seen way too often posing in front of me. "This isn't easy for me to tell you, but I feel it necessary.*"

Whatever he's about to say, I get the feeling I'm not going to like it. I take a deep breath and lean back in my seat but remain silent, waiting for him to speak.

"*Shannon.*" *My hands wrap tight around the armrest of my chair as her name rolls off his tongue. I don't like it. The way he says her name, the way it rolls off his tongue sounds slimy.* "There's something you need to know. Something that happened when she was employed by me years ago that I have to tell you."

"Teresa," *I bark,* "perhaps you should leave."

"No, no, please stay." *My father turns his face to the side.* "Please stay. This won't take long, and I'd like someone with him after I leave."

Teresa nods, but even she's unsure what's about to go down. She looks worried but continues staring at the piece of shit sitting next to her. My father turns back around, looking at me once again, and gives me what I'm sure is meant to be an 'I'm sorry about this' look.

"She was young, quite beautiful, the same as she is today, and I . . ." *He pauses, but I already know where it's going and what he's about to tell me.*

No. It's not true. It can't be.

"I had an affair with her. Only once, but it happened and . . ."

"Stop," *I force out. I won't listen to this. She would have told me. Shannon isn't a liar.*

I hate liars.

"Nicholas, let your father finish. This is obviously hurting him to tell you. Please go on, sir." *Teresa isn't at all the worried woman she was a moment ago. Her facial expression has completely changed. It's lightened up, as if this news is exciting.*

"Nicholas, there's more. It's the more you need to know." *He pulls a piece of paper out of the jacket of his pocket and lays it down on the desk, pushing it in front of me.* "When I told her it wouldn't happen again I felt bad for my part in what I'd done."

Again he pauses, taking a deep breath. When he felt bad? As fucking if. He's been cheating on my mother for years, probably the entire length of their marriage, and he wants me to think he felt bad for fucking a girl.

No, I won't believe it. It didn't happen. He's lying. Something he's brilliant at.

"Shannon tried to blackmail me, well, did actually. If it had gotten out that I had an affair, not to mention with an underaged girl, my career would have been over. She blackmailed me to pay for her college education. And I did."

"I don't believe you. Now get the fuck out of my office." *I'm calmer than I should be at this moment. I should be across the other side of this desk, beating the shit out of him. The heat coursing through my body is scorching. The mere thought of him with my Shannon makes murderous thoughts run through my head.*

She wouldn't. Not her.

"Nicholas, son, I'm being honest with you. Look at it." *He points to the paper lying on my desk, and I glance down. A piece of paper can't prove the truth. He's lying. I know it. I feel it.*

"Get out."

"Nicholas, hear the man out." *Teresa stands, leaning over my desk and opens the folded paper. I look down but don't look at it.*

"Leave. I won't ask again."

"Fine, son, I will. But you need to know who she is. Shannon Taylor is only after one thing, so you need to ask yourself what she is after from you." *He stands and exits my office as I sit, staring at the door he closed behind him.*

It's not true. She isn't the type of person who uses people to gain things. Not Shannon.

"You leave too. Consider our meeting over." *I glance up at Teresa.*

"No, I won't leave you alone with this information, and I won't leave until you look at that piece of paper. Whatever it is, it took a lot for your father to hand it over. Did you see him, Nicholas? He didn't want to hurt you."

I laugh. Of course he did.

I grab the paper off my desk and hold it in front of my face. It's a printed receipt from the University of Southern California for eight semesters' worth of tuition payments.

"Shannon. Marie. Taylor." I read off the student's name displayed on the top as if each word is a sentence and not knowing what explanation she could possibly offer to dispute the colossal fucked-up shit my father just told me.

"Doesn't that tell you something? Your father was right."

I don't want to believe it.

"And you have to see it now, Nicholas. She is using you. LP is publishing her books. She's using you to ensure that continues. She probably knew who you were, knew you were his son, and set out to do this to you. Don't you see it?"

I sit there, slowly crumbling the piece of paper in my hand. I can hear Teresa's voice. I hear every word she says.

Shannon had sex with my own father. She fucked him. The piece of shit, the man I've hated my whole life has been inside my woman. He's had the same part of her I've had. That I've cherished.

Yet I've cherished something that was already ruined. The thought of her and him makes my stomach turn. I want to throw up.

I stand, paper balled in my hand, and drop it back down on the desk before walking out.

"Nicholas, where are you going?"

Without saying another word, I leave, knowing I'm about to end the one thing I've wanted since the moment I laid eyes on her.

Fuck it

Fuck her, and fuck him too.

Love, who needs it?

"Nick, hello?" I look over next to me, seeing Shannon with a look of concern on her beautiful face.

"Yeah?" I question as I shake the images of her from my mind. Images I don't care to remember. It's not Teresa's fault I didn't give Shannon the benefit of the doubt. It's mine and mine alone. It wasn't her who convinced me. It wasn't my father. It was me. And I'm the reason she got hurt, the same as I'm the reason he hurt her last week. I did it all to her, maybe not physically, but I am responsible, and no one will ever convince me I'm not.

"Are you okay? You didn't even pay attention to Jase's fight, which he won, by the way. And . . ." She looks down, so I follow with my eyes. "Your grip is crushing my hand."

I let go.

"Fuck. I'm sorry, baby."

"What's the matter? All of a sudden, you started squeezing my hand, and I look over to see you were a million miles away. I called and nudged your shoulder at least four times before you answered me."

"I'm fine." I shove it off to nothing, not wanting to think about any of it.

"You don't look fine. Do you want me to get you something to drink? A beer maybe?"

"No, I'm good," I lie to her. Whiskey is what I really need.

"So, Jase was awesome. He killed it tonight." She tells me with enthusiasm. No doubt about that. He had this fight in the bag. Doesn't matter if I didn't watch it or not. I could have sat back, closed my eyes, and been able to tell you every move he made. I know him that well.

"Crushing on my best friend now?" I joke, wanting to lighten my mood. She blushes, causing me to do a double take. Her face is on fire; the heat from her gorgeous body is practically rolling off her skin. The pullover she was wearing over her dress is now lying across her lap, and there's a light sheen of sweat below her ear.

Shannon is turned on.

"Should I be worried here?" I'm joking, but maybe I should be. She looks away quickly and then turns back to me, still flushed.

"It's not Jase. It's the whole thing, the scene. It's . . ." She pauses as her cheeks heat. "It's just hot, okay?"

I smile as she turns away from me, embarrassed.

"This"—I lean in as I wave my hand in front of her so she can see I'm pointing down front—"this turns you on? This makes you horny?"

Her head turns, and her eyes are trained on mine as those green marbles glide over my chest and down to my jean-clad crotch. My dick hardens, and her eyes travel back up, telling me what she wants.

I don't know if I can go there just yet. I'm not certain she's ready for that, and if there is a chance she isn't, then I'm not taking anything that far. My cock will have to get over it, and as much as blue balls suck, it is what it is. But she does want something from me. There's hunger in her eyes, and just like that, I forget all about the fight I was looking forward to seeing.

I barely hear the bell sound as I lean over, running my lips from her jaw all the way up to her ear, barely touching her skin. With my right hand, I place it on her knee, just below the hem of her dress.

"Tell me what you want, Shannon." Her head cocks inward toward mine as I whisper the words out. Her eyes cast down to my hand still on her knee. She uncrosses her legs as if inviting me to explore the very territory I can't get enough of.

Shannon rolls her head so that her lips align with my ear and whispers, "I think you know what I need."

"Are you sure? You need to be absolutely certain you want this, here and now."

I have to ask her because if she isn't ready for it, then I could hurt her even more. That's the last thing I want to do to the woman sitting next to me.

"Please," she begs in another whisper. Her voice is barely audible even though she is centimeters from my ear.

"Turn your face back to the fight, baby." She follows my direction as I take my hand off her knee long enough to move her wrap to cover her lap and legs. "Don't take your eyes off the show."

She nods as I slowly maneuver my right hand back to her naked skin, my warm palm covering her knee. Shannon allows her legs to relax, opening for me, but I'm not ready to go up yet. I begin by lightly massaging her knee and lower thigh.

Looking around, I confirm all eyes are on the fight. Honestly, I couldn't care less if anyone sees us; I'm not modest in the least, but I don't want Shannon's friends to see her in this situation.

Inching under her dress, I feel my way upward as slow as possible. I restrain myself from moving to her center, even though it's exactly what I want. I know Shannon doesn't need quick and fast. Besides, I need to watch her facial expressions to make sure I'm not emotionally harming her.

Honestly, I have no idea what's going on inside her head. I don't know if what I'm about to do will help or make things worse. I'm praying it'll help because I want her to move past what happened. I want her to forget.

As I move up and over her inner thighs, she takes a deep breath, bringing in air through her parted lips.

"Remember, baby." I pause, leaning in closer to her ear as I look behind her to ensure people are still engrossed in the fight. They are so I continue my pursuit up her leg. "Do. Not." I allow my tongue to skim the rim of the top of her ear. "Take your eyes off that fight."

She doesn't respond, but I'm certain she heard every word as her legs widen even farther. When I finally breach her center, running my fingers across the bare skin above her pussy, I smile.

"No panties." I make feather-like strokes back and forth. "So fucking smooth."

Curling my fingers except for my index into my palm, I run

the side of my free finger down the length of her sweet pussy, wishing I could taste the juices that coat me.

"You're wet," I declare, making sure I punctuate my words precisely along her ear. I continue a slow rhythm, up and down, up and back down. The more I go down, the wetter my finger gets. The urge to plunge my finger inside her is great, but I can't bring myself to do it. As much as I need a part of me inside her, I can't.

"Fuck," I grit out. "I want to taste you so badly right now."

As I pull back just enough to watch her, the pace of her breathing increases, but just as I instructed, she doesn't move her eyes. They remain fixed on the fight in front of her. I glance at the fight and then back to her face, watching her closely to make sure she's okay.

Her eyes are now a darker shade of green. Her cheek, her ear, and down her neck are flushed. She's hot and sexy as fuck. My dick is straining against the thick material of my blue jeans. I want so badly to unzip them and release myself so she can take me into her soft hands, but there isn't enough of the pullover covering her lap to do so.

This isn't about me, anyway. This is all for her, and I get to be the one who does this to her.

Inching my thumb down into her wetness, I coat myself and bring it back up, maneuvering my finger into her folds. Locating her clit, I press hard, and Shannon's chest expands. She sucks her bottom lip into her mouth, bringing her teeth down onto it.

I look at the fight to see what's going on and lean the side of my head against her. To anyone around us, we look like a cozy couple watching the same fight everyone else is.

I start by moving my thumb in small slow circles, clockwise against her clit.

"What turns you on the most? The hard, solid bodies of the

men down there? Is it the sweat pouring off their skin? What is it that has you so hot, so ready to come for me, baby?"

She doesn't answer me, so I increase the pace as her eyes grow heavy.

"Tell me." She slowly shakes her head.

"I want to know what it is about them that has my girl"—I apply more pressure to her hard spot as I kick up my speed even more—"so goddamn turned on right now."

Again, she shakes her head as the people around us erupt into cheers, screams, and clapping. And as the bell sounds, ending the fight, I go in for the prize. My rhythm is quick, and my pressure against her body is tight, sending Shannon over the edge. Her mouth opens, but her screams are drowned out by the noise around us.

As the crowd dies down and my speed decreases, I turn, capturing her lips with my own. I remove my hand from beneath her dress. Releasing her mouth, I pull back and bring my hand up to my mouth, plunging my saturated fingers inside. Shannon's eyes widen as I pull my fingers back out.

"I love the way you taste, woman."

Shannon's lips turn up, and in a swift move, she leans forward, wrapping her palms around my biceps and kisses me. Her kisses are hard and demanding, forcing me to part my lips to allow her tongue to slip inside my mouth. I know what she wants. She wants to taste herself on me, and I swear my dick just got even harder.

The feel of something, or more likely someone, nudging my shoulder has me releasing the hot lips attached to my own.

"Hey!" Shannon states as I force myself to pull away. Rolling my head to the side, I see Shane laughing and his girl's mouth open, not to mention her other three friends turned around in their seats, gawking at us. When I look back at Shannon, I see I practically have her straddling my lap with my hand cupping her ass.

"Since we paid for that show"—Shane points to the cage—"does that mean we get this one for free?"

"Mind your own goddamn business, asshole."

"Sort of hard to do when you just about laid your woman across my lap to fuck her." He snorts a laugh. "Not that I'm complaining. I mean, if that's what you want to do, I'm game, man."

Had Katelyn not smacked him across the back of the head, I would have punched the motherfucker in the dick.

I may still do that later.

"Hey. I was just fucking with him, babe."

I turn to make sure Shannon isn't too embarrassed. When my eyes fall back on her, she is silently laughing in her seat as she adjusts the top of her dress.

"You okay?"

She looks over at me. "Very okay."

"Good." I stand, and she looks up at me. "Let's get out of here. Jase and Nikki are probably in the back. You ready?"

She nods and stands. Taking her hand, I pull her behind me as I make my way through the throngs of people. Her friends are just ahead of us as we exit the crowded room.

Once we are out of the entrance, I pull Shannon close to my body as the area is packed full of people, and it's easy to get separated.

"Come on. Jase and my sister are probably back there." I point down a long wall off to the side of the lobby, where I know there are private rooms for the fighters to hang out. I pull Shannon along as I search for the door.

Without thinking, I turn the knob and walk through, only to come to a horrified stop and dart my eyes anywhere but the couch in front of me.

"Ah, fuck. Really? Learn to lock a goddamn fucking door." I back out as quickly as possible.

"What's going on?" Shannon tries to duck under me to see inside the room. Before I can tell her she doesn't want to know, she yells, "Oh my God," and clamps her hand over her wide-open mouth.

Pulling her away from the room and slamming the door closed, I stalk off.

Jesus fucking Christ, I did not just see that.

"Was that? I mean, oh fuck, Nick. Your sister. Oh God, did that just happen? No way, right? Wasn't that the guy Jase fought tonight?" she rambles through her laughs.

"Shut the fuck up. Don't talk about it. We are leaving."

Tightening my grip on Shannon's hand, I pull her back down the hall.

"Whoa. Lockhart, hold up." I stop and look behind me as Jase jogs our way, pulling a white T-shirt over his head.

"Save it, brother. Just . . ." I sigh heavily as I look him in the eye. "No."

"Were you, I mean . . .?" Shannon pauses, unsure of what to say to Jase, I'm sure. She doesn't look appalled, but maybe confused.

"Red, could you give us a minute?" Jase asks.

"Red?" she questions. "You're so original, you know that?" Sarcasm oozes out of her mouth, which I have to admit, I'm a bit thankful for at this moment. It's helping the awkwardness of this situation ease away. That is until my sister walks up behind Jase.

"And here I only thought she sassed you, Lockhart."

Looking past my sister's head, I meet Nathan's eyes as he quickly darts them from me and increases his fast pace to a jog as he moves past our group.

"You little slut," Shannon comments with a snicker as she nudges Nikki's shoulder.

I, on the other hand, do not find this funny. There's not one little bit of humor in this. I know my sister. I know the fucked-up shit she and Jase do, but I don't want to see her having sex at all, let alone with two men.

Fucking hell. I'll never get that shit out of my head.

"All of you, just fucking drop it, okay?"

"Lighten up, Nick." Nikki shakes her head like it isn't a big deal.

It's a big goddamn deal, all right. I pin my sister with a stare I know she reads loud and clear. Nikki rolls her eyes and walks off, ignoring it as usual.

That shit is going to rip the two of them apart if she isn't careful. If she doesn't stop it before it's too late.

"Let's go." I tug Shannon's hand and walk away.

CHAPTER FIFTEEN

The following Thursday arrives quickly. It's Shannon's first doctor's appointment, and I had to miss it. She assured me everything would be fine. I didn't need to be there, but I wanted to. From what I've heard, they show you the little shit on some screen. I wanted to see that. I wanted to see our baby.

I can't seem to get caught up from the nearly two weeks I missed from this place. I love my job. I love my business, but sometimes I wish I didn't have to deal with any of it. Anyone who thinks owning and running a company is a piece of cake hasn't ever done it. You don't get to sit back while everyone gets the shit done. Well, at least at Lockhart Publishing, that isn't how things are done.

If anything, my plate is fuller than those who work for me. There's never a slow day or a dull moment. Publications don't stop because the boss wants a break or a much-needed vacation.

The ding on my computer brings me out of my complaining thoughts and back to the present as Teresa's voice pierces my ears through the phone, reminding me I've been on a conference call with her for the last twenty minutes. I doubt she even noticed I wasn't paying attention. I'm the one who called her, and the minute her mouth started running, it never stopped.

Grabbing the mouse, I click on Rachel's email, opening it.

Hey, boss. Shannon's here. Can I send her your way?

I smile briefly as I shake my head from side to side. That girl seems to make me do so every time.

I shoot a quick reply to her.

Yes. Send her in.

As I close out of my email, I hear Teresa clearing her throat on the other end of the phone receiver cradled against my ear. Removing my hand from the mouse, I reach up and take it back into my hands.

"Are you listening to me, Nicholas?" she asks as Shannon walks through the entrance of my office. She is dressed in a white sleeveless shirt that's snug around her tits and loose around her belly. She is showing off a little too much cleavage for a visit to my office, but I'm not going to lie. It's hot. Skimming my eyes lower, I see she's in a pair of dark jeans with a rip at the knee on the left side and sneakers.

"Meeting's over. We can talk later," I say as I motion for Shannon to come in. She doesn't move. Her face and body look as though she is frozen to the spot she stands in as she stares at me.

What's wrong with her? I think to myself as worry runs through me.

"Excuse me?" I barely hear Teresa's reply.

"Continue enjoying your vacation. We will finish this up next week. Bye, Teresa."

I hang up before she has a chance to respond. I couldn't care less if I was being rude. I'm more concerned with the woman standing too many feet away from me, looking sick.

"Are you okay?" I ask as I push my chair back from my desk and stand. I don't like the way she is staring back at me.

Something's wrong. I feel it. My first thought is the baby. Is something wrong with her? I know the kid could really be a he, but ever since the dream I had a few nights ago, it's all I see.

A baby wrapped in a pink blanket.

A girl.

A daughter.

My baby girl.

In a blink of an eye, she grabs her mouth and flees the entryway to my office. Is she sick? Morning sickness, perhaps? Surely not. I mean, I haven't seen her get sick in well over a week, probably close to two weeks now.

When I get to the lobby, I see her entering the door to the stairs, so I run in that direction, pushing the door open and causing it to slam into the wall when it can't open any wider. I take the steps two at a time, trying to catch up.

"Shannon," I call out when I see her on the next set of stairs. She doesn't stop, and I force myself to move faster. When I hit the flat surface on the seventh floor, I'm able to grab her, looping my arm around her waist. "Stop," I command as I pull her back against my chest. I fall back against the wall as I try to catch my breath.

Dropping her head forward, she begins to cry. My body stiffens as I tighten my hold on her. I wrap my other arm around her waist too. Shannon crying isn't something I know how to deal with. It makes my blood boil, and I want to hurt whomever or whatever is making her upset.

"Baby, what's wrong?" I ask as I silently say a prayer to God that nothing is wrong with our baby. It's funny really. I've spent my life cursing God, and now on most days, I find myself begging him for something.

When she doesn't answer, I turn her around to face me. Releasing my right hand from her waist, I tip her chin up to make her face me. I search her eyes for some kind of answer, but I have no idea what I'm looking for. I don't like not knowing what to do.

If she would only tell me.

Speak, woman, I mentally beg.

"I'm going to be sick," she murmurs as her eyes lock onto mine, and I see it. I see what's wrong. *It's me.* Without saying another word, I lift her into my arms and carry her back up the stairs.

Once I reach the eleventh floor, I cross the lobby, still carrying her. Rachel looks up from her desk with wide eyes. "Water," I bark and continue to my office. When I walk in, I take her to the couch sitting off to the side of my office. I place her down gently on the leather in an upright position.

"Do you need the bathroom?" I ask, hoping she isn't about to puke on my couch or the floor. I should've taken her there first. She shakes her head no, telling me she isn't going to hurl.

Kneeling down in front of her, I position myself between her legs.

"I'm sorry," she whispers as I reach up with the pads of my thumbs to wipe away the stray tears.

Why is she sorry, and what the hell have I done now? I notice how pale she looks as she turns her head toward my desk. The sadness in her eyes is still there.

"Shannon?" I say as I reach up, taking hold of her chin to guide her eyes back to me. "What's . . .?" I start to ask, but I'm cut off as Rachel interrupts.

"Here's the water you asked for," she tells me as Shannon and I both look up. I take the small bottle from her hands. "I also brought a cup of hot chamomile tea. I figured it might . . ." She pauses, searching for the right word. "Help."

Shannon reaches up and takes the cup of tea from Rachel. "Thanks," she whispers. Bringing it to her lips, she takes a small sip and then tries to hand it to me. I look down at the cup and then back up to her eyes, indicating that I want her to finish it. She sighs before bringing it back up to her lips.

"Anything else?" Rachel asks.

"No," I say without looking at her. I feel her backing away, and soon the faint sound of the door shutting signals her exit. I haven't taken my eyes off Shannon. Finally, she finishes the tea and removes the cup from her lips. I take it from her and place it on the table behind me. I haven't moved. It feels like it's been forever since I've been this close to her. It's only been a few weeks, but I can't help myself; I place my palms on each side of her jean-clad thighs. My dick twitches as if he knows he's close to what he craves the most. I close my eyes, trying to keep my hard-on from getting any stiffer. After taking a calming breath, I open them back up.

Shannon is looking back at my desk again with hurt eyes. I have no idea what she's looking at. Maybe she's looking in that direction to keep from looking at me. I can't stand not knowing what's wrong with her or what I've done this time to hurt her.

"What's wrong? Why did you run from my office?" I ask her as I gently guide her chin back to face me. She glances at me briefly before casting her eyes down. Another tear falls from her face. I feel myself losing control. My body heats. If she doesn't tell me, I'm going to lose it. I can't stand her tears. They rip at my heart. "Answer me," I demand.

"I'm sorry."

"Stop saying you're sorry and tell me what's wrong. You're freaking me the fuck out," I tell her, hoping that will make her speak. She looks back up at me.

"When I walked through the door . . ." She pauses and looks back down. "I saw it all over again," she tells me, but I don't know what she's talking about. Another tear falls, and I tighten my grip on her legs.

"You saw what?" I ask.

"It all played out in front of my eyes again. You. Her. Both of you," she says as her voice cracks at the end. More tears fall from her beautiful face. What is she talking about?

"Can you clarify? Because I'm not following."

Who's her? Again, what is she talking about?

"Please don't make me say it," she whispers.

"Baby, you have to. I don't know what or who you are talking about." My voice is a bit calmer. Shannon needs the calm and controlled side of me right now, even if it's anything but what I feel. She looks back over at my desk and takes a deep breath as more tears stream down.

"The day I found out I was pregnant," she starts, "I came to tell you."

So that's why she was here. She was going to tell me. I never asked her why she ran from me. She takes another deep breath, like it's painful to talk.

"Continue, please."

She looks down and places her palms face down on top of her jeans. "Rachel wasn't out front, so I came to your office. The door was unlocked. I walked in and saw you . . ." She trails off as tears fall onto her shirt.

"You saw me what?" I say loud, almost yelling but not meaning to.

"I saw you fucking Teresa Matthews," she forces out. My eyes widen, not believing what I'm hearing. She couldn't have seen me. I wasn't in my office that day. Hell, I hadn't been in my office in a week. When I saw her running to the stairs, I was about to walk out of the elevator.

"Excuse me?" I say, not knowing what else to say. What's going on? Shannon looks up, and the crying starts again as her body trembles. I move my hands forward, cupping her ass, and pull her closer to me. I run a hand up her back and into her hair, cradling her head against my chest. "Baby, stop," I tell her, but it doesn't help. She continues to cry.

"I'm sorry. I know . . ." She starts only to stop to catch her breath. She pulls back from me so I can see her face. "I know I don't have a right to be mad, and I'm not." She pauses again through cries. "It just bothers me, and I can't get the image out of my head."

"What the fuck?!" I yell, causing her to flinch.

"I'm sorry," she tells me through her tears.

"I didn't mean . . ." Fuck. "First, stop crying. I can't take it anymore. Please," I beg her, and she takes a deep breath, wiping her soaked face. "Thank you," I tell her as I place my hands on each side of her hips.

"Secondly, I never fucked Teresa that day." Shannon's eyebrows screw up.

"But I saw—" she starts as she looks over to my desk, but I cut her off.

"You didn't see me. I don't know who you saw, but it wasn't me." My voice is forceful, trying to get her to believe me.

"Nick . . ." she begins, like she's about to call me out on a lie.

"Shannon, I swear to God, it wasn't me. The only person I've fucked, had sex with, made love to since you landed in my arms that night at Quaint is you, woman." My voice is loud, and I know I sound harsh, but I don't know what else to say to make her believe me. "Look at me?" I demand, and her eyes are on me in the next breath. "Did you see my face?"

Shannon glances away, looking over at my desk and then down as I guess she is thinking.

"Well, no, but—"

I gently take hold of her chin and lift. "But, nothing. It wasn't me, Shannon." I pause as the reality of what's going on starts to sink in. She saw someone, though, and I'm about to find out who. "And I will prove it to you."

Reaching into the breast pocket of my jacket, I retrieve my phone. After locating the building's head of security's cell phone number, I call him. It only takes two rings for him to pick up.

"Yes, Mr. Lockhart, what can I do for you this afternoon?"

"I need footage from my office pulled immediately." Shannon looks up, confused for a moment before she realizes I have a camera in the room. A look of mortification crosses her face, and I know she's thinking of the time I fucked her on this very couch. I hold up my hand hoping to reassure her.

"Certainly, sir. I can have that taken care of right now. Is there a date and time range?"

"Yes," I stop, trying to remember the date. It was . . . hell, I'm not sure. I look at Shannon as I bring the phone to my chest.

"Do you remember what date it was?

"Um . . ." She too pauses. "The nineteenth, I think."

"June nineteenth," I tell him as I bring the phone back to my ear. "Pull the footage between ten and one," I request as I remember it was around lunchtime when she was here.

Shannon looks at me, her eyebrows pinching together, clearly wondering how I would know that if I wasn't here. I never said I wasn't there, just that whomever she saw wasn't me.

"Of course, sir. I should have that to you within a few minutes."

I hang up, placing the phone down on the table. Shannon is still staring at me.

"I was at work that day, but I hadn't planned on showing up here. I even told Teresa I wouldn't be in that week, but I got tired of thinking about you and what I thought had happened. I thought coming to work would get my mind off you. I was getting out of the elevator, about to head to my office when I saw you running through the door leading to the stairs. I called out to you, but you didn't hear me. I went looking for you, and then I called you. I couldn't find you, so I left to look for you."

She doesn't speak, but she does nods, telling me she heard every word I said. I think she wants to believe but isn't convinced yet.

"Can I have that tea now?"

I pass it to her, and she sips it as she leans back into the couch. She looks around, and I know she is looking for the camera she now knows is in here.

"It only records the view to my desk. It's hidden above the entrance of the door." I hope that eases her, knowing she and I were not captured having sex. "And there isn't any sound. It's simply images."

"Why do you have a hidden video camera anyway?"

"Security," I tell her. "I don't trust many people. It's just a safety measure. Other than myself, the only person who knows it exists is the man I just spoke to."

About that time, my phone chimes with an incoming text message. I lift it off the table and open the message.

John: Check your inbox. Let me know if there is anything else you need.

"Come on," I tell Shannon as I place my phone inside my jacket pocket. "Security emailed me the video. Let's see what you saw."

I know whatever I'm about to view will set me off. I'm trying hard to calm myself. Shannon doesn't need to see that side of me. Neither do the people in my office, but whatever that goddamn bitch did is about to get her ass fired.

Shannon stands; I take the empty cup from her, placing it on the table before walking to my desk. As I sit in front of my computer, I open the email. Just as he said, the video is attached.

Shannon is hesitant at my side. Her body has a slight tremble to it. I reach out, pulling her to me. She comes willingly and sits on my lap.

With a quick click, I open the video, and it starts to play. After a minute or two of nothing, I forward the video until I see two figures. By the time I pause it and play it once again, my anger is boiling over.

"Is that . . .?" Shannon's question is full of shock.

My VP and Jeffery Chaney, I growl inside my head, fuming as my eyes narrow.

"Do you need to see the whole video?" I grit out. I don't mean to be harsh with her, but I don't want to see Jeffery fucking Teresa at the very desk in front of me. Hell, in the goddamn chair I'm sitting in now.

"No. I believe you, but . . ." She slides off my lap, and I'm grateful. I want to get out of this damn seat as fast as I can. "I don't understand."

"Neither do I." I stand and walk around from behind my desk.

"Nick," Shannon calls out, "she called me."

"She what?"

"Teresa. I was about to head up here when she called me that day. She told me the two of you needed to go over details before my book was sent to print. She knew I was coming up here. So why?"

I step back. What is Teresa playing at? Then it hits me. All along, she's been saying little things; she doesn't want us together. She wants to be with me.

That fucking cunt.

"Months ago," I huff, "Christmas. I got drunk, really drunk, at a party. I did, in fact, fuck Teresa, but it only happened once. I knew then it was a huge mistake. I thought we could forget about it. Teresa has had a thing for me for a while. I just figured she would eventually see it wasn't going to happen." I look at Shannon with concern. "Are you okay?"

"Yeah, I guess. Can I kick her ass?" Shannon's voice is laced with heat. Her face is flushed. She's angry too.

"No, pregnant one. I'll take care of it."

"What does that mean?"

"It means I'm going to fire her."

Before I leave, I make sure Rachel sets up a meeting first thing Monday morning with Teresa. I'd like to get it done and over with, but that isn't happening today. The bitch isn't here today, and tomorrow LP is closed for the 4th of July.

Come next week, she is gone.

CHAPTER SIXTEEN

I tried for the last twenty hours to stop thinking about the mess I found out yesterday. I want so damn bad to rip them both apart. Teresa, not physically, because despite everything, I would never lay my hands on a woman.

I know Jeffery hates me for what I did to his brother. It's not like I blame him for that. If someone hurt Nikki or even Jase the way I hurt Daniel, I'd hate that person too. But Jeffery, that motherfucker needs his ass handed to him.

Walking out of the closet, I get dressed. I hear laughter coming from down the hall and music coming in from the windows to the backyard. I know people have already started to arrive.

It's the 4th of July weekend. It might just be the first holiday I'll enjoy if I can put yesterday out of my mind, if only for a few days. The first holiday without my father should be a goddamn celebration.

Before joining the others, I grab my cell phone off the bed, quickly creating a text before I talk myself out of it and send it to Jeffery.

Me: Remember what I said. Stay. The. Fuck. Away. From. Shannon. I mean it, motherfucker.

Shoving it into my pocket, I head down the hall and enter the living room to find Charmin, along with two smaller dogs, on the couch, sleeping.

Where the hell did they come from? My dog looks like a giant polar bear compared to the miniature things next to her.

Looking out the window, I see Shannon engrossed in a conversation with several of her friends and Shane. Jase and Matt are manning the grill. There's noise coming from the kitchen, so I make my way in there to find Nikki chopping an onion.

"Need any help?"

"No, big brother, I'm good. The beer's outside in a large cooler if you want one."

"Good to know, because that is just what I need." I head toward the door that leads to the back deck.

"You okay?" I pause and look back at my sister. "Shannon mentioned what happened yesterday. Need me to teach that bitch a lesson?"

"No, I don't. I want you and that damn redhead out there"—I throw my thumb up, pointing it behind, toward the back door—"to let me handle it. What is it with you two wanting to beat people up? You, I get, but Shannon?"

"Shannon is hotheaded and a firecracker. You should have figured that out by now, and I love her for it." Nikki laughs. "Don't fuck that up, Nick. I've always wanted a sister."

"No, you didn't. Go lie to someone else." I walk over and pull my sister into a hug. I know she's got my back. I get that's what she is trying to tell me, but I also know she wouldn't think twice. She'd beat the shit of Teresa if she thought it wouldn't piss me off.

She peers up at me. "I love you."

"I love you too, baby girl." I take hold of her chin between my thumb and index finger, holding her firmly in place. "But you need to keep your hands and this fucking mouth of yours on your own man and stop the shit you're doing. You're killing him." She tries to pull away from me, but I increase the hold I have on her. "He won't tell you that, but you are."

She shoves me, making me have to release her.

"Stay out of my shit."

Nikki walks past me and out the door. I shake my head but follow her out and locate the cooler. Nikki wasn't lying when she said it was a large cooler. Opening the lid, I reach in, pulling out a Miller Lite.

"Grab me one too," Jase yells from across the deck. I grab another and walk over to where he and Matt are standing.

"Just how many fuckers are we planning on getting drunk?" I indicate to the tub full of alcohol I just left.

"It's a party, man. Enjoy yourself for once." Jase looks happy but also seems lit. I doubt that's his first beer tonight.

Twisting the cap off, I take a long and much-needed guzzle of beer just as warm hands wrap around my waist. Pulling her in front of me and then picking her up off the ground, I kiss my girl. I give her a deep, passionate kiss right in front of everyone, not caring the least bit.

I release her back to the ground and wrap my forearm around her chest, pulling her against my body.

"God, even that shitty-ass beer tastes wonderful on your tongue just now."

"Shitty? There's nothing shitty about this, babe." I hold up the bottle in front of her before taking another sip.

"Well, now there isn't. Not when I can't have any for the next seven months. Anything would taste better than plain water." I look down to see a frown on her face. She is so damn cute sometimes.

"Poor baby," I mock in a playful tone.

"Jerk," she retorts and follows with a jab to my ribs from her elbow. Shannon huffs and walks off toward my sister. Nikki sends daggers my way for butting into her and Jase's relationship, but hell, someone has to help save them.

"What did you do to your sister, Lockhart? Fuck, I'm getting scared just standing next to you." Matt looks away from Nikki and at me. Jase glances at his girl and back to me.

"She's fine," I tell him. Just because I know my sister's kinky shit, and a few other people do too, doesn't mean the world needs to know. Frankly, I want to forget it myself. Looking over at Jase, I ask, "So when do we eat?"

Jase looks over at Nikki once more and then back to me, pinning me with a "what the hell" look before answering, "In a few."

A couple of hours later, I'm pulling out another beer when Jase walks from inside the house. He's furious. It's written all over his face. He grabs my sister by her forearm, getting right in her face to speak. I can't hear their conversation, but I know it's heated.

My brotherly instincts are itching to come out. I want to march over and pull him away from her, but I don't. I know deep down he'd never hurt her; this's the only thing that has me staying put.

"Go take care of that shit, now." His voice rises as he points inside the house. My curiosity kicks up. He practically shoves her through the door before turning and looking at me.

God, I want to deck his motherfucking ass right now.

I see him take a deep breath and shake his head from side to side before he walks over to me.

"I'm sorry, brother." He bends down, reaching into the cooler for a beer of his own as I wait for an explanation. "Your mom just walked in the front door. She's in there talking to Shannon now."

"Excuse me?" Surely, I didn't hear him correctly. "What the hell is my mother doing here?"

"I don't know. I didn't wait around to find out. I'm sure it has something to do with your sister. It usually does."

"Motherfucker. One goddamn day." Why can't I have one day to relax and not think about my messed-up family and my even more messed-up life because of who I'm related to?

"I sent Nikki inside. I told her she needed to make her leave."

"No, I'll handle this shit right now."

I push off the railing and make my way inside to see Shannon, my sister, and my mother seated in the living room. Shannon sees me first and stands. My mother and sister turn at the same time.

"Nicholas, darling." My mother stands up.

"Why are you here?" I slam the door and cross my arms over my chest.

"Nick," Shannon interjects.

"Stay out of this, Shannon. Go outside," I tell her without taking my eyes off the woman I want nothing to do with right now. I don't hate my mother, but I'm far from over her part in what happened. "I asked you a question."

"I invited her."

My arms uncross, and my head swivels to Shannon.

"You did what?"

"Does your hearing need to be checked? I invited her. That's why she's here."

"Excuse us a minute." I stalk across the room. When I reach her, I take Shannon by the wrist and pull her down the hall to the master bedroom.

Once inside, I slam the door closed, surely making everyone aware of just how pissed off I am.

"Want to explain?"

"Want to lose the attitude?"

"Woman," I bark. "Don't start this shit with me. Why is my mother here?"

Shannon crosses her arms together and relaxes her face.

"I thought—" she so calmly speaks, but I interrupt her, being the asshole I am.

"Well, there you go. No one asked you to fucking think."

"I'm going to ignore that." She places her hands on her hips, but I can tell she's pissed off and that little remark will not be ignored. "And you're going to listen to me right now, aren't you?"

"Fine. By all means, speak. I'm dying to know what you thought you were doing." I'm barely able to get the last word out before her palm connects with my face.

"Fuck you, and don't ever speak to me like that again. She was alone, Nick. And you, you need to get over whatever it is she did. I don't know what it is. Your sister won't tell me, but yes, I know it has to do with your dad and me. Whatever she did, she probably thought she was protecting you. She is your mother. You have to let it go. Along with whatever guilt you harbor."

I go to speak, but she cuts me off.

"No. I'm not done. We, meaning me, you, and this baby . . ." She places her hand—the same one she slapped me with—on her belly. "Can't move on together with unresolved bullshit between us. I don't get your guilt, and I know you're keeping something from me, so if you want this, us, then you need to start by mending yourself."

With that, she passes me and walks to the door.

"Shannon," I call out, but she ignores me.

After a few minutes of standing here not knowing what to do, I walk back out. When I enter the living room, my mother is seated on the couch with one of the little rat dogs we have somehow acquired.

She looks up when she realizes someone else is in the room with her.

"Hi," she speaks first. I walk over and take a seat next to her, placing my palms of my knees.

"Mom," I say but stop because I don't know what else to say.

"I'm sorry, Nicholas. I know you are angry with me, and I suppose you have every right to be."

"I am angry with you, and I don't know how not to be."

"Son, I don't know how to get you to understand why I chose to stay silent."

I breathe out one slow exhale, knowing this is about to lead to nowhere, but then she changes the subject.

"Why didn't you tell me she was pregnant? That I'm going to be a grandmother."

"I've only known for about a month, Mother, and it's not like the two of us have been speaking much lately." Yeah, I had to bring the topic back. Shannon wants me to get over it, but I don't think that's possible. Shannon doesn't know what happened. She doesn't know my mother's part in it. I'm not saying my mom is a horrible person. I know she was one of his victims, one of his toys, but she made the wrong decision by staying silent.

Silence gets no one anywhere. Silence only enables a problem. And as I think this, I know I have to tell Shannon everything. Everything I never wanted her to know.

"Nicholas, my son."

"Mom, stop. Look, I am mad, and that's not going to change tonight or tomorrow. I love you. I do and always will. But this, us, our relationship, is going to take time to fix. Okay?"

"I know, son, and I am sorry. I really never wanted to hurt you or her. She does seem like a lovely girl."

I lean over and pull my mother's head to my lips, leaving a gentle kiss on her temple, reassuring her I mean what I say and that I love her.

"Thank you, Nicholas."

"Yeah." I push off the couch and stand, looking around for Shannon, but as I look out the back, I don't see her.

"I'll go and leave you to your friends."

"No." I stop and look down at her. "Shannon was right. You shouldn't be alone, and it's a holiday. Stay and enjoy yourself. I'm sure Nikki is out back, and there's food around here somewhere."

"Are you really okay with that, Nicholas?"

"Yes," I say, resolved before turning and heading out the back door. Looking around, I confirm Shannon isn't anywhere in sight.

"Teller," I yell, and Jase looks over at me before standing and walking over.

"Everything okay in there?" he asks as I see my mother come out. She locates my sister and walks over to her.

"Fine. Did you see where Shannon went?"

"Yeah, she looked upset and took off down the beach. I tried to go with her, but she pretty much told me to piss the fuck off and that she wanted to be alone, so I came back."

"Thanks, man."

I head toward the beach. It's late and growing dark. The sun went down hours ago, so it's going to be tough finding her. I look in both directions but see nothing except darkness, and the only sound is the waves crashing against the shore.

There's a pier close by she likes to sit on. I'm hoping that's where she is.

It only takes a few minutes to walk the distance. When my feet hit the wooden planks, I stop and look out. There's a figure sitting on the ground. I know it's her, so I walk toward the end where she is.

The water isn't calm underneath the pier tonight. It breaks

against the pillars, making loud, crashing sounds. That's about the way my gut feels at this very moment.

What will she think when I tell her?

Will she look at me in a different light? Probably.

Will she hate me and see the monster inside of me? I hope not.

When I reach the opening at the end, I clear my throat to let her know I'm standing here. She doesn't move, so I walk over next to her and stand for a moment, looking out into the blackness of the sea.

"I'd like to be alone, if you don't mind." Her tone is bitter.

"Actually, I do mind." Perhaps I should have chosen different words. "I'm sorry for the way I spoke to you earlier."

"Are you? Are you really sorry, or are you just here to smooth things over with me for now?"

"Yes, I'm sorry, and when I say I'm sorry, I actually mean it."

"Okay. You're forgiven. Now can I be alone, please?"

"No." She blows out a frustrated breath of air, clearly not liking my response. "We need to talk. You said there was something I'm keeping from you. You're right; there is."

It's now or never. Personally, I still wish for the never, but I can't avoid this any longer. She needs to know. She deserves to know.

She turns and faces me.

"You asked me about my problem with Jeffery Chaney." I pause to sit on the ground next to her, crisscrossing my legs. "It's not my problem with him. It's his problem with me. What I did, actually. To his brother."

I take a deep breath and exhale in a gush of air. Shannon may love me now, but will she still love me when she finds out what I did to Daniel? That I'm responsible for what my father did to her? That I'm the reason she was raped?

I close my eyes, and I'm silent for what feels like ages, but she doesn't rush me. This can't be rushed. Hell, if I could lock it up and never have to remember, that would suit me perfectly. But I've tried, and to this day, not a day goes by that I don't think about that day, that moment I changed someone's life forever. But it wasn't just one person's life; no, it was two. I just didn't know it then.

"After I moved out of my parents' house after high school, I only went back for a holiday gathering or breakfast with my mother on my birthday," I start out saying, but I know I'm only prolonging what I really have to tell her. Even this feels like an excuse, and I hate people who only ever offer up excuses for their mistakes, yet that's what I doing. "The morning of my twenty-first birthday, I went over there. I had a fight later that morning, so I arrived earlier than what would have been normal for me."

Why didn't I stop him sooner? I've asked myself that question over and over again, and I still don't have an answer.

"Go on, please."

I open my eyes, realizing I had stopped. Her words are meant to be encouraging, but no amount of encouragement will help me now.

"I knocked, but after a few minutes of no one coming to answer the door, I opened it and went inside. The house was quiet; at least, I thought it was, but before I could make my way to the kitchen, I heard a faint cry. I knew that cry. It was my mother. I grew up hearing that god-awful sound. I turned and ran up the steps to find her."

I pause, sucking in another gush of air as I let the memory of that day filter back into my head. I've tried to forget, but it's impossible to do.

Taking the steps two at a time, I make it to the landing in seconds. I turn right, heading toward my parents' bedroom. I will kill that bastard. I swear it.

"Mom," I call out as I push the door to their bedroom open. I freeze

before I enter the bathroom as my mother looks up at me. A look of mortification passes through her eyes.

"Oh, God, Nicholas. What are you doing here so early?" She quickly looks down as she gathers her baby blue satin robe, closing the opening, but not before I take in her appearance from head to toe. Her knees are red and raw from what looks like carpet burns, a large bruise has formed on the outside of her left thigh, and her nightgown is torn across the top. My mother's blonde hair is falling out of a hair tie as if someone had been pulling on the strands, but her face . . . Oh, God, her face is the worst part and the reason I'm in utter shock.

He's never done damage to her face. Can't let the whole world know about the evil, sick monster that lives inside him. Her lip is bleeding on the right side of her mouth, and her left eye is swollen shut. Her cheek just underneath is red and puffy.

My chest expands as my entire body heats from within. My vision becomes red with hate. Hate for my father, a man I am supposed to love and respect above anyone else.

How could he do this?

How could anyone do this to someone they claim to love?

But the truth is he doesn't love her. He doesn't love Nikki or me. He only loves himself.

"I . . . I was going to call you to reschedule. I never expe . . . I'm sorry, Nicholas. You shouldn't be here. You shouldn't see this," she states as she stands. She's apologizing. Always the one apologizing when it's not her fault.

My heart stops. No words, no breath coming forward. To see my mother like this, it's impossible to describe exactly what I'm feeling or thinking.

"Where is he?" It's a simple question I ask her before I even realize I have spoken it.

"No," she states firmly as she walks to the sink. Looking at me through the mirror, her expression becomes one of seriousness. "You will stay away from your father today."

"I can't promise that, Mother." My voice is relatively calm considering the need to hit something is growing. The beast I carry deep within is itching to come out and play. The beast my father created. He just doesn't know it yet.

She grabs a washcloth and wets it. After wringing it out, she dabs her lips to remove the small amount of blood, but as soon as she wipes it away, more forms in its place.

"This has nothing to do with you, Nicholas. This is between your father and me. You will stay out of it because I am asking you to." She places the rag down on the marble countertop and turns to face me. Her expression is one of sadness. She knows what she's doing. I love my mother, and there is no one, with the exception of Marcus, whom I respect more than my own mother. I would do anything she asked of me. But this is too much. He has taken it too far.

"Mom, don't ask that of me," I yell, not meaning to, but I do, and I can see it startles her. "I'm sorry," I quickly follow.

"No, Nicholas. Your father is under a lot of stress and has a major case to wrap up in court this morning. This"—she points to herself— "he didn't mean it. I know he didn't, and yes, I'm asking you, my son, to let it go. Do. Not. Start anything with your father. Are we clear?" She stands in front of me, placing her hands on her hips.

Is she serious? Every goddamned time, it's never his fault, not in her mind.

Closing my eyes tightly, I try to will the need to pound my fist into my father's face away. With my jaw locked, I suck in air through my teeth and then force it back out. When I reopen them, I look my mother in the face and lie to her, "Yes, Mom, we are clear." Before my facial expression falters and gives me away, I turn away from her and head out of the bedroom.

"Nicholas, don't be stupid."

I don't reply as I take the stairs back down and head out the door, making my way to my black Chevy 1500. Opening the door, I climb in and start the ignition before heading to my father's office.

It's not a long drive, but by the time I make it to the office, my body feels like it's on fire, and my hands are wrapped so tightly around the steering wheel that I have indentions on my palms.

As much as I know going after my father should bother me right now, it doesn't. It feels right. It feels like this moment has been coming for a long time. Growing up, I always knew this day would come. I would stand up to that sorry sack of shit and give him back every cruel thing he ever did and said to my mother. Today is that day.

But it isn't.

When I get inside, I am informed by his secretary that he has already left for court and isn't due to return until late afternoon, if he returns at all.

I leave immediately thereafter, heading over to the gym. I have a fight with Daniel Chaney in less than an hour. Today is elimination day to see which two amateur fighters go on to a paid fight next month. I've worked my ass off for this chance, a chance to prove I can make a career out of fighting. Jase wants it just as badly as I do, though. He has an elimination fight after mine.

It takes a good forty minutes to get all the way across town in midmorning traffic.

I locate a parking spot and park before grabbing my gym bag and heading inside. When I get to the front entrance, my sister is standing at the door.

"What took you so long? I thought you were going to make the trip by Mom's quick?" I don't answer her. This is not the time or place to get into a discussion about that.

"Why are you here? Don't you have class this morning?" I catch sight of my watch, knowing damn well her classes at UCLA aren't over before one p.m. on Thursdays. It's not quite nine-thirty yet.

"Like I was going to miss this?" she tells me like it should have been obvious.

"Whatever," I reply as I storm past her and into the building.

"What's crawled up your ass this morning?"

"Shut it, Nikki. I'm not in a good mood. I'm here to get this shit over with so I can leave. Just leave me the hell alone."

I don't stop and wait for her reply. I head back into the locker room and change.

"You're up next, Nicholas, so get your ass out there already." I look up to see Marcus standing in the doorway as I pull on my gloves.

"I'll be out there when I get out there, okay?" I bark. Shit. That was the wrong move.

"Excuse me?" But he doesn't wait for a response, and I'm smart enough to know not to give one. "No, motherfucker. You'll get out there when I say you get out there. Now get your goddamn ass out there and win that fight."

I bite down on my tongue to keep from saying something that would surely get me knocked on my ass as I brush past him out of the locker room. When I enter the fighting area, I see Daniel already in the ring. I like Daniel. He's an excellent fighter. Has a douchebag of a twin brother, but Daniel has always been a decent guy. We hang in different circles, though. Always have since grade school.

I climb my way up to the step and into the ring. My mind is clouded, and this is the last place I want to be. A far cry from the excitement I felt when I first woke up this morning. This is everything I've been working toward for months, but right now, I couldn't care less.

My father.

I want to see that bastard lying underneath me, begging me for mercy. Mercy I would never show him.

"You here with us, Lockhart?" I look over to see the referee staring at me with concern. Screw that. I need this. Right now, I need to fight.

"Yeah, let's do this," I say and turn my attention to Daniel standing opposite me.

Daniel walks forward and lifts his gloved knuckles, which I bump with mine just as the sound of the bell goes off.

I jump back as fists come toward me fast. Quickly, I duck and *swing my body to the left to miss the punch. Looking back at the man standing across from me, I no longer see my opponent. In Daniel's place is my father. My anger and hatred follow, and I charge the man standing only inches in my path, taking him down to the ground. Using my leg, I pin him down, but not before he swings his left fist, hitting me just below my right eye. I immediately feel the blood trickle out. I don't care though. The pain will be worth it. This bastard will pay for everything he has ever done.*

The first blow to his face feels good, really good. I follow with another to his skull and don't stop. I continue to hit, fighting the anger out of my body.

Every damn day as a kid, I lived in fear of this man. What would he do to my mother next? Would he eventually take it too far? Would I lose my mom? Would he start physically hurting Nikki or me?

I can vaguely hear people shouting all around me. I want the noise to stop. I continue to pound as hard as I can into the still flesh lying underneath my body. It's unmoving, and all I see is red. No longer is it my father. Just a lot of red.

Blood.

There's so much blood.

An arm wraps around my own, yanking me back just as I take another swing,

"Stop, Nicholas. Just stop already." I'm being pulled backward. It's Marc's voice I hear; I know that much, but I wonder where he came from. I try to pull myself out of his grasp.

My father.

I need to finish that piece of shit before he ever hurts another person I love.

An arm wraps around my neck, and I'm forced backward farther until I'm on my ass.

"Stay the fuck down. Do you hear me?"

As if his words pull me back to the here and now, I look up and see people staring at me. Hands covering mouths as if in shock. Jase is at my side in seconds, followed by my sister. Their expressions are the same: shock and disbelief.

What the hell?

I shake my head from left to right, and I look in front of me. There's a body lying on the ground, unmoving, with people hovering over it. As I look closer, it's Daniel.

The fight.

Our elimination fight comes back to me, as does the realization of what I have done. I've just beaten the living shit out of him.

Blood.

Blood is everywhere, covering his face completely.

I vaguely hear someone announce a disqualification, but I'm not really paying attention. I did this. I took out everything meant for my father on Daniel.

I've fucked up.

I've fucked up big time.

I let the vision of my memory fade into the background as I finish telling Shannon just how easily I can lose it and damage a person. I blink once, releasing the tear I've never allowed myself to shed. I'm not sure why. Why now? After all these years.

"Is that it?" Her voice is soft and laced with her own sadness. Her hands are wrapped tightly around my arm. Her palms have moved up above my elbow, and she is resting her cheek on my bicep.

"Daniel was taken to the hospital, where he was put in a medically induced coma for close to two weeks to allow the swelling on his brain to go down. Eventually, he awoke, but there was permanent damage done to his left ear, and from what I heard, he lost complete hearing in that ear. He has a slight speech impediment from being held down by the throat while being beaten."

I take a deep breath and turn, pulling away from her grip and facing her. She doesn't follow me as I back up against the wooden railing. Looking down at the ground, I've never felt more ashamed. This is the first time I've ever spoken about it. I never even told Jase why I did it. I'm sure he guessed. But the damage I did that day, not just to Daniel, but Shannon too, is too much. I'll never get past this.

"Nick—" she starts, but I cut her off. I'm not done. I have to tell her the other part too.

"No, I'm not finished. There's more." I bring my hands up to my face and run my palms over it before placing them inside my pockets and looking back down. I can't even bring myself to look her in the eyes when I tell her.

"After what happened, my father was pulled out of court to come to the hospital. When he found out what I did, he was beyond pissed, but so was I. There, in the hospital, while Daniel lay in a bed hooked up to a bunch of different machines, bandages everywhere and looking like he had just survived a horrific car crash, I told my father if he ever touched my mother again that would be him. The only difference would be he wouldn't survive." I look up at that moment into the most beautiful pale green eyes I've ever seen, and I confess my guilt.

"And you know something? He never did. At least to my knowledge he didn't. Instead, he took his anger, his sick, fucked-up desires out on others, on you." Her gasp rips my heart open, but I force myself to finish.

"He raped you because of me. He was so angry at me. He stormed out of the hospital, but before he left, he told me I would regret what I just did. And you know what? I do. I regret every moment of that day. Taking away the one person he thought he owned and could do all the sick and twisted things he wanted to forced him to find another. He found you. He raped you, and I'm responsible. God, if I could take that day back, baby, I would. I'm so sorry. God, I'm so sorry."

"That's what you think? Is that why you left me?"

"Don't you see, Shannon? I don't deserve you. I'll never deserve you or our baby. I don't deserve to be a part of our kid's life or yours. Look what I let happen. I'm a part of him, Shannon. What if—?"

"No," she yells, and I pull back. "Don't. You aren't anything like him. He was evil. Evil as evil gets, and that isn't you, Nick."

"Shannon, you don—"

"Stop," she shouts, but it doesn't matter. It's the truth, and the sooner she faces it, the better for her and our baby.

"No. It is what it is, and nothing can change it. God, I wish there were. I'd do anything to go back and change the decisions I made that day, but I can't. We all only get one shot at making the right choices."

"Dammit, Nick, stop this self-pity bullshit right now. Yes, there is no changing what happened, but that's life, and you learn to deal with it. I never learned that, but I'm trying now. I'm trying hard, but I can't do that without you."

She wipes a tear off her cheek and pulls in a breath of air through her mouth, but I don't get a chance to say anything as she holds up her palm, telling me to keep my mouth shut.

"I'm not done. It's my turn now, and you're going to listen to me. Got it?" Her eyes are trained on me, hard. She is looking up at me, but she feels so much larger than I am right now. I nod, letting her know I understand.

"Nick, our past is a story. The prologue to where we've been. I finally realized that, and once you do too, the past will no longer have power over you. What that monster did is not your fault. It was never your fault. He chose to . . ." She trails off, pausing to take the breather she looks like she needs. "To rape me. He did it, not you. You have to learn to live with what happened. You have to learn to let it go and move on. I'm not saying forget it because not even I'll never be able to forget, but we have a chance to have a happily ever after. If you love me, if

199

you love our baby, then it's up to you to choose where you go from this moment on."

If only it were that simple.

I do love her, and I love our child growing inside of her. There will never be anything I love and cherish more than them. Not ever.

"Have you apologized to him?"

"Him?" I question, dumbfounded.

"Daniel, Jeffery's brother—have you apologized for what happened to him that day? Did you tell him why?"

"No. I haven't seen him since the day it happened, and before you say something else, I don't think an *'I'm sorry'* is going to cut it for what I did to him."

"You don't have to be a dick," she says pointedly.

"I'm not." For fuck's sake.

"All I'm saying is having a conversation, letting him know why. To let him see how much you regret it might do you both some good."

I breathe and look away.

Well, I never thought about that. I wish it had never happened, but saying I'm sorry, how do I even begin to do that?

"Look, we're hungry. Take us home, please."

"You just ate a couple of hours ago." I'm confused. She did eat. I watched her.

"Your point?"

Not touching that one. I've dug myself a big enough hole tonight already.

"Come on. I'll feed you."

CHAPTER SEVENTEEN

I'm not a coffee drinker, couldn't care less for the stuff. It does nothing for me, yet here I am on my fourth cup of joe this morning, and my assistant, Rachel, keeps eyeing me with suspicion every time she brings me a fresh cup. I haven't told her, or anyone for that matter, except Shannon, what is happening this morning.

I arrived at my office an hour ago, early by even my standards. Typically, Jase and I work out from about 5:30 to 6:30 every weekday morning, but today I blew him off. I guess you could say I woke up on the wrong side of the bed. I woke up pissed off.

It's firing day. That's not the issue I have. I can fire someone at the drop of a hat, provided it's warranted, and not think twice about it. People get themselves fired, so why should I give a damn what happens after they leave my building unemployed?

Teresa Matthews.

The vice president of my company.

Sure, she gets on my last nerve constantly, but she is also great at her job. There's no denying that. I wouldn't have promoted her two years ago had I not believed in her abilities. She is smart, intelligent, and firm. Maybe even a little scary to some people around here.

I'm not sure if I'm more pissed over her meddling in my personal life by trying to fuck shit up between Shannon and me, the lack of respect she has for me, or the betrayal of bringing a man I can't stand into my office and screwing me over by literally screwing him.

I don't take too kindly to being disrespected.

I strum my fingers over the surface of my desk before reaching out for my cup and polishing off the remains of the coffee Rachel brought in ten minutes ago.

If I really analyze this, I'd say it's my own fault. I knew fucking her last year would come back to bite me in the ass. Even drunk off my ass, I knew that, yet I still did it. I'm thirty-one years old. You would think I'd stop thinking with my dick by now.

"So." I look up to see Teresa waltzing into my office dressed to the nines just as she always is. Today she's sporting a red, sleeveless dress with nude heels. The dress hugs her body in all the right places, and I know if I look down, the shoes she's wearing only help to show off her lean calf muscles. "You feel the need to have a conference call while I'm on vacation, and then in the middle, you suddenly have to go. Then I get back from said vacation to a mandatory meeting first thing on a Monday morning. Really, Nicholas, couldn't this have waited? At least until I've gone through all of my emails and messages that came in while I was in New York."

"No, it could not, Teresa."

She sits in the chair opposite me, looking every bit put out that I have her here in my office.

"I saw your lady friend at the coffee shop inside the Meadows building this morning. She . . ." Teresa pauses, and I know it's for a dramatic effect, but I don't give her time to finish. She may have disrespected me and her job, but I will not allow her to disrespect Shannon. She barely even knows her.

"You mean my girlfriend?" The Meadows building is across the street. Why is Shannon over here? She told me she was going to work this morning.

"Right," she bites out. "Anyway, you might want to get her a membership to a gym. She is looking a little plump these days, and I know you like your women fit."

"Well, she's pregnant. What's your excuse?" I retort without thinking my words out before I speak. I don't care that my remark is rude. Hers certainly was, but I need to remain as professional as possible, even if it's hard. Frankly, I would enjoy watching my sister lay her ass out.

"Excuse me?" She's appalled and probably even a little shocked. "Wait, what did you just say? She's—"

I cut her off.

"Enough. We have something to discuss, Teresa."

Covering her shock and ignoring my clipped tone, she asks in a soothing voice, "You aren't going to ask me about my vacation?"

"Why would I care about your personal life or anything you do on your personal time?" Her mouth slackens slightly, and I sit up in my chair. "Oh, that's right. You probably think since you are so damn concerned with mine that I should be with yours as well."

"Nicholas, what are you talking about? Is this not about the contract details we were discussing last week?"

I lean forward, placing my elbows on top of the surface of my desk, pressing my fingers together, and bringing them back against my lips.

"No, it's not. It's about you," I force out as I slam my

forearms down on my wooden desk. Her eyebrows come together, and she's momentarily concerned before her bitch tone comes out.

"What about me?"

"I'm disappointed in you." I shake my head, still not wanting to believe what I saw last Thursday. It's been days. I've had plenty of time to let it all sink in, yet the reality of what she did is so far out there. I don't get it.

"I'm sorry?" She cuts her eyes at me, confused, I'm sure. She doesn't think she heard me right. "What are you getting at?"

"Instead of telling you, Teresa, why don't I show you?" Stealing my eyes away from her, I turn in my chair, facing the computer screen. I rotate it so she and I can both watch it. With a few clicks of my mouse, I bring up the video. I've watched it over and over this morning, so I already have it paused just where I want it. The camera can't see the entrance to my office underneath it, but after replaying it multiple times, I saw the shadow of my door open. I saw exactly what Shannon saw the day this happened.

"What is this about, Nicholas?" She looks away from the screen and into my icy eyes. I have no sympathy or respect for the woman sitting across from me. Why should I?

"Just wait. I think you will be thoroughly entertained, just as I was."

I hit the play button and sit back as Teresa's eyes fall back onto the computer screen. For a moment, she seems taken aback, like I'm forcing her to watch a raunchy porno. Then it clicks, and her eyes widen as she takes a gasp of air, sucking it into her mouth in a rush. Her eyes snap to mine and then back to the screen.

"I—I mean, what the . . .?" She looks all around and toward the door. I'm sure she realizes that's where I have it, right above the door. You can't see it; well, not unless you had a ladder and were looking for it. It's hidden behind an air vent. "You have a camera in here."

Shock is the best way I can explain the look on her face.

"Bingo, we have a winner." The coldness of my voice surprises even me. So much for keeping this on a professional level.

Hatred. That's what I feel at this moment as I stare at this woman, an employee I trusted. Maybe not the same level of hate I had toward my father, but hate nonetheless. Had she not done this, hell, if I had been a few minutes earlier to my office, Shannon would have told me about the baby; she probably wouldn't have been violated a second time.

I know what happened to Shannon isn't Teresa's fault, but as far as I'm concerned, she did play a role in it, whether intentional or not. Our actions always come with consequences.

"Nicholas, I can—"

"You can what? Explain? Doubtful."

"Look, Nic—"

I slam my palm down on the desk as hard as I can, getting her attention, It makes her flinch and scoots back a little in her seat.

"No, you look. I know you set Shannon up so she would think I was the one in here screwing you. What the hell were you thinking?"

"Nicholas, wait," she interjects. "You don't understand."

"You're right. I don't, but what I do understand is that little show"—I point to be screen that is now playing Teresa riding Jeffery's dick in this very chair I'm sitting in—"just got you fired."

"What? No, Nicholas, you can't."

"Actually, I can. Do I need to say it again? You're fired, Teresa. And if that isn't clear enough for you, then hear this: you no longer work here."

"You're firing me over some worthless piece of ass?"

That comment has me up and out of my seat in a flash. Never would I hit a female, but my sister's offer to kick her ass is mighty tempting right now.

"No," I bark. "You got yourself fired, and don't ever speak about someone you don't know again."

"Do you hear yourself right now? Someone *I* don't know? Do you not remember what your own father told you about her weeks ago? No, Nicholas, you are the one who doesn't know who she really is." She stands, throwing her own hands up. "Now she's gotten herself pregnant. Is it even yours? Maybe you need to ask yourself that. Maybe you need to think about what she did to your father and could have done to your family years ago. Remember that piece of information?"

I do, and it was all a lie that I let my father feed to me, and I ate it right the fuck up.

"We are done."

"No, we aren't, Nicholas. Not until I make you understand."

"Understand what exactly? There isn't a way for you to dig yourself out of this hole. It's time for you to go now."

"She isn't good enough for you. Everything I did was for you."

"Like hell."

"It should be you and me, not her. I love you, Nicholas," she declares, but there's no sincerity behind it. She doesn't love me.

"You're delusional."

"Boss, is everything okay?" I look up to see a concerned Rachel at my door and Shannon standing directly behind her. My assistant looks like she's holding Shannon back. No doubt she just heard what Teresa said.

Great.

My little firecracker is pissed. I can see the heat in her eyes from here.

"It will be momentarily." I turn my attention back to Teresa. "This is done. You no longer work here. I suggest you gather your things as quickly as possible, or I'll get security to escort you out."

She stands in front of me, staring and unmoving. Maybe it hasn't sunk in.

"That was your cue to leave. Now." I order.

She does so, turning and walking out. She stops and looks at both Rachel and Shannon.

Rachel backs out of the door to give Teresa room. As she does so, Rachel wraps her hand slowly around Shannon's wrist as if she thinks Shannon may take a swing at Teresa.

Knowing my girl, it's a possibility. One I hope she doesn't act on. She shouldn't even be here right now.

Teresa exits, and Rachel looks at me, confused and concerned.

"Everything is fine, Rachel. As you heard, Teresa no longer works here. Please have her access to the building, computer, and finances revoked immediately."

"Yes, sir." Rachel turns and walks back to her desk, I'm sure to get started on getting everything handled.

Shannon is still standing outside the door, looking in the direction Teresa walked. I have a better view of her now that Rachel isn't standing in front of her. I take a moment to take her in. Her normally straight hair is hanging in loose curls. She's dressed up today, wearing a dark-colored, thin-strapped dress and high heels. From the looks of them, they are six-inch platforms.

Damn, she's sexy. A smile crosses my lips.

"Are you going to continue standing there, or are you going to get your sweet ass in here?"

She turns reluctantly with a scowl still in place on her face as she walks through the door, allowing it to close and lock in place as she passes the entrance. I sink back into my chair as she nears me, relieved the moment I had been dreading all weekend is now over.

"What do I owe this surprise to?" I glance down at my watch. "And so early. It's barely past eight."

"Would you believe I was in the neighborhood?" I eye her, and Shannon gives me an innocent look.

Yeah, sure she was.

"So, what? You just had to come make sure she got the boot?" I chuckle, even though I don't find it the least bit funny.

Shannon shrugs as she walks slowly behind my desk, inching herself closer to where I'm sitting. Swiveling in my chair, I rotate to face her. She looks down at me as she tosses her small handbag on my desk. Once it lands softly on the wooden surface, she bends at the waist and places her lips on mine, giving me a sweet and gentle kiss before pulling away and turning to look around the room.

"I was thinking."

"Were you now?" A smile spreads wide across my face, and I reach forward, holding her by the waist and pulling her back on my lap. She gasps; it's forced and fake, but I don't care. This woman knew what I'd do the moment she turned away from me.

"What has my sexy, exotic pet been thinking about, huh?" I whisper in her ear, causing her to squirm and grind her ass into my cock, waking him up for the party he's been invited to.

"Pet?" she chokes out, surprised I'd say such a thing.

"Yes." I dive my palm into her long locks and lightly tug as I reach low, and with my free hand, slide it slowly along the smooth, hot flesh of her inner thigh. "Everything about you is sexy and exotic, like a rare pet. My pet, that's all goddamn mine, sweetheart."

I'm pretty certain a growl erupts from my throat and into her ear.

Locating her earlobe, I bring it into my mouth, between my teeth, and apply light pressure as I pull it back out. She takes in a deep breath of air through her mouth.

"Nick?"

"Tell me, Shannon. Tell me what it was you were thinking about." I increase the strokes along her inner thigh.

"Wait."

"No, tell me, baby. Tell me now." I kiss down her neck as I adjust the grip on her hair by tightening my fist. My dick is already straining against the zipper of my pants, telling me it's already sneaked its way out of my boxers. Ignoring the discomfort, I continue placing kisses along Shannon's neck and shoulder. Her skin is hot.

"But the camera," she breathes out. I stop and look up. *Shit.* "Can you turn it off?"

"Yeah, give me a minute, will ya?" I release my hold on her and lift her up, spinning her and placing her with ease on the edge of my desk. Quickly pulling a drawer open, I take out a small remote. Aiming at the camera, I successfully shut it off.

I don't need anyone seeing her soon-to-be naked body laid out for someone else's enjoyment.

"Done." I drop the remote back in the drawer and shove it closed before standing in front of Shannon. I grin down at her as I settle between her legs. Her dress is loose, so she doesn't have a problem spreading her thighs, allowing me access. "Now, tell me what it was you were thinking."

I lean in closer, running my hand up both sides of her outer legs, pushing her dress up at the same time.

Reaching up, she slides her palms underneath my black suit jacket and pushes it off, or tries to. I have to assist her in removing it.

"I just thought you could use another memory of what

happened in here." I back away from her and drape my jacket over my chair.

"Did you now?" I turn and ease my way back between her smooth legs.

"And I think I could use another memory too."

"Hey." I cup her face. "I'd never do that. What you thought happened in here. I'd never cheat on you. I love you, woman."

"No, I know that. I know what actually happened wasn't you, but that's not what I mean. I mean . . ." She pauses and looks down, as if ashamed to tell me.

"What, baby? You can tell me."

She looks back up.

"Well . . ." She stops, but I give her the time she needs to speak. "You remember everything I told you? What he did to me in his office?"

I release her face and back away. She's talking about my father and the day he raped her in his own office, the day he held her down and forced himself on her. The day I fucked up and caused him to hurt her.

I fall back into my chair. It's at least a minute before I'm able to look at her. I can never forgive myself for that. The ache in my chest never ceases to exist or ease up.

"What are you getting at?"

She slides off my desk and climbs onto my lap, sliding her legs on either side of mine. Reaching for her, I cup her under her ass. My eyes lift and meet hers. Shannon cups my face just as I did hers a few minutes ago.

"Do you remember?"

"Yes."

"Do you also remember the night I freaked out when you bound my hands together in bed?"

She is going to ask me to tie her down. I know this before she even says it. I can't do it. She freaked out last time, and that's what he did to her. I can't do the same. She can't ask this of me. I won't have her comparing me to that evil.

"Yes, I remember, but Shannon, I—" She cuts me off before I can get the words out.

"Please. Nick, I need this. I need you to give me another memory. It's the only way I can move past it. Please do this for me." She's begging me.

Fuck.

No, I can't. What if . . .? No, I just can't do it.

"Please don't ask that of me."

"I already have. With you, it will be different."

"I can't. Not after knowing what he did. I don't want the chance of you relating that to us."

"I know what I need." Her head falls forward, resting against my own. "I need you to take it away, just as I need to take what happened in here away from you. Please."

I know I have to trust her, but I don't want to do this. It's not that I have a problem showing dominance and binding Shannon; that turns me on, actually, but I don't want to hurt her more than she's already been hurt. I'm not talking about the physical kind. I don't want to damage or traumatize her any more than *he* already has.

I gaze up, looking into her eyes. She wants this. I can see it shining back, hopeful and begging me at the same time.

Trust her. She never asks you for anything.

"You sure?"

"Yes."

God, please don't let this go badly. Please.

Reaching to my left, I pick up the phone and press the button to ring Rachel.

"What can I do for you, boss?" Rachel squeaks out.

"Has she left?"

"Got in the elevator about two minutes ago."

"Good. Postpone my nine o'clock meeting. Move it to one this afternoon."

"Consider it done, sir."

A moment later, the receiver is placed back down, and I'm sliding my hands underneath Shannon's dress.

It's my time to question her.

"You remember this room isn't soundproof, right?" She nods. "For the most part, you need to be as quiet as possible, or at least speak softly. In your case, my little screamer, try not to do that."

She swats me on the shoulder. "I'm not a screamer." I give her an 'are you for real' look. "Okay, maybe I'm a little vocal."

"Okay, babe, whatever makes you feel better." I laugh. She does too, until my hand slides inside her panties. Shannon's breath hitches as I move the top of my fingers back and forth along her smooth pussy.

My pussy.

"You like that, baby?" She bites her lip. "Does it feel good?"

"Yes."

I pull my fingers out. She whimpers, only a fraction, but I catch it. Wrapping my hands around her thighs and gripping firmly, I stand and then deposit her on top of the desk again.

Moving my palm slowly up her body until I reach the back of her neck, I pull lightly, bringing her lips to mine. At the touch of her mouth to mine, a torch ignites within me. With the hand I still have under her thigh, I snatch her forward, making that pussy of mine collide with my now-solid dick.

Running my hand up into her hair, I grip it along the nape lightly, gently pulling her head back. My lips roam down her chin and to her throat, kissing as I go.

"If at any moment it gets to be too much, just say the word, and I'll stop." My words come out against her skin. Shannon doesn't answer me. I stop my advance and make her look me in the eyes.

"Say stop, and I'll stop."

"I will."

"Good. Take your dress off." I back away and sit back in my chair in front of her. Shannon hops off and sheds her dress. "Bra too, but your panties and shoes stay on."

She grins, knowing my affection for her naked but wearing heels. What can I say? It's hot.

"Now get back on that desk." She complies with my request. "Spread your legs."

"Like this?"

"Wider, baby." That's it. "Are you wet?" I can see she is. Her pussy is glistening through the thin material of her panties, and I want nothing more than to have that wetness on my tongue. My cock throbs inside my pants just at the thought of her taste.

"You want to watch me play with myself, don't you?"

"Smart girl."

She moves her hand slowly up her thigh and then between her legs, lightly cupping herself. Then she runs her palm upward before going back down again. On the next upward motion, she pushes the material of her panties to the side and pulls her pussy lips apart.

Jesus, I need to stick my dick inside that.

She presses a finger against her clit, and then, adding another finger, she starts a swirling motion. I let her go for a moment, watching her slow movements.

"Lower." She moves her fingers away from her clit and down to the wet heat I need wrapped around me. A long finger disappears inside her before coming out and then going back in. I lick my lips. The need to taste that sweet, wet pussy is growing inside me as my cock rocks against my pants.

I reach up, loosening my tie until I can pull it from my shirt. I wrap it around the palm of my right hand, as I'm not ready for it just yet. Shannon continues moving in and out of herself, coating her finger in her juices. I reach back up to undo the first two buttons of my shirt. It's suddenly hot inside my office.

"Enough of that," I tell her as I stand and still her hand. Pulling her finger out, I bring it up to my mouth. I release my wrapped fingers around her wrist, but she knows what I want her to do.

My mouth relaxes, and Shannon pushes her finger inside, gliding it onto my tongue. Closing my lips around her, she pulls back out.

"Like the taste?"

"Do you even have to ask?" I move forward, closer to her. "You're my favorite meal, baby." Advancing more, I lean against her, pressing my face into her neck and inhaling as much as my lungs will take in. "And you're the best thing I've ever smelled. Nothing can compare to this scent."

Moving across her neck, I continue my trail of kisses. I gather both of her wrists, bringing them behind her back. Then I kiss up her neck and down to her shoulder. Shannon's head falls backward as she mumbles something inaudible.

Pulling her arms together, I let the tie unwrap from my hand. Gathering it back up, I loop it around Shannon's right wrist, tying it tightly around her skin. Just as I think she's relaxing, her body stiffens. She realizes what I'm doing.

I move to her ear. "Are you still okay? Do you still want this?" I ask in the most soothing voice I can muster. At least, I pray it's soothing.

"Yes." Her answer is quick and breathy, but it tells me she does, in fact, still want this. I pull back so she can see my eyes.

"Relax and know that you can trust me."

"I do trust you."

"Good. Now scoot your ass off."

Her body arches forward as she inches closer to the edge. I lean in a little more, and then I place my hands on both sides of her hips to help ease her down. When her cheek brushes my face, I take the opportunity to nip her jaw with my teeth. Her body shudders, and she lets out a low gasp. Moving to her mouth, I pull her bottom lip into my mouth and nip again as she pulls it away from me. Her heels hit the floor with a soft click. She can almost look me in the eye at this height.

I don't like it.

"Turn around," I command, and Shannon complies. Gathering her hair into a makeshift ponytail at the nape of her neck, I twist it tightly as I snake my left hand around to cup her breast. Using her hair, I tug her body back toward mine and lean in, pressing my hard cock against her hands and ass.

A soft, barely audible moan escapes her mouth.

"Feel that?" My hand roams from her tit, down her belly, and into the fabric of her panties. She's soaking wet. I grip her firmly, pulling her even tighter against me. "This is what you do to me; you make my dick desperate for this sweet, wet pussy right here."

I slide my middle finger inside her with ease. Another moan escapes her mouth, only this time, it's a little louder. Her muscles contract around me as I pull out. As I enter a second time, I add another finger.

"Ooh."

My cock throbs at the sound of her voice.

"It aches for you. Your pretty little wet pussy is the only thing that can make it stop."

I release her hair, placing my hand in the center of her back, forcing her body forward until she's lying across my desk. I rub up to her neck and then back down. I do this several times to ensure Shannon remains calm. On the last downward stroke, I move down to bind her wrists together and grasp my hand over both wrists.

I don't want to tie her down to anything, the desk especially.

I know she says she wants it, but she's doing great with this. I can't push it further. Maybe one day.

Pulling my wet finger out of her, I lean over her body and press my finger between her lips. She takes it all, sucking my finger like the good little cock sucker I know her to be.

I pull my finger away from her mouth and run the tip of my fingers down the length of her arm to her panty-covered ass. I grip the seam. Reaching up with my other hand, I pull the threads holding her panties together apart, repeating the process on the other side.

I gather the material in one hand and snatch them off, sticking them in my pants pocket. I'll discard them later. I'm not a panty sniffer. On second thought, they do have Shannon's juices all over them.

"Spread your legs," I tell her as I reach up and unbutton the rest of my shirt. I need skin-to-skin contact with her. "Wider, baby."

I undo the buckle on my belt, followed by the button and zipper. My pants fall to my ankles and pull my boxers with them. My cock springs forward, hard, solid, and ready for this sweet pussy laid out in front of me.

I look down; my cock is an inch away from her beautiful round behind. I run my palms down each side of her warm, smooth skin, spreading her cheeks apart.

Lifting and then bringing my right palm down, I smack her solidly on the ass. She yelps, but for the most part, she holds it in.

In a swift motion, I push forward and slide into her heat.

"Ahhh." She bites down on her lower lip. My girl is working hard to be quiet.

"Fuck." Her warmth makes my head spin. I still myself inside her to ease my dizzy spell.

Once I'm able to see straight again, I rear back and slam

forward, harder this time. Every time I pull out, her muscles tighten around me, and if I don't keep a slow, steady pace, she'll pull the come right out of me; I'm sure of it. I was ready to blow the moment she pulled her panties to the side, and I saw sweet heaven.

I push forward again, and as I do, I lean over her, diving my hand into her hair once again and pulling it taut. Most of the curls have fallen now, but I don't care. I want her to look like she's been fucked.

She is mine to fuck, to love, to drive crazy.

No one else's but mine.

With a fist full of long, red hair, I guide her up and off the desk, against me as much as possible. With my other hand, I wrap around her front, her belly. Knowing there is another person behind my hand is weird. I can't lie. I never thought this would happen, but knowing it's mine is scary and thrilling at the same time.

I bring Shannon's face close to mine. I release her hair and place my hand loosely around her neck, cupping her face on both sides of her jaw.

I push forward again, and her eyelids fall shut. When she opens them, I turn her face to look at me the best she can.

"I love you. You know that, right?" I retract myself and with force, push inside her again.

"Yes." It comes out rushed and louder than I know she wanted it to.

"And do you trust me? Do you know I'd never hurt you?" Her eyes cast to the side and away from me for the briefest moments, and her reply is hesitant.

"Yes." She just lied to me. Perhaps not on purpose, and maybe she doesn't want to believe I'd hurt her, but somewhere inside her, she does.

Can I really blame her?

I'll just have to work harder to earn it, but I won't lose her, them. I won't.

Lowering my head, I kiss her shoulder as I move my hand from her belly to her hip and pick up the pace. I won't last long going at this speed. Hell, I'm surprised I've lasted this long.

Shannon's moans increase from slow, drawn-out sounds I could barely hear to shallow, quick spurts that increase in volume as I pound into her.

Her body stiffens, and her insides grab onto me, squeezing for dear life. Thank the Lord because I'm about to come. I have zero control over myself around her.

When I feel her body shudder, I move my hand away from her neck to cover her mouth, and just in time. Her screams are muffled. Just as my own explosion ripples through my body, I bite down on her shoulder to hold back the curse words this woman forces out of me.

I still and relax onto her, causing Shannon to fall forward onto the desk. My dick slackens inside her, and I pull out.

"You're amazing, baby. If you want to clean up, there's a bathroom over there." I point off to the side of my office to a closed door as I pull up my boxers and pants.

Shannon twists to face me. "Good . . ." She doesn't get a chance to finish before I pull her to me and kiss her on the lips. I move my hands behind her to untie her wrists and retrieve my tie.

"I need this back."

"Ass."

"Yes, I am. Now off you go." I swat her lightly on the behind. Shannon bends to pick up her dress and bra, then turns to head in the direction I instructed her a moment ago.

While she's gone, I button my shirt, tucking it into my pants, and finally, loop in my belt and buckle it in place.

Shannon exits the bathroom a few minutes later. I'm standing against the edge of my desk, waiting on her.

"Are you okay?"

She strolls up to me and smiles.

"Better than okay. Thank you." Her smile is genuine, and I say a silent thank you to God. "Don't stay here too late today. I'm cooking you dinner."

I burst out laughing. That's the funniest thing she's ever said to me.

"Hey." She slaps me lightly on the arm. "I'm serious."

"Damn, I thought that was a joke."

"I resent that remark." Her eyebrows scrunch together.

"Sorry, babe, but you know your place is far, far away from a kitchen." I laugh again. Man, my day has improved already.

"Stop being a dick."

"That will never happen. It's time for you to go. You're too much of a beautiful distraction." Shannon smiles at my compliment. "Seeing how I just fired my second in command, I now have a shitload of work piled on top of me."

"You're smart. I'm sure your delegation skills are exceptional." Not really, but I'm not going to tell her that. I've just been a believer that if you want something done right, you do it yourself.

I kiss her once more, and then she exits my office.

CHAPTER EIGHTEEN

Leaving the door open, I walk back into my office and head over to my desk. Dropping into my chair and leaning as far back as possible, I take a deep breath. The two-hour meeting I just wrapped up has left me drained. Leaning forward, I unbutton the sleeves on my shirt and roll both sides up, well as far as I can without exposing the ink on my left arm.

I'm not conservative with my body art, nor am I ashamed of the array of ink that covers me. I wouldn't have them if I didn't like them, but I will always remain professional here. I expect this from my staff, and I'm certainly not excluded.

"Is there anything I can get you, boss?"

I look up to see Rachel standing in my doorway. She looks . . . I don't know . . . frazzled, maybe. No, that's not it. Ever since I told my team that Teresa was no longer employed by Lockhart Publishing, along with the events that took place inside my office, my assistant has been off.

That conversation was awkward and led to a long meeting. People were in shock. Some seemed relieved that she's gone. But the last thing I want is for anyone on my staff to slack in their job duties. I know I have to replace her quickly.

The only tenured person is Matt, and I know he's going to hate the idea. That's a discussion for later, though.

"Not unless you have some alcohol stashed in your desk."

Rachel doesn't catch my joke for a moment, which tells me something is wrong with her. "I'm sorry?" she finally clues in. Rachel is normally light, full of spunk, and probably the only person who would even attempt to bring humor into our conversations.

"What's wrong?" I ask, allowing my attempt to make her smile fade away. "You know I don't think what happened is your fault, right?"

She walks farther into my office. When she nears, she looks like she may be on the verge of tears.

"I think maybe it is."

"What are you talking about?"

It can't be her fault; she had nothing to do with it. This is absurd. Rachel takes a seat in front of me, her eyes cast down so she isn't looking at me.

"I've been seeing him," she starts, leaving me with a feeling in the pit of my stomach I don't like. By him, I assume she means Jeffery. I know I shouldn't be mad; she's an adult and free to see whomever she wants. Except she's my assistant, and he's an enemy. Hell, competition, in fact. "Just a fling, I guess you could say, for the past few months. It's nothing serious, but that particular day, I had planned lunch with him. He knew you weren't in the office. I think I even mentioned that. I told him I could take a longer lunch since you weren't here, and well, everyone else usually did too, so I didn't think it mattered if I was late coming back."

I take in what she's told me. He used her. Maybe he hadn't

planned what would happen, but I'm certain he's been using her from the beginning.

When I don't speak, she looks up. I can see the sorrow in her eyes. She shouldn't feel responsible, not for that. It was in no way her doing. Certainly, I can't lie; I would rather her not discuss me or LP with him. Hell, if I'm honest, she can do so much better than that douche fuck.

"Don't blame yourself in any way for what happened. Nothing is your fault." I pause, allowing my words to penetrate her ears. "Why don't you take the rest of the day off and go enjoy yourself? I know it's nearly five, but take the next two hours and go do whatever it is you do to make yourself happy. In fact, head over to Serenity at The Cove. Treat yourself on my account."

Finally, a smile, half a smile, but a smile nonetheless. I'll take it.

"Don't you know? You don't own that place anymore. You can't just order them to squeeze me in. Their appointments are booked out for several weeks."

"I have pull," I state. I may have sold the place, but people are still loyal to me, and when I tell them to do something, it generally gets done, no matter if I'm in charge or not.

"Okay, boss. You're not mad?"

"No, Rachel, I'm not, but if you don't get out of here, I might reconsider that."

A noise draws my attention away from my assistant. I glance over to my desk, where my cell phone has been lying since early this morning. The sound indicates I have a voice message waiting for me.

"Go on," I tell Rachel as I flick my wrist, and with my other hand, I pick up my phone. She exits my office quickly, and I look down at my phone. Looking at the missed calls list, irritation and anger envelop me. This fucker needs to be dealt with too.

Jeffery Chaney.

How dare he come into my building, into my company, into my goddamn office and . . . I can't even think it out.

Motherfucker.

I press the play button and hold the phone up to my ear.

"Did you misplace something of value, Lockhart? Perhaps the sexy and oh so fuckable redhead I watch walk into the lobby of my building just now? Don't worry, I'll take care of her for you. I'm sure you've heard just how much I love to restrain and play with my toys."

Then I hear the clicking sound of the call ending.

I will rip that bastard to pieces.

What is she doing there? She promised me she wouldn't work for him. She promised me she would stay away.

Shoving my phone into my pocket, I leave my office.

I will rip him the fuck apart if he touches her.

And her . . . Just what the hell am I going to do with her? She's going to give me a heart attack at this rate.

I don't bother with parking in the underground garage. Instead, I pull up out front of the building, parking alongside a no parking sign, and get out.

I know his office is on the fifth floor. As I enter, I walk directly to the elevator in front of me and slide inside just before the doors close.

"What floor do . . ." someone starts to ask, but I don't bother with a response. I reach in front of him and press the button for my floor.

As soon as the doors open again, I exit into the lobby. Before entering the office, I notice the large, bold letters of C & S that mark the building's name on the wall. C stands for Chaney, and S stands for Smith, his partner's last name. Sounds more like a collection agency than a competing publishing company.

As I walk through the frosted glass door, I see a receptionist out front. She's busy on a phone call. I don't intend to speak to her anyway. I know where I'm going.

I veer to my left, making my way down a long hallway before coming to a wooden door with his name on it.

"Sir, excuse me?" The young brunette behind the front desk calls behind me, apparently finished with her phone call. I ignore her and push the door open.

As I open the door wide, a man's voice hits my ear. It's deep, full of force.

"Hey," he calls out.

The first thing I notice is Shannon standing too close to a man I can't stand. Jeffery's hand is wrapped around her wrist, and she's pulling away, but she stops when her face turns to meet mine.

I can practically hear the gasp that comes from her mouth. That's when I notice the other man for the first time. The man who spoke a second ago.

"Release her, Jeff. Now."

Daniel. Jeffery's twin brother.

I walk in with purpose. Jeffery releases Shannon's wrist as I near.

"I see you got my message."

Shannon turns to look at him; her eyebrows pull together, and her head cocks to the side. She then realizes he set her up. He wanted me to walk into this.

"I told you once. Don't make me repeat myself. You stay the fuck away from her."

I grab Shannon, probably a bit too roughly, pulling her to me. I need to feel her to know she's okay, to know they're okay. If I'm honest with myself, I can't imagine Jeffery harming her, well not unless she asked him to. However, the motherfucker hates me, and he might do anything to get at me.

"She came here on her own." He turns to look at her. "Didn't you, Shannon?"

She says nothing.

I move forward, getting into Jeffery's face.

"Don't even speak to her." I turn and stop for a second, staring at Daniel before pulling Shannon from the office and the building.

Once outside, I finally take a breath of air and then turn on her.

"What the fuck were you thinking?" I shout, knowing I'm being too hard and not giving the least bit of a shit.

"Nick, let me—"

She doesn't get to finish before I'm inches from her face. "No, you promised me. You promised me you wouldn't have anything to do with him." How could she come here? She knew damn well I'd be pissed. Oh, I'm pissed all right, baby.

"Would you let me explain?" She backs up so I'm no longer in her face.

"Explain what exactly? Why you lied to me? Are you serious?"

"I didn't lie. Would you—?"

Again I cut her off. "The hell you didn't. You know what? I can't deal with this shit right now." I hate fucking liars. Why?

"Nick, stop." I turn, ignoring her pleas.

"You can take your fucking lies to someone else."

Without looking back at her, I walk to my car, which is parked out front, get in and drive off, leaving her standing there.

CHAPTER NINETEEN

Almost a week after my confession to Shannon, I finally have the balls to speak to Daniel in person. Shannon was right when she suggested it, but that doesn't make it easy. I still haven't the slightest clue what I'm about to say to him, but my life can't go on like it is now.

My head is beyond fucked up. Three days ago, I walked away from Shannon yet again. Saying I'm sorry just isn't going to cut it this time. I've tried to drown myself in work; with Teresa's shit piled on top of mine, there isn't a shortage, but I can't focus.

I didn't let her explain.

I'm a douchebag, no doubt about that.

I didn't give her a chance to tell me why she was there in the first place. I jumped to a conclusion yet again. Why do I do that with her? I've always been the type of person to hear people out and then decide whether I believe them or not.

I've slept at my house the past two nights, if that's what you'd call it. More like laid there and thought, put a couple of holes in a wall or five, and thought some more. Soul searching is good, being destructive is nothing more than childish behavior, but the fact remains: I can't sleep without her next to me. I don't want to sleep without her next to me. I need her. I need them both.

Telling her what happened to Daniel, what I did to him, was the scariest thing I've ever had to do, but at the same time, it lifted a weight off my chest. A small amount of weight, but a weight nonetheless. I just hope the same can be said when I walk back out of this place. I can't even attempt to tell her I'm sorry and beg for her forgiveness until this is finished. Until I make amends.

Yeah, like that is likely to happen.

I pull the door open to a place I never thought I'd enter again. Walking inside Jackson's MMA, my old gym, I look around and see nothing is the same as it was ten years ago. All the equipment is newer and state-of-the-art. The mats are now located in the far left corner instead of the middle. The boxing ring is set up in the far back, and there is a welcome desk that didn't exist back then.

"Hi." I'm greeted with a warm, sweet smile from a young girl, probably in her early twenties. "Can I help you, sir?"

"Yeah, I guess you can. I'm here to see Daniel."

"Okay," she tells me as she turns and walks behind the counter. "Is Danny expecting you?"

"No, he isn't."

"Okay, well, let me call up to his office to see if he's available. Your name?" She picks up the phone and dials a phone number.

"Nicholas Lockhart."

She pauses and looks up with shock across her face.

"I-I'm sorry, s-say that again?" she stutters. It's obvious she knows my name, which tells me she knows the history too.

"You heard me correctly, honey. Tell him it's Nicholas."

"Right." She places the phone down on the receiver. "There wasn't an answer. If you'll excuse me, I'll go find him."

She rushes from behind the counter as quickly as her feet will move her. She turns and looks back at me once before disappearing through a door off to the side. Last I remember, that's the hall leading down to a massive room that houses the MMA cage. The room where I ended Daniel's fighting career.

Within a few minutes, I look up to see Daniel Chaney walking toward me. He looks relatively the same, older, and much better than I expected. There isn't major damage to his face like I thought there would be. Multiple scars characterize his face, but most are faint. Only the large one near his jaw is prominent, noticeable from the surgery he endured.

"What are you doing here, Lockhart?"

Yes, the question of the day. What exactly am I doing here?

"Can we talk?"

"Look, I'm sorry about Jeff. I didn't know he was pulling that shit with your girl."

"It's not about Shannon." I shake my head. But I will be dealing with Jeffery soon enough. The image of him with his hand wrapped around her wrist as she was pulling away from him crosses my mind, but I quickly push it back.

"All right then, I'll ask again. What are you doing here?"

"I told you. I just want a word with you, please, in private." I add as the young woman walks back up front, eyeing me with what I assume is hatred.

Daniel stares me down, trying to read my intentions. I'm sure of it. My expression is blank, giving nothing away, so I know he's unsure of me right now.

"Very well. Let's go up to my office then."

"Danny?" the girl calls out as I move to follow him.

"Everything is fine, Lily. Stay your ass put."

Once we make it up the steps, Daniel opens an office door and gestures me inside. I walk in, taking a seat in one of the chairs in front of a messy desk.

"So you bought this place from Jackson, huh?"

Daniel sits down in the large black chair across from me.

"I did, but I'm sure that's information you already know, and I also doubt that's why you're here now." He looks at me pointedly, but I don't see the hatred behind his dark blue eyes that I see from Jeffery or even the girl downstairs. His eyes are the only things that differ from his twin brother's. Daniel has warm, almost inviting, dark blue eyes, and Jeffery has cold gray eyes.

"Yeah, I suppose you're right."

"Why are you really here, Nicholas? What do you want?" He leans back in his chair and waits for me to speak. I'm silent for a moment.

"An explanation I guess. What happened. What I did to you and why."

"Now? A fucking decade later? Are you serious?" He's surprised.

"Yeah." I lean forward, my elbows on my knees, and I lace my fingers together.

"Let me ask you something." He leans forward, elbows digging into the wooden surface of his desk. "Can you honestly say you were meant to be a fighter? If what happened had not happened, you hadn't gotten banned from the cage, would you have made it a career?"

"What?" Where the hell is he going with this? Sure I would have. It was everything I wanted to do back then.

"Just wait, hear me out a minute. I listened to your bitch-fest a second ago. Now it's my turn." Now I remember why we were never friends. He's more of a ball-busting asshole than Jase is. "Nicholas, you were a good fighter. I'll give you that. Hell, you probably still are, but you always lacked what a great fighter has to have."

Is he serious? I'm here to grovel and say I'm sorry, to beg for his forgiveness while he's sitting over there trying to coach me on my fighting skills.

"What are you getting at?"

"Control. You never had it. Maybe you have it today. I don't know. I saw a bit of control the other day in Jeff's office. I know you wanted to cream him, yet you didn't."

"Excuse me?"

"Shut it for a sec, would ya? Just listen." He pauses and shakes his head. He's pissing me off. "I knew that ten years ago. I even knew that fifteen years ago, back in high school. Everybody knew you didn't know how to control yourself or rein in your temper. If someone pisses you off, really pisses you off, you lose it. Nicholas, The Loose Cannon, Lockhart, remember?"

"Are you going to make a point?"

"Yeah, if you will shut the fuck up like I asked."

"Careful, Chaney, I don't take well to people bossing me around."

"Exactly, you just made my point."

"Well, I guess fucking enlighten me because I have no idea what you're even talking about."

"What happened, happened for a goddamn reason, man. You were never meant to be a fighter, Nicholas. You were always meant for the suit and tie shit you're doing now. The boss, and from what I've heard, you seem to have excelled at it." I look down at my attire and glance back up at him. "And me, I was never meant to be a career-long fighter either. My place was always here, coaching and training other fighters, helping them hone their own skill. Had what happened never happened, then I might not have ended up here. That's what I'm getting at. Granted, it would have been nice not to have to go through multiple facial surgeries and complete dental reconstruction, and I'd love to have full hearing in my left ear."

Is he telling me he's okay with what happened with what I did? Surely not.

"I don't get it. You're glad it happened?"

"No, I'm not glad, yet in a way, I'm thankful. Grateful even. Fuck, man, I'm happy. I have a great life today and a girl I plan to make my wife real soon. I don't have any ill feelings toward you. I don't hate you, Nicholas, and honestly, I never did. I stepped inside a ring, a cage, or onto a mat daily, every time knowing full well that if I got hit or kicked wrong or fell in some strange way, that permanent injury was a possibility, even death. Anyone who doesn't realize that is stupid. So no, I did not hate you then, and I don't hate you now."

I peer up at him. I didn't expect to hear this from him. I try to take it all in, everything he's told me.

"If forgiveness is what you're seeking, then okay; you got it. I forgive you, Lockhart, but if you ask me, it's not me you need forgiveness from. It's you. You have to forgive yourself and move past this. It's in the past, so put it there and let it go."

I laugh.

"Yeah, you were definitely meant to be a coach." He's right. Every word, but forgiving myself? I don't know that it's possible. He doesn't blame me, but what I did, there just isn't any excuse. "The girl downstairs, the feisty one, she's yours, isn't she? Lily, right?" I ask, even though I know the answer. I could tell she loves him, wants to protect him, and hates me as she should.

"Yeah, Lil is mine, but feisty? You want to talk about feisty? I met your girl the other day. That woman is something else. I've never seen anyone get right in Jeff's face, well, except maybe you, and threaten to beat his ass. And that girl was serious too."

"Say what?"

"Shannon? That's her name?" I nod. "She told you why she was there, didn't she?"

"No," I confessed. "I didn't exactly give her the chance to speak after I yanked her from his office."

Why do I get the feeling I'm about to feel like I'm the biggest jerk in the world?

"She called him, asking if she could have a word with him, and he eagerly agreed. She showed up within ten, maybe fifteen minutes. Jeff loved the fact that I was there. In fact, he had planned to take the opportunity to tell her about you and me. I may not hate you, but my brother's a different story. He can't get over what happened. It changed me for the better really, but not in Jeff's eyes. Anyway, she walked in and proceeded to ask him why he did whatever it was he did in your office with some chick. I don't know what he did, and I don't want to know, but she was pissed off. Got right in his face and told him if he even thought about the name Nicholas Lockhart again, she'd make him regret it." Daniel laughs, remembering the moment I obviously missed.

"Jeff isn't used to anyone, let alone a woman, asserting dominance. He got pissed and grabbed her by the wrist. That's when I stood up and yelled at him. About that time, you walked in. He really wouldn't have hurt her. You know that, right?"

I'm a jerk all right.

"I don't know. He hates me like you said. I'm not sure what he's capable of when it comes to me."

"My brother is a dick, a true sadist, but he isn't an abuser. He'd only hurt a woman if she asked him to, and even then, she would have to beg, and he'd have to believe her. He may be fucked up in the head, he may crave certain sexual desires that normal people don't, but he isn't a monster, Nicholas."

"So you say."

"So I know." His tone is firm, and as much as I don't want to believe him, I know he's right. Jeffery Chaney and I will never be more than enemies, but that doesn't mean he's a bad person, not like my own father was. "Are we done here? I have shit to get done."

"Yeah, we're done." I stand and extend my hand. "For what it's worth, I am sorry."

"I know you are. I can see that." He takes my hand in a firm grasp. "And even though I don't carry any ill will toward you, I think I needed this closure, so thank you."

I turn, opening the door to exit with Daniel behind me.

"I'll show you out. I wouldn't want Lil to jump you as you leave."

I chuckle as we both make our way down the stairs.

"You have a lot of nerve coming here again." I look up as I register the voice.

Jeffery.

"This has nothing to do with you, brother, so stay out of it." Daniel slides past me and turns to look at Lily, standing next to Jeffery. "Are you responsible for this?" He gestures toward his twin's presence.

"What did you expect me to do?"

"To do as your boss instructed you and stay put."

"Well, girlfriend status trumps employee."

"And both of those statuses can be changed. I'd suggest you make yourself scarce."

Lily rolls her eyes.

"Get off her ass, Danny. She did the right thing in calling me." Daniel ignores his brother.

"Now," Daniel barks out. She cuts her eyes at me as she storms past.

Daniel turns to me, extending his hand once again. I'm certain it's for a show in front of his brother. I extend mine and grasp it.

"What the fuck?"

Daniel releases me and looks at his brother. "Do I need to tell you again? This has nothing to do with you, so why don't you leave? I'm sure Lil pulled you from something more important."

Jeffery looks my way, ignoring his brother and staring me in the eye.

One day.

One fucking day, we will come to blows. Mark my word.

"Stay away from Danny, and do not ever come back around here again. Do you understand what I'm saying?"

"Or what?" I spit out as I move forward, coming to a halt when Daniel places a firm palm on my chest.

"Watch it, Lockhart," he tells me before turning to look at his brother and then addressing the both of us together. "If you two have something to settle, then take it the fuck outside. This shit isn't happening in here."

"I don't have anything to settle with him." Okay, that's a lie, but this isn't the time or even the place. Daniel is right about me. I don't control myself easily, and that's something I need to work on. "But I do have something to say."

I look Jeffery in the eye, which he returns. I want him to know I'm serious, and if he doesn't follow through on what I'm about to tell him, then he and I will have an even bigger problem.

"Stay away from Shannon. I'm not asking. I'm telling you. Do not go near her again. She's pregnant, and if I even think you're messing with her, then I won't hesitate to come after you. And Rachel, stay away from my assistant. She isn't built for that twisted shit inside your head. Leave her the fuck alone."

"You're so full of orders. Funny thing is, I don't take them from anyone, Lockhart."

"Then you better learn."

Daniel's other palm flattens across his brother's chest as he inches closer. "This is over." Daniel's voice booms. "Leave, Nicholas."

I do just that.

CHAPTER TWENTY

As I pull into the driveway, I come to an abrupt stop. I can't park in my normal spot next to Shannon's Panamera. Jase's Jeep is in my way, so I park behind his truck and turn off the ignition, wondering what he's doing here in the first place. Opening the driver's door, I hop out and ease the door closed. Being one-thirty in the morning, I don't want to shut it too hard and disturb anyone. Neighbors aren't too close, but I don't want to scare Shannon, either.

After unlocking the door and walking inside, I drop my car keys into the front pocket of my blue jeans. The lamp on the other side of the room is on, and that's when I notice Charmin. She glances up at me before placing her head back down on the cushion and shutting her eyes.

She's a good dog, but she isn't Niko. He was always happy to see me. I miss throwing his ball to him. I miss him bringing it back to me, wrapped in all his slobber; I miss him.

As I make my way down the hall to Shannon's bedroom, I don't know what I'm going to say. I'm the ass. I'm always the motherfucking ass, and as usual, I know I assumed something without giving her the benefit of the doubt. I blew up and walked away.

What is wrong with me?

Her door is slightly ajar, so I push it open, expecting to find her asleep, but what I find instead has me feeling like someone reached deep down into my throat and pulled out all the oxygen from my lungs.

She isn't alone.

My head, the logical part screaming *don't overreact*, is telling me, no, he would never in this lifetime do this to me and neither would my sister. Sure, they have a fucked-up lifestyle, hell, an even more messed-up relationship, but they wouldn't.

Except logic went out the goddamn window the second my eyes landed on his hand wrapped around her belly protectively. His fingers splayed out covering most of the surface.

Shannon is lying in between my sister and best friend, asleep. All three of them are. Shannon is facing Nikki, their foreheads touching and their hands clasped together. Jase is behind Shannon with his dick pressed up against her ass. Maybe it's just his crotch, but the same difference in my book. His right arm is underneath both Shannon and Nikki's heads, and his left arm is the one I want to rip off right before I put his head through a wall.

She looks like perfection with her long red hair and fair, uninked skin as she lies surrounded by colorful, tan, and muscular bodies.

Just as I clutch the frame of the door with my right palm, Jase stirs, as if sensing someone in the room. His head lifts and our eyes meet. A couple of seconds later, not soon enough though, he looks down as if realizing the murderous look in my eyes. He quickly removes his hand.

Without making a noise, he brings his index finger to his lips, telling me not to make a sound. When he gets out of bed, he reaches down to the floor and produces a T-shirt. He quickly pulls it over his head.

Oh, there's going to be a sound all right, the sound of my fist coming in contact with his bones any second now. Never in my life have I wanted to actually hurt my best friend. Sure, we've gotten into it a time or two over my sister, but even then, there was a level of love and respect. Now though, right this very moment, there is only anger and the need to inflict pain on Jase.

Slowly, he moves his right arm out from under the girls and climbs out of bed. The look on his face is angry; his eyes tell me he wouldn't mind going toe-to-toe with me too.

I don't know what his problem is. He's the one in here in bed with my woman and has his arm wrapped around my kid.

"Out," he mouths as he points behind me. I squeeze the wood even harder as I pull in air through my mouth. My jaw is locked so goddamn tightly I'm surprised my teeth haven't broken. "Go, Lockhart, now."

I turn and make my way back into the living room. The rhythm of my heart is pounding a tattoo in the center of my chest, almost loud enough to cause me to lose my train of thought.

"Kitchen," Jase whispers from behind my back, although it comes out more as bark than anything else. Before I make it there, I spin on my heel, grabbing him by the shirt and propelling his back into a hard wall. I hold him there, looking him in the eyes with what I'm sure is fire reflecting at him.

"Whatever is working inside that head of yours, turn it the fuck off."

"Don't." It's all I'm able to grit out. As much as I want to hit him right now, hurt him, I can't bring myself to do it. He's my best friend. He's my brother.

"No, you don't, motherfucker. Get your hands—" Jase is cut off by the booming sound of my sister's hard voice.

"Nick, what the fuck are you doing? Let him go, now."

"Take your hands off me." We both ignore my sister's presence as we stare each other down. Finally, I open my fists, releasing the material of his shirt, and step back.

"What the hell, Nick?" My sister walks up next to me, and as I turn my gaze to her, I don't see his fist until just before it connects with my jaw. I manage to catch myself with my hands before my face hits the hardwood floor beneath me.

Oh, it's on. I turn to jump up, but Jase squats down and gets inches from my face, shoving his finger in front of my eyes.

"That was for leaving your woman alone and terrified, you stupid son of a bitch. You have your panties so far up your ass right now you can't see, let alone think straight."

Reaching out, I shove Jase backward, making him lose his balance and land on his ass. I take the time to jump up.

"What are you talking about?" I don't wait for his response. I'm not entirely thinking about what he's saying anyway. As I'm about to lunge for him, my sister steps into my path, halting my advances. "Move, Nikki."

It gives Jase enough time to get back to his feet.

"Would you stop, please?" my sister begs. It's highly unlike her and makes me take my eyes away from Jase to look at her.

"No, Nikki, let him. If he wants to do this, then let's fucking do this, *brother*."

"Both of you stop, now." Her order, full of lethal venom, forces us to stop and listen. "She doesn't need this shit."

Shannon.

"Want to explain to me what's going on here?" My question is directed at my sister. I can't look at Jase without the need to inflict massive amounts of pain on him.

Nikki opens her mouth, but Jase speaks first. "Oh, now you want to let someone have a word." Sarcasm drips from his lips.

"Now you want to let someone explain. You're unbelievable, dick face."

"If you have something to say, then just . . ." Nikki's elbow jabs my ribs before I'm able to finish what I'm saying. I look over at her, but she's looking in another direction. When I turn, I see Shannon standing at the entrance to the hall looking a bit pale, more so than usual. I move my eyes up to meet hers, but they aren't focused on me. She's tired. Her eyes are heavy, and her body is bowed slightly. The same feeling the night she first met me washes over me as I realize what's about to happen.

I'm at her side within moments of her body nearly hitting the ground. My knees crash to the hard floor as I wrap my arms around her limp body.

"Shannon?" It comes out in a scream.

Panic.

This is what panic feels like. It's crushing, sucking the life out of your own body.

I flip her over with ease, my sister kneeling down next to me as I brush strands of hair away from her face.

"Baby," I call out, but she doesn't respond. I know she's just fainted, but I have to check for a pulse anyway. It's there, and it's strong.

Nikki kneels next to me, her eyes cutting to mine before lowering to Shannon.

"I told you to make her eat something last night." My head snaps up to see Jase pinning my sister with a hard stare.

Shannon hasn't eaten. What the hell is going on? If there is one thing I know about my girl, it's that she loves food and does not miss a meal. She did look weak when I first saw her.

"What did you want me to do, exactly? Force feed her? Yeah, right." Nikki takes Shannon's wrist into her hand. She peers up at me, staring at me through dark eyelashes. My sister is pissed off, and it's directed solely at me.

"What's your fucking problem? And why hasn't Shannon eaten? Is she sick?"

"You're my fucking problem."

I snatch Shannon's hand from hers as I gather Shannon into my arms, lift her, and stand up. I quickly move over to the couch and lay her down before kneeling beside her.

"Will you get her a glass of water for when she wakes up?" I look over at Jase. He nods before walking into the kitchen.

"Why don't you move out of the way and let me handle her?"

Like fucking hell I will.

"Why don't you lose the attitude, Nikki?" I snap back.

"Why don't I not?"

"Then leave, goddamn it." Can't she see I'm dealing with a lot of shit right now?

"You leave, asshole."

Is she five years old again? Fuck me.

"Both of you need to cool it. You're getting on my last nerve." Jase walks back in, water in hand.

"Stop! All of you." Shannon squirms, and I breathe.

"Fuck, you scared the shit out of me," I say as I lean over her and rest my forehead against hers. She's okay. Well, I hope she is. She is pregnant. I know Jase said she hadn't eaten, but maybe this isn't a fainting spell. What if something's wrong with the baby?

She squirms again, and I lift myself up.

"Can you sit up?" I say to her. She looks at me; there's anger in her eyes. There should be. I deserve that.

I pull her into a sitting position on the couch. Jase hands the cold glass of water to me, and I push it in front of Shannon. She takes it from my hand. That stare is still killing me.

"What are you doing here?" she asks after downing most of the contents in the glass. I take it from her and set it on the table behind me.

"Are you okay? Do you think you need to go see a doctor?" I'm not ignoring her question. I just don't want to discuss us in front of Jase and Nikki. I want to talk to her alone. I have to make this right.

"I'm fine. You can leave now." Her words cut like a knife in my chest. Leave? I don't ever want to leave again. I won't ever leave again.

"Shannon, let's discuss that later. Let me make sure you're okay."

"No, let's not. I'm fine. Now, get out."

Fuck, that hurts.

"Baby, I'm not leaving. I know I fucked up and I'm sorry. I'm so—"

"She wants you to leave, Nick, so do it." My sister's words are nasty, hurtful even. She's never spoken to me this way. Hell, she's always had my back and been in my corner no matter what the situation.

"Stay out of this, Nikki." I train cold eyes on her. She's on the edge of pissing me off. "Got it?"

"Enough," Shannon yells. She stands, making me back up. After a few steps, she turns to face me, and I stand. "I'm done doing this, Nick. I won't wait around or tread on eggshells for you, anticipating the next time you decide to lose your shit and leave me."

"I won't."

"I don't believe that, and the next time you do, I might have our baby, and I will not put my kid through that. This is done, Nick. You and I are over."

No.

I'm pretty certain my heart just broke in half.

Shannon pivots on her heel and leaves me standing alone. Jase and Nikki are here, but inside, I'm completely alone.

"No," I choke out. I can't lose her, but Shannon doesn't stop.

She continues walking without so much as a glance back in my direction. "Shannon," I call out her name.

Nothing.

I don't know how long I stand here, willing her to come back to me. She doesn't. Eventually, a large presence comes up behind me. I know it's Jase. He wraps a hard arm around my chest, and the other hand he places on my shoulder.

"Give her some time, brother."

"I can't walk away. I can't leave."

"You have to. This isn't going to solve itself today."

"She fainted. She needs to eat. She might need to go to the hospital or something. I don't know."

"I got that."

No, I got that. It's my job, not his or anyone else's.

"We'll make sure she and the baby are fine, but you have to leave for now."

I shake my head.

"Come on. Let's walk outside."

Jase pulls. I don't budge. He practically drags my pathetic ass out the door. We get to the end of his Jeep, and he stops.

"You two will work your shit out, but give her time, okay?"

"Why were you and Nikki here? Why were you both sleeping with her?"

"You know that in there was just sleep, man." I don't say anything. I need him to tell me more than that. Yes, I know he'd never touch my woman, at least not in an inappropriate way. "Last night, she called Nikki. She had a nightmare, so we came over. Nikki went to bed with her, and I slept on the couch. An hour later, she woke up screaming. It took another hour to calm her down. Nikki asked me to get in bed with them. She thought someone being on both sides of her would comfort her. It did."

"What kind of nightmares? Why didn't someone tell me?"

"What kind do you think? And as far as telling you, your sister would have cut off my dick."

My father. The bastard is still hurting her from the grave. I suppose I am too.

"I know you know I'd never go after what's yours. Not today, not tomorrow, and not ever. Shannon is hot. I'm not blind, but I don't want your woman. Let's face it; she isn't my type, brother. My type begins and ends with that crazy ass sister of yours."

We both laugh.

Yes, it does, as unfortunate as that is. I love my sister, and I love my best friend. I'll never tell him, but I think he's a fool for sticking with her. I know he loves her, the whole heart and soul kind of love, but Nikki has a lot of her own demons to make right in her head. I just don't know if she ever will, and if she doesn't, it's going to kill Jase one day.

"Do I need to say it again?"

"What?"

"I got that." He points to the house. "At least until you both figure shit out. She loves you, man. Don't doubt that."

I shake my head. I don't want him to take care of what's mine. It should be me. I really messed up this time.

"Just make sure she eats and that she and the baby are okay."

We say our goodbyes. Not so manly goodbyes, but fuck it. I need a goddamn hug right now.

I get in my car and drive away, not knowing when or if I'll get them back, but one thing I do know for sure. I'm going to try.

CHAPTER TWENTY-ONE

I t's been three weeks since I've seen or spoken to Shannon or even my dog. Feels more like three months. I've been alone inside these walls all twenty-one nights. I'm going insane. I've managed not to create any new holes this go around. That has to be a sign of improvement.

With the exception of work and my weekday morning training sessions with Jase, I've mostly kept to myself. I saw my mother yesterday and had lunch with her, in fact. It was pleasant, an awkward pleasant, but nice all the same. Our shit isn't fixed and won't be fixed any time soon, but I know we'll get there. I can't hold this over her forever. It's not her fault.

It's his fault.

All of it is his fault.

I've had plenty of time in these last three weeks to take a step back and really see things for what they are. It's like Daniel said, things happen for a reason. Do I think if I had known certain things I could have changed them? Sure. Had I handled things differently years ago, would things today be different? Yes, I believe that wholeheartedly.

But I no longer wish things had gone in a different direction. I might not have ever met Shannon if they had. She is the best thing that's ever happened to me.

And I miss her.

I don't blame her for not giving me another chance. Why should she? But that doesn't mean I'm going to stop trying to get one. I'll beg. I'll plead, and I'll do whatever it takes to get her back, get *them* back.

The sound of a light knock on my front door brings me out of my thoughts. I'm sure it's her.

I asked her earlier this morning to bring Charmin over, and she agreed. I'm praying everything goes perfectly as planned.

There's another knock, but I remain standing next to the mantel where our pictures sit. This space was bare before I met her and she quickly filled it with photographs. There's one of us, her in my arms and looking up at me. One of Nikki and Jase, with Jase's arm wrapped around my sister's chest. Another of the dogs, Niko and Charmin, sleeping next to each other on the sofa, and the last one on the far end of the mantel is of me hunched down and Niko sitting next to me.

I miss my dog.

The sound of the doorbell chimes throughout the house. Shannon has a key. Probably doesn't want to use it given the fact we aren't exactly together at the moment, but she has it, and I want her to use it.

And she does. Well, at least someone is inserting a key at the moment. The only other person who has one is my sister. Nikki isn't speaking to me and hasn't for weeks. She isn't speaking to Shannon either. She thinks we're both stupid.

"Nick, I know you're home," she calls out at the same time Charmin comes running through the living room. She hasn't been here in forever. I'd bet she doesn't even remember this was her first home. "Your car is parked out front."

"I'm in here," I answer while bending down to pet an excited Charmin at my feet. She's gotten so big in only a few weeks' time. The puppy in her is harder to see.

"Right. When do you want me to pick her back up?" I look up to see Shannon looking at everything but me. Her eyes look all around the living room and then the kitchen as if she's never seen the place. She's avoiding looking at me for a reason.

I smile as I take in her appearance. Shannon doesn't know it, but she's just told me I have a chance. And it's a chance I intend to use to my full advantage.

"I don't."

"What?" She turns to look at me for the first time. Fuck, she is beautiful. She steals my breath away every time. I could look at her for the rest of my life and never tire of this sight. "What do you mean you don't want me to come back to get her?"

She's dressed in a navy sleeveless dress and nude high heels, with no stockings, making her legs bare. Her skin is glowing. I'm itching just to get my hands on it again, so I stick them both in the front pockets of my jeans.

"I can bring her home tomorrow if need be." I don't want her to think I'm taking the dog from her. I'd never do that. Shannon loves that dog. Charmin has come to be hers.

"Oh." Her eyes darken again. "What's that smell?"

Shannon turns and walks the short distance into the open kitchen. So far, everything is working out well.

"Crab legs."

She turns her head back to me, her eyes wide, and her face lights up. I've got her attention now. Moments later, her excitement wanes. "I don't think I'm supposed to eat that. Something about, um . . ." She pauses, trying to remember why.

"Shellfish is fine, actually, and shrimp." Her face beams. "Yes, I have shrimp too. It's low in mercury. It's fine. I checked." And I have. I've been reading up and researching baby shit. You'd be surprised by the wealth of information out there. There's a book on everything. I've learned that my company has even published a couple. Something I should have already known, but now I do.

"I'm sorry." Her face falls. "I didn't mean to invite myself. Were you having company over? There's a lot of food in here."

I can hear the disappointment in her voice and maybe even a hint of jealousy. Surely, she doesn't think I'd go on a date with another woman. Wait, she better not have been on a date with another man.

Chill, Lockhart, just chill, man. You need to play this cool.

"Just you."

"Me? Did you plan this? Nick—" I cut her off before she tries to shut this down. That isn't going to happen.

"It's one of your favorite meals, and besides, you can't feed my baby takeout every night."

"I don't think this is a good idea."

"It's just food, Shannon. A simple meal. Let's eat. I can hear your stomach rumbling from here."

"You're standing three feet from me." And not nearly close enough.

She pulls out a stool from underneath the island and climbs on it. I turn and fetch the plates.

Once I have our meal plated, I set hers in front of her. I've gone ahead and cracked all the legs, so she shouldn't have a problem getting the meat out.

Shannon gives a forced smile as I take a seat across from her. We eat in silence for the longest time.

"Would you like something to drink?"

"Water would be great."

Again, we go back to silence.

"You're quiet." She's too quiet.

"So are you."

"Right."

"I don't know what to say, Nick."

"What do you want to say?"

"I don't know. What do you want to say?"

I push my plate away. I'm done eating; even she has stopped eating what remains on her plate. There's so much I want to say, yet I don't.

"Maybe I should go."

I don't think so.

I stand, and she does the same. When she turns to leave, I round the corner and take her hand in mine.

"What are you doing?"

"Don't leave just yet."

"Nick, I don't—"

I cut her off. No way will I be letting her leave. If I have to tie her down, I will, in fact, do just that.

"Just wait a minute." I pull her into the living room and over to the mantel.

"What are you doing?" I stop in front of the very pictures I was looking at earlier. I pull her in front of me, pulling her back to my chest.

"Nick, stop. This isn't—"

"Hush."

Taking the remote control out of my back pocket, I hit play before she decides to challenge me.

"Just look," I whisper into her left ear as I point to the picture of us, "and listen to this song. That's all I want."

"No Matter What" by Papa Roach starts playing, followed by the soft, soothing voice of Jacoby Shaddix. I bet no one has ever described his voice like that, but Shannon does. This is her favorite song and the perfect song for us.

Every word he says at the start of the song is everything I feel for the woman in my arms. I need her to know it as much as I want her to feel it. I'd do anything for her. Anything.

After about a minute into the song, about the time the second verse starts to play, Shannon relaxes against me. I tighten my hold on her and brush her hair to the right as I tip my head down. Running my lips over the edge of her ear and down the skin on her neck, I reach my favorite spot. On the second chorus, I kiss her there, gently pulling her skin between my lips before moving back up to her ear.

By the third verse, I say, "I love you. I need you, Shannon. I want you both until my last breath." I move my hand down and cup her belly with my palm.

After another minute, the song ends, and with a click of a button, the stereo is turned off. Shannon sniffles as liquid drops onto my forearm and runs down, eventually landing to the floor.

My intention wasn't to make her cry. In fact, I can't stand it when she does. I feel helpless and shitty.

After placing the remote onto the mantel, I reach back into my pocket and retrieve the small ring I've been carrying around for a while now. I take my hand out and turn her to face me. Her nose is a rosy color. With my left hand cupping her jaw, she closes her eyes, another tear falling. I bend down, kissing her on the lips. It's been far too long since I tasted her.

Reluctantly, I release her lips, pulling back from her mouth. Her eyes remain closed as I go down onto my knees in front of her. After a couple of seconds, her lids open. Eventually, her eyes locate mine. Realization dawns on her, and the greens widen.

"Will you marry me, Shannon?"

Air exhales from her mouth in a gush before she rushes to take more in. At least she isn't saying no, but she isn't saying yes either. She isn't saying anything, and she is unmoving. She's staring down at me as I peer up at her.

Sweat forms above my brow. How long is she going to leave me hanging? This is killing me, but I'll wait forever for this one.

She's it.

I could have gotten her in my bed at any point tonight, the second she walked in my door if I really wanted it. This isn't about that. I want her in my bed every night. I want forever.

"An answer would be nice."

"Well . . ." She pauses. Her expression is unchanged.

Well? She said *well?* It wasn't a yes, but it wasn't a no either.

Fuck, she really is going to be the death of me.

"It would be nice to get Nikki and Jase out of my bed. You'd be surprised how much room that man takes up, and your sister, she's a cover thief."

"What?" I shake my head and play back every word Shannon has just spoken.

Is she?

Is she saying?

"What are you saying, exactly?" I need clarification on this one.

"Yes. Yes, I'll marry you." There's excitement and joy in her voice.

Music to my ears.

"So you might want this then?" I hold out the ring I have between my thumb and index fingers.

She said yes.

Fuck, yeah.

CHAPTER TWENTY-TWO

I'm standing on the warm, sandy beach about ten yards from the water. When the tide comes in, it almost reaches my bare feet but never quite touches them. I'm looking down with my hands crossed in front of me. It's amazing how I got here. I keep wondering if this is real. Charmin looks up from the ground next to me as if something has caught her attention. Right before I raise my head to see, I hear the soft melody of music. As I gaze up, a smile forms across my face.

There she is.

My beautiful, smokin' hot girl.

Mine.

They are about to be all mine.

"God fuckin' damn." I hear coming from my left. The words are drawn out, long and slow. My eyebrows pinch together, and my smile fades as I swing my head to the side. My best friend's mouth is gaping. No, that's not the right word. Jase's mouth is dropped open so far apart the bottom half might as well be taking up space on the sandy surface below. I follow his eyes to see what's so clearly caught his attention.

Shannon.

My bride.

Is this motherfucker seriously trying to get knocked the fuck out? He can't take his eyes off her. Yeah, she's drop dead gorgeous as she walks down a short set of stairs, landing her bare feet on the sand. She is walking in my direction. Her right arm is looped through Ben's as they make their way to me.

"Don't make me punch you in the dick."

"Huh?" He turns, looking at me, confusion on his face, and I nod in the direction of Shannon. Jase looks back, and realization dawns as he shakes his head.

"I got nothin', brother. Fuck. I'm sorry, dude, but damn, she's fuckin' beautiful."

Yeah, damn. I can't disagree with him there. She's perfect, but she is my perfect.

"Do I need to remind you of my sister's bat-shit crazy jealous streak?" I know Nikki won't hurt Shannon; she loves her. Those two have grown very close.

"No, man, I'm very familiar with it." He swings his head, looking past me to the right where his girlfriend is standing. She's Shannon's maid of honor, just as Jase is my best man. She isn't paying him a lick of attention. She is staring at Shannon too. Nikki's face is all smiles, but I know her, and it's her masking technique. The one she puts on to make people think she's fine. She's not. She's uncomfortable and a little bit sad. I can see it. No one else can, but she is my sister, and deep down, I know what her problem is. Even if she won't admit it.

It's my wedding day, so I don't want to focus on Nikki's issues right now, but I know no matter what happens, the shit's about to hit the fan with her and Jase. That's a pile of crap I'm not sure even I'm ready for. She's my baby sister, and he's my best friend. Hell, he's my fucking brother.

Shannon and Ben make their way in front of me, and we all turn, facing the man who will make us husband and wife. Ben kisses my girl on the lips, and if it were any other man, I would have decked him. He releases her to me and walks to stand next to a few other people who are witnessing this event.

Shannon and I didn't want a big wedding. Hell, I'm not even sure if this would be considered small. Besides the minister standing in front of Shannon and me, there are only maybe ten people present. It's fucking perfect.

"Nicholas and Shannon, have you come here freely and without reservation to give yourselves to each other in marriage?" The minister looks between the two of us.

"Yes," Shannon and I say in unison.

"Will you honor each other as husband and wife for the rest of your lives?" Again looking back and forth between us both.

"Yes," we say again at the same time. I look over at the woman who will be my wife in only a few moments. She is breathtakingly beautiful. I cannot believe she is about to be mine. *Both of them*, I think as I glance down at her belly. There's a small bump underneath her dress. Even if no one can see it with the empire-style wedding gown she's wearing, I know it's there, and it brings a smile to my face.

"Will you accept children lovingly from God and bring them up according to the law of Christ and his church?" I chuckle and see Shannon's face blush. She glances in my direction, and we look at each other for a moment.

"Yes," we both say. I hear Jase's low chuckle behind me. If I weren't standing in front of a man of God, I would punch him in the gut.

"Since it is your intention to enter into marriage, join your hands, and declare your consent before God and your friends." I take Shannon's hands into my own and turn to face her. She is smiling, her bright smile I love so much. I will never tire of the face in front of me.

"Nicholas, do you take Shannon to be your wife? Do you promise to be true to her in good times and in bad, in sickness and in health, to love her and honor her all the days of your life?"

"I do," I declare, remembering everything we've been through in the short time we have known each other. Remembering the pain I still feel, knowing everything Shannon has endured. Remembering my father. If given a second chance, I'd do it all over again. I know it was wrong, but I'm not sorry, and one day I'll have to answer to the man upstairs for my own sins, and I'll take whatever punishment He decides.

"Shannon, do you take Nicholas to be your husband? Do you promise to be true to him in good times and in bad, in sickness and in health, to love him and honor him all the days of your life?"

Shannon smiles and closes the short distance between us. She's smiling, but there's something else hidden behind those eyes. I haven't the faintest clue what. My eyebrows knit inward. She stands on her tiptoes, leaning forward and up to my ear so that only I can hear what she is about to tell me.

"I love you, Nicholas Lockhart, but . . ."

Why is there a *but*? I take a deep breath, not sure what she is about to tell me. *God, please don't let her call this off.* He hasn't announced us married. She hasn't said "I do." She can still change her mind. Surely, she isn't changing her mind. She did start with an *I love you.* That's a good thing, right? Fuck. What do I do if she tells me she doesn't want to be my wife?

"The next time you decide to use my car in the middle of the night and not tell me, I expect you to place the seat back in its original position."

What is she talking about? I haven't driven her new car, and the last time I drove the nine eleven was ... *Oh, shit. She* ...

"I do," she announces after taking a step back. My eyes widen as she gazes up at me with a knowing look. She knows.

"I now pronounce you Mr. and Mrs. Nicholas Lockhart." I barely hear the minister's announcement. Oh, hell. She knows, and she still married me. She knows I killed him. I killed my father, and she still chose me.

"You may kiss your bride." I hear the priest, but it doesn't fully register. I'm frozen where I stand. She knows.

Shannon closes the distance between us once more and again stands on her tiptoes. She places her hands on my shoulders and whispers, "It doesn't change the fact I love you. If anything, I love you even more, Nick. You made me feel safe. You took away a monster. Because of you, no other woman will ever be hurt by him again. Now, please kiss me. Kiss me and make me your wife."

Moving my hand to her hip and my other behind her head, I pull her forward into a deep, passionate kiss.

She is mine; they are both really mine.

Forever.

EPILOGUE

SHANNON LOCKHART

I've been sitting in this hard, rather uncomfortable metal chair for almost two hours now. I mean, how long does it freakin' take to get a tattoo done? Granted, I realize a lot of work is involved, but come on. How much longer do I have to sit here?

This is so not how I imagined the start of my honeymoon going. I had at least thought I'd be cock deep in some way by now, but no. It's not like I'm sex deprived; well, at least not in the last few weeks since Nick finally realized it's perfectly okay to do me. However, it's my damn honeymoon, and so far, saying "I do" hasn't paid off.

Did I yet mention the crasher we have tagging along with us? Oh, yes, Nikki and Jase are along for the fun. I'm complaining, but all in all, I'm completely cool with it. Weird, I know, but it's only for tonight.

After the ceremony, the four of us boarded a small private jet that took us from Los Angeles to Las Vegas. Apparently, this is Nick's favorite place on Earth. Not really sure why; I mean, it's fun and all, but we're in the desert. Tomorrow, we leave for the real honeymoon in New Zealand. I cannot wait to get to our destination. The tourist in me is itching to come out. Plus, I have so many photoshoots planned.

This honeymoon is going to be epic. That is, if I ever get out of this tattoo shop.

The moment we landed in Las Vegas, Nick turned his cell phone back on, and it started ringing. I remember he ignored it, but then it rang a second, and the third time, I recognized the number. It was the detective I spoke to a few months ago. The one handling Nick's father's murder. To say I'm worried is an understatement, but I can't stress over that right now. I do want to enjoy this. It is, after all, still my wedding day.

The backs of my legs are drenched in sweat. I can feel it, and it gross. Had I known this was something I'd have to endure, I probably would have dressed in something other than shorts. A nice long, cool summer dress, in fact, but then I wore a dress all day long and wanted something different. Something that didn't have "preggers" stamped across the front.

At just over four months pregnant, I look and feel like a whale. Twenty extra pounds will do that to a woman. Nick doesn't seem to notice, but then, that's his job. He's supposed to make me feel sexy. And he does a damn good job of it too.

I look over at the door Nick and Jase walked through hours ago, hoping one or both of them will come through. After staring at the closed door for a few minutes, I turn to watch Nikki chatting with the older-looking woman I met when I first walked in.

Miriam.

I'd say she's in her late forties, maybe her early fifties. Not that I'm judging, but I just wouldn't have placed her here being an older lady. It's not that she doesn't fit in; she does with her jet-black hair, piercing green eyes, and the array of tattoos decorating her skin. Both of her arms are covered in amazing inkwork, and at her age, she rocks it.

I want a tattoo so badly. I always have, but I can't get past my fear of needles to go through with it. I can admit it. I'm a chickenshit when it comes to anything to do with a needle. I shudder just thinking of them.

The sound of a bell chiming draws my attention to my left. In walks a thin woman, and from the looks of her, I'd say she's three or four inches shorter than my five feet seven inches, with strawberry-blond hair that has bright red streaks at the end. She's looking down as she enters the shop and plunders through one of the many bags she is toting across her shoulder. Running my eyes over her, I see that everywhere on her body, where there is exposed skin, is a work of art. That's the only way to describe this chick. She is beautiful.

"Hey, Mir, is my cli . . ." She halts, and there's a moment of silence before an overly excited screech bubbles out from this woman's mouth. "Holy shit-balls! Why didn't you text me to let me know you were coming to Vegas?"

"Surprise, bitch." Nikki turns and echoes her excitement.

The woman, who obviously Nikki knows well, places her large bags on the ground carefully, as if the contents are fragile, and then stands before running up to Nikki. Grabbing her with both hands, she plants a kiss right on her lips. I cock my head to the side to watch as I contemplate if tongue is currently being involved.

I'm not shocked. Shocked was a few months ago when I saw Nikki getting double-teamed. No, the shock has worn off.

Who would've thought?

Not me, that's for damn sure.

I've come to learn Nikki isn't bisexual, but from what she's told me, she likes to "play" as she calls it, and doesn't mind the third member of the trio being female.

Yep, definitely tongue.

As much as I'd like to deny it, and I totally would to my husband, watching this play out is hot.

Really hot.

I should totally be ashamed of myself.

The swapping of spit stops as the woman pulls back and places her arms around Nikki's shoulder.

"I can't believe you're here. Please tell me, my Jasey Pooh is here too?"

Jasey Pooh?

Someone seriously just called Jason "Rockstar" Teller, Jasey Pooh.

No way. I had to have heard that wrong.

Just, no. Jasey Pooh, really?

"Of course he is," Nikki says with a devilish grin across her face.

"And what about the sex god himself? Please tell me your brother tagged along."

Whoa. Both of my eyebrows arch up.

"There's no other man who has ever made me cream my panties the way Nicholas Lockhart can. And man, I certainly haven't been properly fucked since the last time I saw him."

Oh, my God, I'm going to strangle this bitch where she stands. Nikki looks over at me. She looks like she's about to fall on the floor laughing.

This isn't funny.

In no fucking century is this funny.

"Just thinking about that beautiful cock of his in my mouth and down my throat. Damn, I'm wet already." She licks her lips.

She just doesn't shut up.

Albeit, his cock is beautiful, but it's my cock and for my pleasure and enjoyment only, dammit.

"Ew, gross." Nikki's smile changes to disgust.

"Hey, don't knock it till you try it, babe."

"Again, ew, yuck, and gross. My brother, remember tramp?" Nikki shudders.

The new girl turns, noticing me for the first time. She gives me a once-over from head to toe and then draws her eyes slowly back up the length of my body. If I didn't want to pummel the bitch, I might appreciate the seductive smile she's throwing my way.

"And who's this? She with you?" She elbows Nikki in the arm. "Does she have virgin skin?"

"Um . . ." Nikki ponders. "Don't know, actually."

"Got any ink, sweetheart?"

"No."

"Why does she look like she wants to rip me apart?" She turns back to Nikki, who is trying to hold back a laugh. "Should I not have kissed you or something?"

"Or something is more like it." Nikki can no longer hold her laughter back. "My God, this shit is priceless."

"What? Please tell me already."

"Let me introduce you." Nikki reaches out, grabbing me by the arm and pulling me close. I quickly jerk out of her hold and cross my arms over my chest. Better safe than sorry. If I don't hold my fist firmly in place against me, I'll hit her. "Eve Matthews, I'd like you to meet Shannon Lockhart." Nikki pauses for effect, I'm sure. "My sister-in-law." Another pause as it registers in Eve's head. "Nick's wife. I think the two of you have a lot in common."

Nikki can no longer contain herself. She's belly laughing, tears rolling from her eyes.

"No shit?" Eve's eyes widen, though not in an angry you-just-stole-my-boy-toy-away-from-me way. Shock, yes, but not what I expected. She laughs. "No. There's no way Mr. I-don't-fuck-a-chick-twice got hitched."

"He fucked you more than once, didn't he?" Nikki spits out.

"I'm different."

Oh, she's about to be different, all right, different with a black eye.

"So is Shannon."

"Apparentfuckingly." Eve laughs aloud again. "You lucky bitch. I hate you." Again, I don't hear a snootiness behind her words. She isn't mad, but she isn't apologizing for her earlier statements about Nick and his beautiful cock, which she's apparently had more than once.

I really want to hate this woman, but for whatever reason, I don't, and I'm unsure why, because I really want to.

"You and I are going to be the best of friends." She grabs me and pulls me flush with her own body as she wraps her arms around my neck and squeezes.

"Watch it, Matthews. That position is already filled." There's a serious tone in Nikki's voice, which registers with Eve as she pulls one of her arms free. Now she drapes her right arm over my shoulders. "She is my BFF."

Yes, Nikki and I have become really close, extremely fast even. I adore Nick's sister. I love her, in fact.

"So where are the guys anyway?" Eve changes the subject.

"In the back with Chance. He's probably still working on Jase's piece," Nikki replies.

"Well, what are we still doing out here? I want to go see my boys." She is way too excited.

"Your boys?" I reel back, eyeing her without realizing my question came out bitchy and accusative. Her arm slides off my shoulder.

"Yeah, what?" She cocks her head. "Are you the jealous type, honey?"

No. I. Am. Not.

"Careful, Eve. This one has a wicked right hook," Nikki declares.

"You a fighter, babe?"

What the hell is with all the pet names?

"No, *babe*," I bite out.

Why am I being such a bitch? This is not like me. Sure, she's sucked my husband's cock, probably had it shoved inside her too, but really is that any reason for my bitchiness?

"Oooh, sassy. I like this one," she says to Nikki before turning back to me. "And by boys, I mean my boys, in the back that work here. Come on. I'll introduce you. Chance is going to be in love with your canvas."

Canvas?

Huh?

She grabs my hand, lacing our fingers together as she picks up her bags and pulls me toward the door I was watching earlier. I look over to Nikki, who shrugs, telling me to go with it. Eve pauses before pushing through.

"Mir, where's my client?"

Miriam looks at Eve with the same irritated look I've seen my mother give me a time or two.

"If you would check your messages once in a while, you would know I sent you a text over two hours ago to let you know he had to reschedule."

As if no big deal, she says, "Okay," and pulls me along.

"You're a tattoo artist too?" I ask, smoothing my voice. I really shouldn't act like a total bitch to her. She hasn't done anything wrong. I'm sure there are plenty of women Nick has slept with in his past.

"No, sweets. I'm nowhere near that talented."

"Oh, please," Nikki gushes. "She is very talented. Something else you two have in common. Eve's a photographer, too."

"Shut up," we both echo at the same time.

Well, that explains all the gear she's carrying around.

"Would I have seen your work?" Eve asks.

"Doubtful."

"You have, actually," Nikki interjects. "You own a collection of her work."

"She does?"

"I do?"

"Yeah, stupid. Those kickass birthday presents I got you three months ago, the skyline of LA and that photograph of a building in graffiti."

Eve's mouth drops.

When did Nikki purchase those? I don't even recall an order for them.

"No fucking way." She turns to me. "You're Shannon Taylor? As in *Sights of the City of Angels* Shannon Taylor? Seriously?" She jumps up and down.

I don't get it.

"Yeah."

"I love your work. Come on. Chance is never going to believe this shit."

When we enter the back, I see it's a large room with multiple stations set up. An array of people sit in chairs and lie on tables back here. More than I would have thought. Only one other person came back here after Nick and Jase, but all surfaces have a body on them.

Looking around, I spot Nick; he's standing next to another guy who's hunched over. I don't see Jase, so I assume he's the large body mostly hidden.

"Chance," Eve yells. The tattoo artist halts what he is doing as Nick turns to look our way. I look at my husband, who isn't looking at me. His eyes widen, and he has a deer-caught-in-headlights look across his beautiful face. He's looking at Eve.

"I'm busy, Evie." He turns and pulls her into an embrace as he kisses her on the temple and then releases her.

"Whatever. Do you know who this is?" Eve pulls me forward with a hard jerk, her excitement shining bright like the lights on a Christmas tree.

Jase lifts his head to look up at all of us. His eyes are heavy, as if he was asleep. Surely, not. Not with someone stabbing his body with a needle over and over and then over some more.

Chance, who I'm standing in front of now, gives me a once over, then does twice more times with his diamond-blue eyes. He's wearing a black T-shirt and blue jeans, but I can tell by his hands, arms, and neck that he too is covered in tattoos, just like Eve here. He glances up at Nick, who is now boring hard eyes down at him.

"Judging by the look on Lockhart's face that tells me he wants to punch me in the gut, I'd say his wife."

"Eve," Nick says as he takes his eyes off Chance and looks over at her, nodding at her and then at me. "I see you two have met."

"Shut up, Nicholas. I'm not speaking to you," Eve says. Everyone except Eve and I laugh. She then turns back to Chance. "Shannon Taylor!" The excitement in her voice returns as she tells him my name.

"Lockhart. Shannon Lockhart," Nick corrects, and Eve spins her head in his direction once more.

"Didn't I tell you to shut it?"

"Damn, dude. I'm pretty sure Evie just dropped you for your wife."

Nick quickly reaches out and pulls me to him, wrapping his arms around me tight.

"Mine."

I swear if one more person pulls or jerks on me, I'm going to knee someone in the crotch.

Nick turns me around, repositioning me in front of him with my back against his front, and then splays his palm across my belly. He loves to do this and does it often.

He really is going to make a great dad. I just know it.

"She could be ours?" Eve shines a devilish grin my way. Did she just proposition me for a threesome?

"I don't share, Eve," Nick's voice booms. Eve rolls her eyes and turns back to Chance.

"That piece you were working on last night. That black crow that turns into a tree. It would look killer on this one." Eve points to me. "Take off your shirt, love."

"Pardon me?" Everyone turns to look at me, so I step farther into Nick's warm body.

"A modest one?" Eve glances up at my husband with a confused look. I'm not modest, but I certainly don't know these people. Without waiting for Nick to respond, she turns back to face Chance. "And she has virgin skin."

The corners of Chance's lips turn up in a sexy grin.

"I've just fallen in fucking love. Now take that shirt off, sweet thing." What the hell is wrong with these two? When I continue to stare at him as if he's grown two heads, he looks up at Nick again. "Tell her it's okay?"

Nick removes his hands, and I'm instantly cooled off.

"It's cool, baby. Humor him and take it off." I never imagined these words coming out of Nick's mouth. He obviously trusts these people, perhaps a little too much. Hell, even Jase is lying on his stomach, peering up with his chin placed in his hands, patiently waiting. Am I missing something here?

"Sweetheart, I'm a tattoo artist. I see half-naked chicks hourly. I promise I won't get a hard-on. Now, off with that shirt."

Reluctantly, I lift my shirt over my head, wondering why the hell I'm doing this. I might want a tattoo, but it is not going to happen.

"Holy hell, you knocked her up too. You're a busy man, Lockhart." Chance laughs. "Come closer, sugar."

Nick shoves me forward, and I turn my head and look at him as Chance reaches for me.

"Spin for me, darlin'." I do so, and he stops me as I'm facing Jase, or my chest is facing Jase and my side in front of Chance.

"Hey, have those gotten bigger?" Jase lifts up a little farther as he looks at my boobs and tries to hide a snicker.

Perfect, a stellar honeymoon this is.

"Do you need me to punch your lights out? I don't think Chance has finished that piece on your back yet." Nick steps forward, and Jase looks up at him.

"I'm good, brother. Just enjoying the view."

"Baby, put your shirt back on before someone in here gets their ass kicked." Nick pulls me gently away from Jase. I lift my tank top, pulling it over my head and back into place.

"You have perfect skin, beautiful." Chance smiles at me. I've never in my life been called multiple pet names before tonight. It doesn't irritate me, though. I actually like it. "After you drop that calf, you have to let me have it. I need a new canvas, and you have a blank slate for me to work with. Your body is divine."

Had he not just called my baby a calf, that might have been the sweetest compliment anyone has ever given me.

"She might not want any ink, Chance," Nick tells him.

"Do you, love? Do you want me to ink that flawless skin of yours?" His eyes are hungry. Not in a sexual way; well, at least I don't think so. I don't get that vibe from him.

"I don't know." Maybe, but the needle . . . I'm certain I couldn't handle that part of the process, and that part seems like a pretty large chunk of it.

"She does," Chance decides.

"Do you want me to get a tattoo?" I twist and look up at my

husband's face. Nick has a lot, and judging by that bandage on his wrist, he added to his collection tonight.

"That, Shannon, is entirely up to you. You are perfect the way you are now, but you would still be just as perfect with ink."

Aww . . . he melts my heart. Okay, now that was the sweetest compliment I've ever received.

"I'll say this though, if you do want one, Chance here is the best. Most of Jase's and mine were done by him. Every piece of work on that one"—he lifts his finger and points to Eve—"was done by Chance."

"You too?" I look at Nikki.

"Nope, my guy's Bryan. See the blond over there?" I turn in the direction she is pointing. "He's done most of my work."

"So you don't think Chance is the best?" I ask, now curious why she gets someone different to do her tattoos.

"I didn't say that. Bry and I just work. Chance has done a piece on my side, but I fit with Bryan. That's all."

"Yo, Nicolette, when you gonna bring that sweet ass over here and show a brother some love?" Bryan yells across the room. I look over to Jase to see his reaction. He seems unfazed. Guess they do have an open relationship.

"I'll get over there when I get over there. You look busy, loser."

"I'm never too busy for you."

"Look, sorry to shut this party down early, but it's time I get my bride naked." Nick squeezes my hip.

"You know my number if you two get bored and want some company," Eve chimes in.

"We won't," Nick says back. "But I'm sure Jase and Nikki can occupy your time. Let's go, baby."

Nick pulls me from the tattoo shop, and after a ten-minute walk, we make it to our hotel. As we enter the building, his phone rings. I have a sickening feeling it's that detective. As Nick removes his phone from his pants pocket, my suspicions are confirmed when his happy, carefree smile fades. He looks up at me and then answers the phone.

I say a silent prayer as we maneuver through the lobby and to the elevator.

Please, God, let this be news I can handle. News he can handle. I don't want to lose him. I just got him, and I want forever.

The call ends quickly, and I hope it's a good sign. I mean, if the cops were going to arrest you, they wouldn't call to warn you first, right?

Nick presses the button for elevators, and seconds later, they open.

"Nick, you're killing me. What did he say? I know who it was. Please tell me. Tell me something."

He enters the small area, and I follow him. He's hard to read sometimes, and I have no idea what's going on inside his head. When he looks at me, I see it.

Relief.

I think that's what I'm seeing.

"They're closing the case. He called to tell me personally. I . . ." Nick stops speaking. He's in shock. This is the best news. This I want to celebrate.

The elevator comes to a halt and the doors open. I walk out with Nick following. Moments later, we enter our room, and I turn to see a completely different expression on Nick's face.

His carefree, fun, and sexy demeanor is back.

"Are you hungry?" Nick asks me.

"Starved," I declare, knowing of only one thing that could satisfy the hunger inside me.

"I'll order room service. What would you like?" Nick closes the door and turns around to face me. I lower my gaze down his chest to his package covered in denim that has been the topic of discussion tonight. I need to reclaim him. I need to make sure it's still mine. Nick chuckles as he registers my need. "And what you're hungry for, I assume, isn't on any menu then?"

"Oh, what I want is on the menu, just not any menu you've ever ordered from."

I walk forward, palm outstretched, and I press it against Nick's chest, applying pressure so he takes a step back. Then another step, and another until his back is against the door we walked through. Pushing myself up onto the balls of my feet, I lean in and claim my husband's lips as I reach in front of me and pop the button of his jeans loose.

Within a few seconds, I'm pushing his pants and boxers down.

"Shirt off, now," he demands as he releases my lips. I lower myself and pull my tank off before placing my hands on his hard, thick length.

I lower my eyes until I see the object of my desire. My mouth waters the instant it comes into view. Just looking at his perfect, beautiful cock has me wet and ready for him.

Going down to my knees, mouth level with his cock, I run my hands over his smooth, scorching skin. I jut my tongue out, licking the salty tip of pre-cum. Nick's body tenses at the contact, and he pulls in a quick breath of air.

"Mmmm," I hum and then look up. His eyes are on me. I love it when he watches me.

I'm ripped from that glorious cock all too soon, causing a whimper to bubble from my mouth. Nick doesn't give me a chance to pout. Within an instant, my husband pivots, and I'm pushed up against the same door he was moments ago. My shorts and panties are gone in a flash.

"But I . . . oh God." Nick pushes inside me, balls deep before I realize it. The air from my lungs forces out of my body in a rush. "Shit."

"Fuck, I love the feel of your heat surrounding my dick, baby."

"Easy," I gasp out. "You're going to squash our daughter."

"This is something my little princess will have to get used to."

I'd laugh, but my husband is completely serious. Oh, shit, I'm going to come quick. I can't hold it, not when he's inside me.

"I love you, Nick."

"Woman, I love you so much."

BONUS SCENE
MICHAEL MANNING

My tired eyes stare at the computer screen another second longer before I lean back in the same raggedy leather chair I've sat in for fifteen years. Looking up at the dirty ceiling, I mull over the years I've served this city.

What do I have to show for it? Not jack shit.

I've spent twenty-four years doing everything by the book. Going after the bad guys only to watch most get off on a technicality. Some rookie screws up my hard work and a criminal is set free to walk the streets of LA. Nine times out of ten, that same dirtbag will do something worse the next time around. Domestic violence, sexual assault, murder... To them, it's all the same. They don't care. They don't have a conscious.

Sometimes, I wish I didn't have one either.

I lean up and my eyes land on the plaque hanging on the wall. Serve and Protect.

A long time ago, I thought that was my calling, but what have I accomplished in all the years I've been a cop? Damn near half the men and women I serve with don't respect that statement. And the ones who do, the good cops, they'll be jaded eventually, too.

Movement at the entrance to my office catches my attention and pulls me from my depressing thoughts. My eyes glance over as Brie sticks her head around the corner.

"Hey, Mike, I need you." Her long, brown hair is down tonight and half-covers her face as she leans inside. "Got a situation. A woman left her infant kid up front. Claims the baby is Drago Acerbi's and she's scared for the boy's safety."

The eldest son of LA's notorious and alleged Italian-American mob boss, Alessandro Acerbi. Yet another failed case. Another criminal free in a long list of cases stamped closed without being solved.

One more year of this bullshit and I'm done. Twenty-four fucking years I've served. I've followed all the right rules only to come down to a year before retirement, and tonight's the night I join The Dirty Blue. Fucking great.

"Give me five, Brie. I have a case to wrap up." I sigh louder than I intended, making Detective Brianna Andrews's face turn from serious to concern. "Then I'll handle what you have, okay?"

"Sure, boss." She hesitates, making me think she wants to say more. She doesn't. Instead, she vanishes from my door, leaving the same emptiness I feel in the pit of my stomach.

I outrank her and all the detectives in my unit with my seniority, but I'm far from her boss or anyone else's. Though she refuses to stop calling me that. For some odd reason, even the captain gets a kick out of it. Brie is one of the good ones. I was just like her in the beginning when I received my promotion to detective. I thought I would make a difference. Help change this city for the better.

I was delusional.

Picking up the phone, I glance down at the file on my desk to locate the same number I've called multiple times today. I've wanted to get this over and done with for hours. Then I can leave and down a bottle of Jack.

After punching in the numbers on my desk phone, it rings. To my surprise, he answers.

"Hello." His voice isn't the usual self-assured I'm accustomed to when speaking to Nicholas Lockhart.

"Mr. Lockhart, this is Detective Manning with the Los Angeles Police Department. I'm glad I finally caught you."

"I'd apologize, Detective, but I got married today. Accepting phone calls wasn't on the agenda."

"Congratulations then." I'm aware of his marriage to his pregnant girlfriend, Shannon Taylor. I met her a while back, at the start of my investigation. Upon uttering the murdered victim's name, her body language changed. The detective in me knew she was keeping something hidden behind her eyes, which prompted me to look into her background. What a cluster of history did I discover . . . "I'll keep this as brief as possible so you can get back to your lovely wife."

"Thank you, Detective. I appreciate that." He sounds weary. I'd imagine the guilty should. It must be exhausting.

I don't have to put on a game face for what I'm about to do. Lying is technically part of my job. I can act naturally in any situation.

"As much as I hate to tell you this, the investigation into your father's murder has come to a close without resolution, Mr. Lockhart. We have exhausted all efforts and leads. We don't have any viable suspects. I'm sorry."

"I-I understand."

"The case is now closed. I will be letting your mother know tomorrow."

"Well, I appreciate the call."

"Good night, Mr. Lockhart. Congratulations once again. I wish you well."

When the line goes dead, I remove the phone from my ear and place it back on the receiver. Then I glance at my computer screen once more, at the paused video I've watched over and over so many times I now have every frame memorized.

The same video that was taken from a surveillance camera of a parking lot in the early morning hours when the dishonorable Judge James Lewis was murdered.

The same video that clearly shows the face of the man I just got off the phone with. The man I have no doubt murdered his father.

Reaching for my mouse, I move it until the cursor hovers over the "x" to close the video. Once it's closed, I drag it to the trash can on my computer. And lastly, I empty the trash.

Gone.

Case closed.

An unsolved murder in a long list of unsolved murders in this city.

Pulling out an old tattered file from under the Lewis file, I open it to see a photo of a much younger Elana Lewis. Bruised. Beaten. Broken.

A tired sigh escapes my lips.

For the life of me, I'll never understand why she stayed with that bastard. I tried hard to get her to tell me he was the cause of her injuries. Instead, she stuck to her story of falling down the stairs. How fucking cliché.

In the end, it seems the motherfucker got everything he deserved—beaten to death by his son.

Was it justified? I don't know.

I looked into Nicholas's past. I know what he did to Daniel Chaney. He obviously has anger issues, but I'm choosing to look the other way. I'm choosing to cover up a crime. Destroy evidence in a murder investigation for my own selfish reason.

I failed her all those years ago. This time I won't. She doesn't deserve her son taken away. Even if he is a murderer. Justified or not, murder is still murder.

DIRTY BLUE
Brie and Drago's story is now available.

ALSO BY N. E. HENDERSON

SILENT SERIES:

Nick and Shannon's Duet

SILENT NO MORE

SILENT GUILT

MORE THAN SERIES:

Can be read as standalones but not recommended

MORE THAN LIES

MORE THAN MEMORIES

DIRTY JUSTICE TRILOGY:

DIRTY BLUE

DIRTY WAR

DIRTY SIN

THE NEW AMERICAN MAFIA:

Must be read in order for the complete story

BAD PRINCESS

DARK PRINCE

DEVIANT KNIGHT

STANDALONE BOOKS:

HAVE MERCY

ACKNOWLEDGMENTS

You, my reader—thank you from the bottom of my heart for reading my story and taking a chance on me. Thank you for sticking around and I'm sorry I left you which such an awful cliffhanger in Silent No More. I'm sorry I didn't get this book published sooner, but I had to make sure it was perfect; Nick's story was perfect. And to me, it is. I hope you enjoy it. Thank you again!

Joe and Michael—my world. Thank you both as I know my writing takes my time away from you guys. I love you guys so much.

Sabrina—thank you for everything. Without you, I don't know if I could have finished this story. Thank you for the advice and encouragement. Thank you for the many texts and helping me make this story better.

Lindsay—I'm so glad I met you through my writing and the book community. Thank you for beta reading book 2. I appreciate your help, thoughts, advice, and proofreading.

Teri and Sue—thank you for beta reading this book. Your comments were amazing. Thank you for pointing things out and making me think. You guys are awesome and the BEST!

Bloggers—I'm not sure where to begin. Thank You is fitting, but not enough. There are so many of you that's helped me over the last few months and I thank you. Two Unruly Girls with a Romance Book Buzz, Love Between The Sheets, A Risqué Affair,

Bookworm Betties, and SO many more. Thank you guys so much!!!

Papa Roach, because your music and lyrics inspire me. I've never discovered another band, artist, etc. that when I listen to them, I feel the words inside me. Thank you for gracing the world with all of your talents. Yes, I am probably cheesy fan-girling here, but it is what it is. Thank you and I love your music.

ABOUT THE AUTHOR

N. E. Henderson is the author of sexy suspense and new adult romance. When she isn't writing, you can find her reading some form of romance or in her CanAm Maverick, playing in the dirt. This is Nancy's second book.

For more information:
https://linktr.ee/nehenderson

31474486R00166